A DR. BANNERMAN VET MYSTERY

PRAISE FOR
PHILIPP SCHOTT

The Accidental Veterinarian

"Few books . . . approach the combination of fine writing, radical honesty and endless optimism found in Winnipeg practitioner Schott's . . . Laugh until you cry — and believe, as he says, that all that really matters is that the heart of the pet (and its owner) is pure."
— *Booklist*, starred review

"Schott's writing is engagingly conversational and showcases his colorful sense of humor . . . Educational, entertaining and compassionate, this confluence of happy accidents is a must-read for anyone who is, loves or works with a veterinarian."
— *Shelf Awareness*

The Willow Wren

"Philipp Schott pulls off the considerable feat of creating empathy for his characters without ever resorting to easy excuses for their sometimes indefensible choices . . . a fine, nuanced storytelling achievement."
— Frederick Taylor, historian and bestselling author of *Exorcising Hitler: The Occupation and Denazification of Germany*

"This beautifully written tale alternates between displays of sardonic humour and setting some truly poignant and heart-wrenching scenes. Morally complex and nuanced, this book is a must-read for anyone who wants to understand a difficult period in German history."
— Dr. Perry Biddiscombe, historian and author of *The Last Nazis: SS Werewolf Guerrilla Resistance in Europe 1944–1947*

How to Examine a Wolverine

"An engaging study of the behaviors of pets and the people who care for them. Schott's tone is warm, friendly and folksy in his storytelling and his conversations with pet owners; even in the most stressful times, he's a compassionate and level-headed guide. *How to Examine a Wolverine* is an essay collection that celebrates the love of animals."

— *Foreword Reviews*

"Schott's writing style is conversational, which makes *How to Examine a Wolverine* an easy and enjoyable read."

— *Winnipeg Free Press*

"While the stories here are blue-ribbon perfect for anyone who loves four-footed, furry creatures, author Philipp Schott takes this book a few dozen hoofprints past your everyday household fur-kids."

— *Goshen News*

FIFTY-FOUR
Pigs

FIFTY-FOUR
Pigs

A DR. BANNERMAN VET MYSTERY

PHILIPP SCHOTT DVM

This book is also available as a Global Certified Accessible™ (GCA) ebook. ECW Press's ebooks are screen reader friendly and are built to meet the needs of those who are unable to read standard print due to blindness, low vision, dyslexia, or a physical disability.

Purchase the print edition and receive the eBook free. For details, go to ecwpress.com/eBook.

Published by ECW Press
665 Gerrard Street East
Toronto, Ontario, Canada M4M 1Y2
416-694-3348 / info@ecwpress.com

Cover design: David A. Gee
Cover artwork © Joey Gao / www.joey-gao.com

LIBRARY AND ARCHIVES CANADA CATALOGUING IN PUBLICATION

Title: Fifty-four pigs / Philipp Schott.

Names: Schott, Philipp, author.

Description: "A Dr. Peter Bannerman mystery."

Identifiers: Canadiana (print) 20210381248 | Canadiana (ebook) 20210381272

ISBN 978-1-77041-614-7 (softcover)
ISBN 978-1-77305-913-6 (ePub)
ISBN 978-1-77305-914-3 (PDF)
ISBN 978-1-77305-915-0 (Kindle)

Classification: LCC PS8637.C5645 F54 2022 | DDC C813/.6—dc23

This book is funded in part by the Government of Canada. *Ce livre est financé en partie par le gouvernement du Canada.* We acknowledge the support of the Canada Council for the Arts. *Nous remercions le Conseil des arts du Canada de son soutien.* We acknowledge the support of the Ontario Arts Council (OAC), an agency of the Government of Ontario, which last year funded 1,965 individual artists and 1,152 organizations in 197 communities across Ontario for a total of $51.9 million. We also acknowledge the support of the Government of Ontario through Ontario Creates.

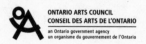

PRINTED AND BOUND IN CANADA

PRINTING: MARQUIS   5 4 3 2 1

MIX
Paper from responsible sources
FSC® C103567

For Lorraine

PROLOGUE

They were unsettled. The routine had not changed — the lights came on at the same time and they were fed at the same time — but other people were here this morning. Yesterday as well. Visitors came from time to time, but rarely in the winter. And there was something different about these visitors. They could not see the visitors, but they could hear them and smell them. Something undefinable about the visitors caused anxiety to ripple through the barn like a wave. But they couldn't act on these uneasy feelings. Instinct said flee. But the doors were closed. And besides, it was very cold outside, and there was no food out there when the world was white. They knew that. Here, inside, it was warm, and more food would come. More food always came. Yet they were still nervous, so they shuffled and jostled and made noise and sought comfort in each other. Then it was loud, so loud, and bright, so bright. Then dark. The world ended.

CHAPTER
One

P eter heard it before he saw it. A deep, percussive thud from somewhere ahead and to the left. Beyond Baldurson's woodlot. Loud enough to be heard over the rattle of the truck on the washboard gravel. Unexpected enough to startle him. His immediate thought was that it sounded like something massive had been dropped from a great height.

Whump.

Like a whale or a cement truck.

Pushing those thoughts aside, he glanced at the clock on his dashboard.

8:33 a.m.

Then he saw it. Pillows of smoke began vaulting one over the other, as if scrambling to get a better view, the rising column of battleship grey sharply contrasting the bright blue Manitoba January sky.

"Shit," Peter said to himself as he brought the truck to a stop on a rise that afforded the clearest view. The smoke was definitely coming from the other side of Ed Baldurson's place. Perhaps three kilometres away.

That would be Tom's farm.

"Shit!" he said again.

He was due at Tom's later that morning, but was expected at Bill Chernov's first.

Forget that. One of Bill's heifers had a cut on her leg, but that could wait.

Peter put the New Selfoss Veterinary Services truck in gear and spun the tires as he accelerated toward the intersection, turning left instead of right as planned. As he did so, he voice-activated his phone.

"Hey Google, dial 911."

After a brief pause and two rings, an operator answered. "911. What is your emergency?"

"An explosion and fire at Tom Pearson's farm nine kilometres south of New Selfoss, about two kilometres east of Provincial 59."

There was a brief pause and the click-click-clack sound of rapid typing on a keyboard.

"I have your coordinates. Are you at the fire?"

"No, I'm about three kilometres southeast of it. New Selfoss volunteer fire department will know where Tom's place is." 911 calls in rural Manitoba were all routed through the Provincial Public Safety Answering Point in Brandon, almost 300 kilometres away. Their variable ability to accurately pinpoint the locations of emergencies was a perennial subject of coffee shop deliberation.

"Are there people in the building?"

"Well, I'm not there yet, so I don't know for sure." Peter tried not to sound irritated by what struck him as a silly question. "But I don't think Tom would be home and he lives alone."

"First responders will be on their way shortly."

Peter took a deep breath to steady his nerves and then sped up as he neared Tom's farm.

Peter was right. He could see the source of the smoke as soon as he turned the corner past the trees and arrived at the bridge over Yellowgrass Creek. Tom Pearson's hog barn was on fire. The smoke was thick, too thick to get an immediate sense of how big the fire itself was. He knew that the amount of smoke did not necessarily indicate the size of the fire, but still, this looked like a big one. Barn fires were not uncommon, but why an explosion?

The manure pit.

There had been a massive hog barn explosion two years ago near Altona because of methane build-up in a manure pit combined with some poorly considered welding work. But Tom was careful and smart. And Tom would not be there doing any welding, or anything else that could generate a spark, because he was always at Rita's Coffee Shop in New Selfoss by 7:45 at the latest, except on Saturdays and Sundays. And it wasn't a Saturday or a Sunday. It was a Tuesday.

Peter skidded to a stop in the farmyard and yanked the truck's door open.

The pigs! Those poor pigs!

There were no other vehicles in the yard. Tom's might have been in the garage, but there's no way he would have slept through the explosion. Tom must be at Rita's, as Peter had assumed. It was up to Peter to save the pigs. He jogged a few steps toward the barn before he hit an invisible, pulsating wall of extreme heat. He couldn't force his way through it. There was no way. He realized that he had probably parked the truck too close, so he jumped back into the cab and reversed 20 metres at high speed to the far side of the yard.

Then he got out and stared at the unfolding catastrophe.

Flames were now shooting out of all the barn windows. A door on the east side of the barn appeared to have been blown out by the force of the initial explosion, creating a cone-shaped blast pattern in the snow, toward an aspen bluff that the pigs were sometimes pastured in. Fortunately, this was away from the house and the other outbuildings, which were across the yard to the west.

Then, with a suddenness that made Peter jump, the roof collapsed in a deafening boom, sending fiery embers straight up into the air as if from a squat prairie volcano. Peter was glad that he had moved the truck. Tom's hog barn wasn't one of those modern, fully sealed, high-tech, steel-clad porkchop factories, but rather an old wooden one, repurposed for his pasture pig project. Only in January in Manitoba there is no pasture, so the pigs need a cozy straw-filled refuge out of the wind and the snowdrifts. Old wood plus dry straw equals tinderbox. This was going to be nothing but ash and char in a matter of minutes.

Those poor pigs.

Peter had known some of them personally. They all had names. Fifty-four of them, if he remembered correctly. And Peter usually remembered correctly. He got out of the truck again, slower this time, and leaned heavily on the hood, unable to take his eyes off the conflagration. Unable to think of anything else to do. The only sounds came from the fire, a crescendo and decrescendo of roars and crackles, following some complex infernal rhythm. Even the crows were silent. Six of them roosted in the big elm with the tire swing beside the porch, all six watching the fire with intense interest. Normally they would be cawing at Peter, but not today. Peter had left his gloves in the truck, so put his hands into his parka pockets and drew in a deep breath.

Peter wondered who would arrive first. He hoped it would be his brother-in-law, Kevin. He often felt self-conscious around people he knew less well. He was well aware that his arms seemed slightly too long for his already long frame and that his head stuck forward, as if he was peering at something. (In fact, it was likely the result of a lifetime of ducking and stooping.) This gangly effect was enhanced when he moved, which made him look like he was still learning how to use his body. Graceful was not a word that was often, if ever, applied to him. His dark brown hair was usually unruly too, so well-groomed was another word that was not often applied to him. He knew that it was a joke among his friends to begin describing him to someone as tall, dark and . . . trailing off so that the listener would helpfully insert the customary completion of that phrase. "No, not that," they would say. "Definitely not that." Peter was in early middle age — 41 to be exact — and could reasonably be thought of as young, or as old, or as in-between, depending on the light and how he had slept and how hard he had been working. He also knew that many people misinterpreted his smile. At a casual glance, it tended to be read as genial, but a significant minority, if they had the vocabulary, instead thought of it as enigmatic or cryptic or inscrutable. This had the effect of dividing people into two camps — those who found Peter amiable and those who found him unnerving. For the latter group, he radiated . . . something. He knew he was amiable, but he wasn't especially troubled to be thought of as enigmatic instead. He just wished his body wasn't so awkward.

After a couple of minutes of watching the flames and smoke Peter pulled his gaze away and began to look around. There were several tire tracks in the snow-covered yard. It had snowed one or two centimetres yesterday, stopping at around six in the evening. Tom had obviously not had the snowblower out since then. The tracks overlapped with each other and appeared to be from three different vehicles, but it was difficult to be certain. One would have been from Tom leaving this morning. Tom lived alone now, but he was very social and did get a lot of visitors, especially in the evenings, so the others could have been from last night. Perhaps Tom's '80s cover band, The Newer Waves, had a practice last night? Otherwise, there was nothing else of note to see. And certainly nothing that hinted in any way at what might have happened here. The manure pit still seemed like the most likely answer, although Tom's was quite small compared to that one in Altona, and Peter was sure that it was well ventilated.

Peter knew that the RCMP would arrive first and that, because it was a Tuesday morning in January and likely not much else was going on, they would be able to come straight here. The fastest they could drive on these roads would be 90 kilometres an hour, so allowing for two minutes to get into the car they should be here eight minutes from when Brandon 911 dispatch contacted them. This was five minutes ago now, so . . . Peter cocked his head and listened. Yes, there it was. The fire was still loud, but he could hear the siren now.

Three minutes later an RCMP Ford Interceptor skidded into the yard and, to his relief, Peter's brother-in-law jumped out. Peter knew it was Kevin before the car stopped. Kevin Gudmundurson's bright red hair made him a cinch to identify from a distance. His thrice-broken nose and the fact that he was built like a bear trained to wrestle professionally, and was almost as hairy as one, completed the picture. Up until the previous summer the Mounties had prohibited beards for most members, but that policy changed, so now Kevin also sported a lavish Viking growth on his broad chin. Or, at least as lavish as the force would allow. There were still limits. Kevin's dream was to let it grow to chest-length and then fork it into two long braids. This would have to wait until retirement.

"Holy Toledo!" This was one of Kevin's favourite expressions, but it was said with particular vehemence this time. "When did you get here?"

"Ten minutes ago. I heard the explosion while driving to Chernov's."

"Explosion? Are you sure?"

"No question. I heard it from three klicks away. And look at the east side of the barn."

"Right." Kevin nodded. "I suppose it could have started off as a fire and then set off a gas line or something . . ."

"Maybe, but the fire would have to have been small because there was no smoke in the sky until after I heard the explosion."

Kevin grunted, scanning the yard with his hand shielding his eyes against the brightest part of the fire. "Anybody else here?"

"I don't think so. There's just the tire tracks leaving from the garage and maybe two others here in the yard."

"Yeah, I see that."

They were both quiet for a moment.

"Volunteer fire should be here soon. Nothing else for us to do until then," Kevin said as he began to jot a few details down in his little coil notebook. Then he looked up and smiled at Peter. "Mmm, smells like bacon, though, eh? Had breakfast yet?"

"Shut up, Kevin, that's not funny."

"Sure it is!"

"Can I go now? Bill's expecting me."

"Yeah, go on. I know where to find you if I need some more details or a statement, and I'll see you soon regardless." Kevin smiled. "In fact, Sunday dinner at the latest, eh?" Peter's wife, Laura, invited her brother over most weeks on Sunday evenings.

As Peter drove out of the yard, he saw the red flashing lights of the New Selfoss Volunteer Fire Department's old pumper truck in the distance. It looked like they would meet on the narrow Yellowtail Creek bridge, so he pulled over just before it and waved at Dan, Dave and Brian as they raced past. Soon after he crossed the bridge, he saw another vehicle approach at high speed. It was Tom Pearson's black pickup truck. Peter raised his hand in greeting as they passed each other in a whirl of snow, but Tom did not seem to notice as he stared straight ahead.

Poor Tom.

CHAPTER
Two

Peter was in the minority in New Selfoss in that he was not of Icelandic descent. He was mostly Orkney Scot on his father's side and Ukrainian and German on his mother's. John Bannerman, his great-great-great-great-grandfather, had been recruited by the Hudson's Bay Company to row their York boats and man their trading posts in the remote wilderness of Rupertsland. On retirement, he settled in the Red River Colony like so many of the other Orkney Scots he worked with. This wasn't so much a choice as a necessity because most of them were unable to afford the passage back to Orkney. The Germans in Peter's mother's background came from the plains of Mecklenburg and were likely the source of his height, whereas the Ukrainian ancestors accounted for his dark complexion. Many of their descendants, including his mother, had what his grandmother described as the "Mongol spot" on their backs. It was an oval patch of slightly darker skin just below the shoulder blade, about the size of a loonie. According to his grandmother it was the result of an errant gene passed on from when Genghis Khan's Mongol horde rampaged across the steppes of Ukraine in the early 1200s. She said that it was a good thing, although she never explained why. Peter didn't have one and had always felt a little bereft as a result.

As proud as Peter was of his own heritage, he was equally proud to be connected to the dominant community through Laura. Laura and Kevin were "new New Icelanders." The original New Icelanders had first settled around Gimli, on the other side of the lake, but then there was a leadership dispute, and a group broke off to found New Selfoss on this side. By chance, New Selfoss was featured in an extremely popular mid-20th-century Icelandic novel called *Forest Heart Kingdom*. On the strength of that fame, it attracted a steady trickle of new immigrants from Iceland. These were the new New Icelanders, often dreamers and idealists and misfits of various descriptions. Kevin and Laura's parents were firmly in the dreamer category. Their father, Egil Gudmundurson, was a kindred spirit of Peter's. In fact, Peter sometimes wondered whether that had played a subconscious role in Laura's initial attraction to him. For example, like Peter, Egil nurtured a passion for forests. However, this was an idiosyncratic passion in Iceland, a country where the largest tree would be classified as a sickly shrub anywhere else. Egil dreamed of a land of big trees. He dreamed of vast forests. He dreamed of lakes fringed with pines and hills crowned with tamarack. He dreamed of rivers cascading through stands of spruce. In short, he dreamed of the New Selfoss described in *Forest Heart Kingdom*. Their mother, Katrin, was no less a dreamer. Her dreams were of wild animals like bears and wolves and moose and beavers and elk and martens and wolverines. Iceland had only a few Arctic foxes and no other wild land mammals. She too dreamed of New Selfoss.

Introduced by mutual friends, they both knew within minutes what the future held for them. Two weeks later they eloped to Canada, to New Selfoss. There they not only found the animal-rich, sylvan dream-world described in *Forest Heart Kingdom*, or at least strong enough echoes of it, but they also found a community that *Maclean's* magazine later named "Canada's Quirkiest Town." Being quirky themselves, this cemented New Selfoss as home. They loved New Selfoss and, by extension, they loved Canada, so when their children were born, they decided that they should be given the most Canadian names they could think of. It was the mid-1970s. Hence Kevin and Laura.

Although the Gudmundurson siblings shared red hair and a pale complexion, they could not otherwise be more unalike. Whereas Kevin was beefy, loud and temperamental, Laura was slight, quiet and calm. She was often described as elfin. The tops of her ears even stuck out very slightly. She was pleased by this description. Better an elf than a barbarian, she would tease her brother. Laura was ambivalent about her hair, though, which she usually described as looking like an unpeeled carrot. In one of Peter's rare forays into poetic language, he said, "No, not the colour of carrots, but the colour of the sun in the autumn woods, the colour of rare treasure and the colour of joy and optimism." They did make a striking pair — Peter tall and dark, Laura small and pale — but there was a kind of complementarity and unconscious synchronization that made it seem right to everyone who saw them together.

Peter and Laura did not have children and there was little chance of any appearing in the future, so it was impossible to guess whether the Viking red would be able to fight its way through Peter's genetic mix, or whether the Mongol spot would ever reappear.

The rest of the day was thankfully more routine. At least in comparison to the way it had started. The cut on Bill Chernov's heifer's leg was not as deep as Bill had feared, and there were no catastrophes at the local animal shelter when he paid a call to examine and vaccinate the latest batch of puppies that had been dumped there. Catastrophes were not an uncommon occurrence at the shelter. Following the calls, the afternoon of appointments at the clinic also flowed smoothly, except when Bruiser the Pomeranian lifted his leg and peed on Peter's shoe. But if that was the worst that was going to happen, it was a good afternoon. Actually, Bruiser could have nipped him too, and it would still be a good afternoon in comparison to the morning.

When he got home Laura was out, so he was only greeted by their dog, a cheerful black and white lab-husky-border-collie mix named Pippin whose outstanding feature, next to his mismatched ears — one erect and one floppy — was his nose. Not the appearance of his nose, but its prowess. Even by the exalted standards of his species, Pippin had an extraordinary sniffer, able to detect two molecules of cheese at 500 paces, or so it seemed. To Peter's surprise, scent training Pippin had become one of his favourite pastimes, rivalling even cross-country skiing and watching *Dr. Who* reruns. At first it was just for fun and to see how good Pippin really was, but when Peter realized that Pippin was much more than merely good, he began to enter him in competitions. Normally Peter avoided formal events and clubs and other such gatherings whenever possible, but he was curious to get a more objective measure of Pippin's talent in comparison to other dogs. To his surprise, Peter enjoyed the competitions, and Pippin seemed to enjoy them as well. He won each one he entered, and then last year he took gold at the Western Canadian Scent Dog Association championships in Moose Jaw. Peter was now thinking of taking him to the world championships in the Netherlands in the fall.

Pippin gave Peter's pants a thorough olfactory inspection, learning lord knows what all about his day. Once this was done, and Peter had finished the customary scratch behind Pippin's ear and the equally customary two liver treats, he set about making tea. He selected decaffeinated lapsang souchong. It was that sort of a day. The kettle had just started to whistle when his phone vibrated in his pocket. Irritated that the call would disrupt the timing of his tea making, Peter allowed it to go to voicemail. Steeping needed to begin two minutes after boiling, when the water temperature had dropped to 93°C, and then the tea ball needed to be immersed for three minutes. Taking a call now would be too risky. There was nothing that couldn't wait for ten minutes — five minutes to make the tea and five minutes to take the first calming sips. Even checking now to see who the caller was or, worse still, listening to their message would derail his thoughts, which were currently focused on the rituals of winding down from the day.

Once the tea was ready Peter went into the living room, followed by Pippin. This was his oasis. The house generally was an oasis from the irrational world, but the living room was the oasis within the oasis. The house was over a hundred years old, built in the Edwardian style by New Selfoss's first full-time doctor. It was the very definition of a "character home" with squeaky hardwood floors, leaded glass windows and an abundance of charming nooks and crannies. It even had a small round turret in the southwest corner from which you could catch a glimpse of the lake when the leaves were down. The house had sat on the market empty for a couple of years before Peter and Laura bought it, derided by everyone as a money pit, but they were bewitched. For once in his life, passion overruled reason and Peter agreed with Laura that this was the only house for them. After ten years there were still many renovations to be made, but the living room was perfect. The one concession they had made to modernity was to put a large window facing east, as the magnificent view across their meadow and out over the forest had for some reason been ignored by the original builder. Otherwise, the living room had light umber-coloured walls and carefully restored dark oak wainscoting. Assorted oriental rugs covered the worn hardwood and an eclectic assortment of furniture was arranged in a loose semi-circle around the large stone hearth. An antique rolltop desk sat in one corner beside an antique globe on a stand. The room was decorated with mementos and photos from their travels, as well as curios related to their shared interests in fantasy and science fiction.

This was home.

Peter inhaled the smoke-scented steam from his lapsang souchong and briefly forgot that there was a voicemail to listen to. Pippin had fallen asleep beside his chair. The house was silent.

Peter took several long sips and then remembered his phone. The message was from Kevin. All he said was, "Call me right away."

Curious, Peter set his tea aside and called.

"Hi Kevin, it's Peter."

"Hey Pete, thanks for calling back." Only Kevin was permitted to call him Pete, and then only under sufferance.

"What's up?"

"I'm going to have to ask you to come down to the station to give a formal statement."

"Oh?"

"Pete, there were 55 bodies in that barn."

"But Tom's only got 54 pigs."

"That's right, I know. But I said 55 bodies. I didn't say what species. They were burnt all to hell, mostly just bones left, so it was hard to tell at first, but one jawbone is definitely human."

CHAPTER
Three

Peter was finished giving his formal statement and they were now chatting in Kevin's chaotic, paper-strewn office, sipping that horrific Mountie coffee. It had a weird solvent aftertaste. Peter pined for the delicate smokiness of his lapsang souchong, sitting forlorn and undrunk on his kitchen counter back home. The very thought of it put him into a reverie.

Peter Bannerman was not religious or spiritual in any sense of the word, and he thought of himself as a flexible freethinker, but this did not stop him from holding several firm beliefs that struck others as devotional in their own way. He believed that loose leaf black tea should be steeped for precisely three minutes, except for East Frisian, which should be permitted to steep for no longer than two minutes and thirty seconds lest too many tannins be extracted. He believed in the benefits of the Japanese practice of "forest bathing," wherein one was expected to feel better by wandering through a forest and breathing in the molecules released by the trees. He believed that acutely felt emotions were primitive throwbacks that were rarely helpful. He believed that the division of the Prairies into three separate provinces was arbitrary and inefficient. He also believed in the fundamental truth of the Latin phrase "solvitur ambulando" — it is solved by walking — and said it often.

But most fervently, Peter believed that to call something "random" was to either be lazy or stupid. He believed that everything in the universe could be explained by mathematics. Admittedly, much of this math was of a complexity far beyond the ability of any human to calculate, but he was confident that eventually computer intelligence would master even the apocryphal effect on the global climate of a single butterfly's wingbeat deep in the Amazon. Consequently, Peter snapped out of his daydream and bristled when Kevin said, "The amount of power a manure pit explosion produces is random."

"You don't mean that. What you mean is that you are unable to calculate yet how powerful it could be," he said, trying to keep the edge out of his voice. "And even if you can't calculate it with precision because there are too many variables, like exactly how full the manure pit was and how well the venting worked, you can at least rationally estimate probabilities. Just calling it 'random' and leaving it at that is lazy."

Kevin rolled his eyes. "Yeah, yeah, sure. That's what you always say, Pete. But it doesn't matter anyway. We do know that the explosion was strong enough to blow that door out and start the fire, and that's probably good enough. Jawbone was right there, although behind a cement partition that was still standing, but probably close enough to be knocked out by the blast and therefore not be able to escape the fire. Either that or Jawbone was either already unconscious or restrained. Forensics will figure that out without us having to calculate pig shit detonation ballistics."

"Restrained? Really? How likely is that?"

"Not very, but we have to cover the bases. Probably the force of the blast was enough to knock him, or her, out. If I had to guess right now, I'd say we were dealing with a transient who picked the wrong place to hole up and have a smoke."

"But guessing isn't how this works."

"No. There are lots of other decent guesses. Accident, manslaughter, murder . . . all possible. We'll have to wait and see."

Both of them were quiet as Peter considered this for a moment. "You don't suspect Tom's involved, do you?"

Kevin looked at him warily. "Maybe. He has an alibi, but then almost everyone does. At least at first."

"It's impossible regardless. Tom would never do that to his pigs, let alone another person."

Kevin closed his eyes, rubbed his forehead, and sighed. "I know you and Tom are pals. You can't be objective about this. I shouldn't be talking to you about any of this anyway, especially since this could end up being a murder investigation. The folks from D Division in Winnipeg will be here tomorrow."

"I'm always objective, Kevin," Peter said with a smile, but it was that particular smile of his. It didn't matter to Peter anyway. He knew that Kevin would eventually tell him more, in part because he wouldn't be able to help himself and in part because he knew that Peter could be trusted with confidential information. And, although Kevin would never admit this, there was a third reason: Peter's hyper-rational brain had been useful to him in the past.

As if Kevin had been reading his mind, he said, "I know why you're smiling that weird smile of yours. Stop it. This is not a missing crazy cat lady. It's way outside of your lane."

Peter shrugged. He knew not to push.

Kevin was referring to Edna Carson, who had been reported missing last fall by her nephew when he came up from the city for his weekly visit. As Edna bought all her cat food for her 17 cats from Peter, he knew exactly what she bought and when she bought it. She would buy in bulk every month or so. By weighing the cats, comparing to their previous weights on the medical records, determining how much food they had access to (two large bags, chewed into by the cats after about two meals had been missed) and calculating their metabolic rate, he was able to say that Edna had last fed them between 20 and 25 days prior. The nephew had stated that he had last seen her alive on his previous regular visit, exactly seven days before. When Kevin confronted him with Peter's cat calorie math and how that indicated that she had already been dead for at least two weeks at the time of that alleged visit, he broke down and confessed. He took Kevin to the buried body. The motive was obvious: inheritance. A cliché, really.

And then soon after that Peter had helped with a missing persons case. Or, more accurately, Peter and Pippin had helped with a missing persons case. Melody Prince, a 15-year-old girl from the nearby Yellowgrass First Nation, had disappeared and was assumed by the RCMP to have run away to the city, but her family felt very strongly that this was impossible. Peter had done some work for the band council to help deal with the stray dog population and the girl was the daughter of one of the councillors. Curious and concerned, Peter volunteered to help figure out what happened. A combination of Pippin's sniffing talent and Peter's application of rigorous logic led to the discovery of Melody's body in the lake, trapped by rocks. The coroner concluded that it was an accidental drowning. Kevin had appreciated Peter's help with the cat lady case, but Melody made the Mounties look bad and that created some tension between the brothers-in-law. Even so, Peter felt emboldened to try to help with another disappearance from Yellowgrass, a young man named Leonard Alexander. He and Pippin did their best, but they were unable to find any additional clues. He tried to keep these efforts quiet from Kevin.

Small towns being what they are, Edna's and Melody's stories circulated, and not long after, Trish McWilliams came into the waiting room of New Selfoss Veterinary Services around Christmas time without her dog, quietly asking to see Dr. Bannerman "about a personal matter." She was suspicious that her husband, Marv, was having an affair with Wendy Sigurdsson. She was embarrassed to ask, but she wondered whether Peter had any ideas how she could prove it. Marv was careful and left no evidence around the house. Trish had tried to check his phone when he left it unattended, but it needed a fingerprint to unlock it. Peter did have an idea, and his idea worked. It was a straightforward matter of getting Pippin to track Marv's scent to Wendy's cottage on Salk Bay one evening when Marv was supposed to be at a late meeting in Winnipeg.

Peter found he really enjoyed this type of problem solving and, if he were honest with himself, he also enjoyed the coolness of being thought of by some as a quasi-P.I. He had no trouble persuading himself that detective work and veterinary medicine were a perfectly logical pairing. In fact, he thought, it was astonishing that it didn't happen more often! Most veterinarians already used detective metaphors when describing how they made diagnoses on limited budgets with uncooperative and incommunicative patients. Being a private investigator was just applying those skills to prise secrets from the affairs of uncooperative and deceptively communicative humans.

Laura was in the front hall when he got home. From the look of the bags beside her, it seemed that she had just returned from the local Home Hardware store.

"New project?" Peter asked.

"Yeah, I found a chair at Krafts 'n' Things that I'm going to restore. It's in the car still. I needed some sandpaper and varnish and stuff. But you've had an exciting day, I hear?"

Pippin and Merry, their tortoiseshell cat, were in the front hall now too, so it was becoming crowded. Peter stepped around them to take off his boots and coat before remarking, "Word does get around fast."

"Of course it does!" Laura laughed. "Alice at the shop knew about Tom's barn, and Kevin called me looking for you when you didn't pick up right away."

Peter grinned — his brother-in-law had many positive traits, but patience wasn't one of them. He gave Laura a kiss on the cheek and said, "Oh yeah, exciting is one way to describe it. I've been in desperate need of tea. I'll make a fresh cup of decaf lapsang and then will tell you all about it."

Later, when he had gone to bed, Peter realized that the coffee in Kevin's office had been a bad idea. Not only because it tasted foul, but because Peter found that he was increasingly sensitive to the effects of caffeine. He had meant to ask Kevin for decaf but got distracted by the disorder in his office and by the fact that he could almost make out details from another case on the computer screen over Kevin's shoulder. Of course, he knew he shouldn't snoop, but mysteries, riddles and problems always drew his eyes as though they emitted tiny tractor beams. It was something about a poaching ring, but he couldn't make out much else. In any case, the combination of the fully caffeinated coffee and the excitement of the morning events, plus a few stray but recursive thoughts about poaching, prevented Peter from sleeping very well that night.

He always pictured his insomniac thoughts as hamsters running on wheels. The hamsters were now jazzed up on coffee. When he had trouble sleeping like this, he would recite the list of English monarchs in his head, starting with King Egbert of Wessex in 802, until that bored the hamsters into submission. That night, however, he was at King Aethelred the Unready (978) when the hamsters started listening. They cocked their heads as they ran and began chanting the names along with Peter. To his dismay, this spurred them on, and they ran even faster. From experience, Peter knew that if they weren't at least a tiny bit sluggish by the time he hit William the Conqueror (1066), then it was hopeless. Speeding up at poor old Aethelred definitely meant that it was going to be a long night.

The next morning was clear and bright and cold again. The weeks of high blue skies and tongue-freezing-to-lamppost cold that had characterized Peter's youth on the Prairies were rare now. The cold snaps had become shorter, and sometimes even sharper, but definitely shorter, and were interspersed with cloudy warm spells that felt like intrusions of eastern weather. Peter loved the legendary dry cold, so despite the sleep deprivation, it felt like a good day. Laura slept a little later most days, so Peter usually had an hour to himself in the early morning. Even when he needed the sleep and even without setting an alarm, he was up at six more or less on the dot, every day. Some of this was Pippin's doing, but some of it was simply the way Peter was. His biorhythms were rigid, as Laura would say, or reliable, as Peter preferred to think of them.

Their house, on a low hill at the northern edge of New Selfoss, faced east and offered a clear view to the horizon. In late January at this latitude actual sunrise wouldn't be for a couple hours — 8:07 a.m. to be exact — but astronomical dawn was at 6:15 already. This is when the first stars near the eastern horizon disappear, heralding the approach of the sun. Peter would make a pot of Irish Breakfast tea and sit by the big picture window with all the lights off and look at the stars. Normally he was not a proponent of blends, but the Irish Breakfast had sentimental appeal as he and Laura had honeymooned in Ireland and had been back a few times since, each time beguiled by the place. He took his tea clear, and always in a cracked vintage CBC mug, and then sat and watched the stars wink out, one by one. Usually Merry hopped up onto his lap when he sat down. She'd stand and purr and knead for a moment until Peter gently forced her to lay down. Pippin would be dozing nearby, having been fed breakfast and briefly let out for his early morning toileting.

Then all was still.

Sometimes the aurora borealis would ripple across the northern sky and sometimes, depending on the time of year, Venus, the morning star, would slide up over the horizon, preceding the sun like a demure courtier. If it was cloudy, he would surf news sites on his phone while he drank his tea, but on clear mornings he just sat and looked at the sky.

Nautical dawn, when the horizon would become visible — hence the name, as this had obvious importance for sailors — followed at 6:53. In late January this was around the time when Peter should be properly starting the day. His quiet hour of tea and contemplation would be done well before the third and final pre-sunrise stage of civil dawn, when it was light enough to see details outside without artificial light. By that time, he'd be walking Pippin, or feeding Gandalf the goat, or making breakfast, or having a shower, depending on what sequence of activities the specific morning permitted or demanded. Peter often pointed this out to Laura as evidence that he could, in fact, be flexible when it was logical to be so. And each time Laura rolled her eyes.

Just as he was taking his last sip of tea, Peter noticed movement at the edge of the trees that defined the eastern limit of their yard. A deer, perhaps? Or a coyote? The distant horizon was becoming more clearly defined, but everything in the foreground was a murky play of shadows layered on top of other shadows.

Then one of these shadows moved again and, for the briefest moment, stood in sharp relief against the horizon.

It was a human shape.

It was very still. Peter felt sure that it was directly facing the house. He realized that as there were no lights on in the house, whoever was out there could not see him. They probably assumed that everyone was still asleep.

Peter froze, unsure what to do. Nobody was out walking at that hour in the winter, and certainly not at the eastern edge of their property. There was no good explanation for this. Should he go out and find out what was going on? Probably. He couldn't just ignore it. The dead body in Tom's barn notwithstanding, New Selfoss could in no way be considered a dangerous place. There would be an innocent explanation. He just could not at the moment imagine what it might be. In the dark, his hand found his phone, but he didn't make a call.

Later he would think back to that moment's hesitation with regret. So much could have been different. A life might have been saved.

Before Peter could get to the door, he heard an engine, probably a truck. Swivelling to the front window he saw two red tail lights disappear down the road. The house was on a dead end, so it couldn't be through traffic. It had to be the mystery visitor.

Peter decided not to tell Laura for the time being.

CHAPTER
Four

It was a Wednesday and a full day in the clinic with no farm calls. Normally this meant more of a leisurely departure from home, but Peter wanted to get to the clinic early to read up on a case that had been bothering him. He could do that at home, but he liked to keep the separation between home and work as clean and sharp as possible.

The clinic was a pleasant 20-minute walk away, downhill going there, uphill going home. There had been an option to build their house adjacent to the clinic, but again, that separation was important to him and Laura. He preferred to walk, but in an emergency, he could be there in three minutes in his truck. The staff had long since stopped being surprised at the weather he walked in, but he still got comments from clients who saw him come in, looking like an Arctic explorer. His standard reply when he was queried about his sanity was to quote the British adventurer Ranulph Fiennes: "There is no such thing as bad weather; there are only bad clothing choices." It's not clear whether that answer always settled the question regarding his sanity, but everyone smiled and chuckled good-naturedly anyway.

That day he came in before any of the staff and immediately headed to his desk in the small doctor's office, beyond the far side of the waiting room. As he walked through the waiting room, he passed the elaborately framed portrait of his predecessor, Dr. Irwin McSorley, which hung on a feature wall beside the reception desk. Peter had never met the man, but he felt a kinship to him and often gave the picture a little nod as he went by. The clinic had originally been built by the Manitoba government in 1965 to encourage a veterinarian to set up practice in New Selfoss. Up until then the district had been served by vets in Selkirk and Beausejour, but New Selfoss town council was adamant that their town deserved its own veterinarian and lobbied the province intensively. Gimli, they argued, a smaller and less important town, had had their own veterinarian since 1958! Not only was animal health at stake, but civic pride. Whatever their rival across the lake had, New Selfoss had to have too. It not only had to have it, but it had to have a better, more modern version of it. Consequently, when New Selfoss Veterinary Services opened with the requisite ribbon-cutting ceremony on a stormy July day in 1965, it was the most state-of-the-art practice in Manitoba, complete with x-ray equipment, gas anesthesia, an in-house laboratory and a waiting room that would not have been out of place at a high-end professional office in Manhattan, with its wood panelling, Danish modern teak chairs and tasteful abstract art (Klee and Kandinsky). Dr. Irwin McSorley, a well-respected and experienced veterinarian, was recruited from Ontario and a new era in animal health care began.

McSorley rapidly became a local legend, pulling off feats of endurance, selflessness, diagnostic savvy and therapeutic innovation that by 1970 had tagged him with the nickname McSupervet. The community was bereft when he died suddenly of a burst aortic aneurysm in the middle of a C-section on a heifer in 2004. "Are you resting, Doc?" the farmer had asked to his everlasting regret. Nobody was able to imagine New Selfoss Veterinary Services without McSupervet. Various associate veterinarians had come and gone over the years, but it was mostly a one-man show, and now that one man was gone. It was into this environment that Peter had stepped. He was the un-McSorley. Where his predecessor had been passionate and voluble, Peter was reserved and rational. However, he also had the advantage of being clad in rhinoceros hide. The first few years of harsh judgment from the McSupervet fan base pinged off of him like so many pebbles. But then very slowly, client by client, people began to learn to appreciate what Peter brought to the practice. And equally slowly, the legend of McSupervet began to fade as it became increasingly clear in whispered acknowledgements that McSorley had in fact been a bit of a quack. An amiable, hard-working quack, but a quack nonetheless who had coasted on his early successes and his backslapping hi-how-are-ya charm.

Objectively seen, Peter's desk was actually almost as messy as Kevin's, but to Peter's eye there was a logic to it, albeit a particular and obscure logic. Non-priority management paperwork was at the far left, priority management paperwork was at the near left, priority patient-related paperwork was at the near right and non-priority to the far right. The laptop computer sat in the middle and the telephone behind the patient-related paperwork. The corkboard above his desk was festooned with patient photos, photos of Laura, Pippin, Merry and Gandalf, and a few key do-not-forget memos. Peter woke up his computer and set about logging into the Veterinary Information Network to refresh his memory regarding the ins and outs of high calcium levels in old cats. He remembered many technical facts for life on having learned them once, but certain specific facts felt Teflon coated and needed to be relearned each time he tried to recall them.

Before he knew it the clinic was open, and he was being told that the first appointment was ready. Hypercalcemia had been a wormhole into which 45 minutes disappeared as if they had been 45 seconds. This first appointment was Ranger Valgardson, a black lab with itchy skin, and the second was Tammy Edwards's two cats, Maxi and Mini, for their vaccinations. So far, so routine.

The third appointment was less routine. Elton Marwick was an elderly gentleman who did not have a pet, but who Peter recognized from the coffee shop and the pub. They had been introduced by a mutual friend once and had exchanged a few friendly words. Mr. Marwick had immense, unruly eyebrows, like grey caterpillars who had been given electric shocks, and as far as Peter could tell, he always wore a tweed flat cap and a natty herringbone blazer. He apologized several times for taking up Peter's valuable time, but he wanted his help in figuring out who had broken into his garden shed last week and why they had done so. The police weren't interested as nothing was stolen, but Mr. Marwick was unnerved. He played darts at The Flying Beaver with Tom, Chris Olson and Ken Finnbogason and they had suggested that Peter had an eye for details others missed and a taste for unusual puzzles. Peter said he'd come and have a look in the next few days.

The fourth appointment was the most interesting. It was Michelle Nyquist, Tom's first ex-wife. He had three ex-wives, although that sounds worse than it was. The second ex was ex because she died in a hunting accident, and the third, Angie, left him and Tom was widely regarded as the wronged party. Michelle owned a trio of enormous, regal Russian wolfhounds. The effect was striking when she walked with them because she was a short and rather round woman — stout, polite people said — so the dogs looked like a phalanx of bodyguards, tall enough to mostly shield her from view. When she stepped out from among them, she made a strong impression all on her own as well. She was generally considered the best-dressed woman in New Selfoss, which was admittedly a fairly low bar, but even by urban standards she was stylish and well put together. She made up for her unfashionably squat and rotund genetic endowments with her more fashionable cash endowments as heiress to a sweatshop fortune. Predictably rumour had it that Tom had married her for her money, but this didn't make sense to Peter as he knew that Tom had happily signed a pre-nup and then when his eye landed on Sandra, the late ex number two, he was as quick to leave the marriage as he had been to enter it. Michelle, Tom, Peter and Laura had been firm friends as couples for a while. Laura's estimation of Tom declined substantially after he left Michelle for Sandra. Michelle could be annoying, but loyalty was one of Laura's key values.

Michelle only had Parker, the smallest of her behemoths, with her that day. He had been feeling a bit off since yesterday afternoon. Michelle would be at Peter's door if any of her boys so much as sighed too loudly. While he examined the dog, she said, "So, I hear you were at Tom's place yesterday when the barn blew up?"

"Mm-hmm." Peter was trying to listen to Parker's heart with the stethoscope, so he did not want to encourage conversation. Why people instinctively seemed to start talking right then of all times was a mystery to him. Maybe it was because they couldn't tolerate the silence.

"Oh, sorry. I'll let you finish that." She patted Parker on the head while Peter completed the auscultation.

"You were saying?" he said as he straightened up.

"Just that I heard you were at Tom's yesterday. You saw the fire?"

"Yes, I did. It was quite something." Peter went on to explain hearing the explosion and seeing the smoke while driving, and then what he saw when he arrived at the farm.

"Wow. Those poor pigs."

"My thoughts exactly." Peter suppressed the temptation to share the news that it was not only pigs that suffered and died. It was not public knowledge yet.

"Do you know what I heard today?"

A rhetorical question. Peter hated rhetorical questions, but he sat down on his stool and asked, "No, what did you hear?"

"Apparently Tom's been going around town saying that eco-terrorists blew up the barn!"

"Eco-terrorists? In New Selfoss?"

"Well not exactly eco-terrorists I suppose, but direct-action animal rights types."

"Oh? Like who?"

"I guess there's a group with a branch in Winnipeg called the Global Animal Defence Army. GADA. They've been sending Tom threatening emails for a few months now." Parker looked mournful at being ignored during all this human blah blah blah. Peter reached over to the treat jar and pulled a large freeze-dried liver treat out for him.

"But why Tom? His pigs are, relatively speaking, really well looked after. I get being opposed to industrial agriculture, but that's not him. They should target those barns with 1,200 hogs at the Poplar Rose Colony."

"The emails weren't about the pigs. They were about his bear hunt sideline."

Tom Pearson liked to think of himself as a Renaissance man and he dabbled in a wide range of businesses and hobbies. Michelle was referring to the guiding he did for rich Americans, Europeans and Asians during the spring and fall black bear hunting seasons. He apparently had quite a reputation in that world and had been written up in a couple of big-game hunting magazines.

"But why blow up pigs to save bears? Or at all if you're an animal rights person? It makes no sense." Peter furrowed his brow and gave Parker a scratch behind his ear.

"Tom is saying that they planned to release the pigs as a kind of two-for-one action. You know, punish him for his bear hunting and save some pigs at the same time. He's saying that they must have accidentally caused an explosion. Maybe dropping a spliff in the manure pit or something."

"What? That makes even less sense. Release pigs in January? Aiming marijuana joints into sewage lagoons? Tom's a smart guy. He must be distressed and not thinking straight to come up with a wacky theory like that." Although as he said it, Peter considered the jawbone. Accidental self-immolation by a GADA member? But why didn't they flee? Maybe first knocked unconscious by the explosion like Kevin suggested?

"You think Tom's smart?" Michelle interrupted his reverie. "I know you guys are friends and maybe, in some ways, he is smart, but he's also an asshole. He knows that people are going to think he did it for the insurance money. I, for one, sure think that's what happened. He's up to his eyeballs in debt. He'd say and do anything to deflect attention."

"He loved those pigs," Peter countered, unable to imagine Tom deliberately doing harm to them. Well, except at slaughter time.

Michelle snorted. "Tom loves Tom. That's it."

Peter wasn't always the best at reading people or stickhandling his way through delicate social situations, but he did know it was best to move on from this conversation. He nodded to Michelle and then turned to his patient, "Hey Parker, how about another treat and then we'll have a peek in your ears?"

CHAPTER
Five

Peter loved his hometown. He loved the fact that New Selfoss was a different sort of town right from the beginning. When Mount Askja erupted in Iceland in 1875, it caused widespread famine and pushed a quarter of the population of the little country to emigrate across the Atlantic. Sigtryggur Jonasson had arrived three years earlier and persuaded a large number of these refugees to settle on the west shore of Lake Winnipeg, establishing the semi-autonomous Republic of New Iceland, centred on the town of Gimli. "Gimli" is the Icelandic word for paradise. Soon 2,000 Icelanders were living there. But it was not paradise. The harshest winter in memory was followed by a spring and summer that featured Old Testament plagues of noxious insects. Moreover, it was a deeply religious place and that began to cause some settlers to chafe. God had abandoned them in Iceland and now God was abandoning them in Canada. In the eyes of these settlers, God was either unworthy of worship or the product of the largest scam in human history. The self-appointed leader among these skeptics was Arne Sigurdsson. Arne had a vision of an atheistic utopia. Almost 150 years later, this still had resonance for Peter. He knew the story by heart.

If you can say "messianic atheist" without it sounding like an oxymoron, then that's who Arne Sigurdsson was. Standing at a roughly sawn-and-nailed pine podium on the beach at Gimli, framed by wind-ravaged Lake Winnipeg, with his long, dirty-blond hair flying, in his trademark booming voice Sigurdsson quoted Percy Bysshe Shelley, Arthur Schopenhauer, Friedrich Nietzsche and other prominent 19th-century atheists, and lampooned the dour local Lutheran ministers who had, in his considered opinion, only offered feeble prayers against the eruption of Mount Askja, and yet more feeble prayers against the smallpox epidemic, which had raged through New Iceland the previous winter. He swatted a blackfly and held it up in the air.

"Can those god-botherers pray these pests away? No! Of course, they cannot! They will see us suffer every horseman of the apocalypse! Each time they say that it is God's will! Each time they say that he moves in mysterious ways! It is time for the mystery to end! Religion is the dark mysterious night of the past! Science is the light and truth filled day of the future!" Arne thundered. "In this place we will continue to suffer under the leadership of men from that darkest past! I have seen the future, the brightly lit future, the brightly lit scientific future, and it is yonder!" He turned dramatically on his heel and pointed directly across the vast lake. On a clear sunny day, the far shore would have been just visible across the narrow south basin, but it was windy and grey, so his audience of followers and curious passersby strained their eyes and only saw a jagged horizon of convulsing green-brown water.

Fortunately for Sigurdsson's vision, living conditions were truly miserable in Gimli, even if far less of the blame could be laid at the feet of the church than he proclaimed. An exodus was already beginning, mostly to Winnipeg, or south of the 49th Parallel to the Dakota Territory, but a few dozen hopeful families were persuaded to follow Sigurdsson around to the far side of the lake. He had selected a peninsula jutting north between the wide estuary of the Winnipeg River to the east and the open lake to the west.

At first it was just called Selfoss, after Sigurdsson's Icelandic hometown. He argued that it was perfect because Selfoss means "seal waterfall" and the nearby Winnipeg River had many otters, which were similar to seals, and had many rapids, which were similar to waterfalls. The settlers were too tired and hungry to disagree, or so goes the story today. The New was added when Selfoss moved to higher ground after three consecutive years of terrible spring flooding. It also signified new leadership, as Sigurdsson was found to have an unacceptable interest in young girls and was driven out of the settlement. He eventually died in the Yukon, having been swept up in the Klondike gold rush. As with so many people who are able to maintain a cordon sanitaire between delight for the art and disgust for the artist, the good burghers of New Selfoss remained committed to Arne Sigurdsson's modern atheistic and science-oriented principles. In fact, its first church didn't open until 2008, and then only after a divisive referendum and the threat of an imminent Charter of Rights and Freedoms challenge.

Eventually the Icelanders were joined by a large contingent of Finns who came to work in the forestry industry and then slowly, as the town grew more prosperous and needed to attract skilled labour, people from almost every fragment of the Canadian ethnic mosaic settled there, but Icelandic-Canadians remained in a slender majority, and as *Maclean's* magazine had recognized, the town remained a unique and eccentric place. It was never clear whether the double meaning of the New Selfoss motto, "Curious, By Nature," was an intentional, winking acknowledgement of that or not.

On Thursday morning Peter drove past that first church, a small Northern Lights Pentecostal chapel, on his way to Rita's Coffee

Shop. He only managed a visit there every couple of weeks or so when he didn't have any early morning calls. He hoped that Tom would be there so that he could offer his sympathies regarding the loss of his pigs and his barn. As a rule, Tom was always there with Brian and Brian, but perhaps recent events had upset his schedule.

Peter turned from Pasteur Avenue onto First Street and parked in front of Olaf's Hair and Nail Salon because it wasn't open yet and the parking at Rita's was always inadequate during the morning coffee rush. Rumour had it that Tim Hortons was eyeing a location on the edge of town, beside the Pentecostals, as it happened, but there was strong opposition in town. Everyone could see that New Selfoss was gradually becoming like every other Manitoba small town, but that didn't mean they had to like it. One thing that wouldn't change, though, is how narrow the streets were compared to most similar towns, so Peter looked carefully before swinging his door open and unpacking his long legs, long arms and long back. He had once lost a door and caused grievous damage to the front of Rachel Berkowski's Chevy Cavalier by not checking first.

Rita's was packed as expected, and Tom was there, in his customary booth in the far corner, his tightly curled grey hair visible over the edge of the divider. The taller of the two Brians was facing toward the door and spotted Peter. He smiled and waved him over. This Brian, Brian Palmer, was fully bald and sported a precisely trimmed Van Dyke goatee. He was the local dentist and liked to think that he and Peter had a special kinship as the types of doctors who some people thought of as somehow lesser than MDs, but the truth was that Peter did not like him. There was always something very slightly oleaginous in his manner of speaking and he always leaned in a little too close for Peter's liking, fumigating him in excessively minty breath odour. But Tom and Brian were good friends, so Peter tolerated him. Brian was Tom's hunting and fishing buddy, two activities Peter fastidiously avoided. Peter enjoyed Tom's descriptions of Brian's gear, though, as he always bought the most fashionable and most expensive versions. His fish finder did everything but place the hook in the fish's mouth and his hunting clothing made him look like he was modeling for the cover of *Field & Stream*. Tom joked he could practically still see the price tags on the stuff. He also ribbed Brian that he was, as they say in Texas, "all hat and no horse." But when Brian wasn't around to hear him, Tom admitted to Peter that he was actually a really good shot.

The other Brian, Brian Windham, the town's mayor and the first non-Icelander to hold the position, had apparently already left. He often often received calls which compelled him to bolt. Or perhaps he hadn't come this morning.

Peter slid into the booth beside Brian, opposite Tom. "Hey Tom, how are you holding up?"

Tom looked awful. His normally jovial, round face was blotchy and saggy, like a partially deflated pink soccer ball, and his unwashed black curls stuck out at odd angles. He was wearing a torn black Guns N' Roses concert sweatshirt, stretched tight over his paunch, and grey track pants.

"I'm doing OK, thanks." Tom smiled, but it looked forced.

"I hear you think it was the animal liberationists?" Peter was not one to beat around the bush or make small talk.

"Yeah, that's the best I can figure out."

"It seems bizarre, though. I mean, planning to release pigs in January? What kind of liberation is that?"

"These aren't genius-level people," Brian chimed in.

"But still, isn't it a stretch?" Peter countered. He wondered whether either of them knew what he knew about the bones.

"Maybe, but it's less of a stretch than the other rumour going around, that I did it for the insurance!" Tom sounded bitter. "I haven't updated my policy in years. The payout isn't going to come anywhere close to covering the value of those pigs. As you know, some were rare heritage breeds. Priscilla, that Red Wattle sow, alone was worth three or four grand! And with any suspicion that I was involved it'll be years before they pay, if ever. I'm screwed, man, no matter how this shakes out."

"No, no, I believe you. I can't imagine you doing this. But animal rights warriors don't make sense to me either." Peter paused to catch the waitress's attention and order a coffee and a bran muffin. "I'm curious, though. A fire is one thing, but the explosion is another. Why did it blow up?"

"I have no idea, man. That's why I'm thinking a terror or sabotage angle. Those GADA people have been threatening me with some sort of action for almost a year now. You should see some of the emails! Just nuts!"

Brian nodded in a fashion that indicated he had seen the emails and agreed that they were just nuts.

Peter pursed his lips and shook his head. "Well, regardless, what a devastating loss."

"Devastating is right," Brian said. "Dan, Dave and I couldn't save anything. It went up like a stack of newspapers at a blowtorch party. Bet those nutjobs dowsed the place in gas."

"Well, the cops will figure that out pretty quickly. But seriously Tom, I'm so sorry."

"Thanks. Yeah, I don't know what I'm going to do now. Maybe rebuild, but maybe just pack up and move on. Maybe life is telling me something. First the divorce with Angie and now this. I don't know."

"Don't make any rash decisions yet. I'm here for you, Tom. Whatever I can do to help, just ask."

"Ha, well, if you want to use your Sherlock routine to find out who did it or how it happened, I'd owe you big time!" The way Tom laughed made it clear that he was joking. Brian joined in the laughter and slapped Peter on the shoulder.

Peter laughed too, but he knew he'd be thinking about what happened at the barn until there was an answer.

CHAPTER
Six

It was a quiet morning and the first farm visit wasn't until 11, so Peter decided to call Elton Marwick and see if he was home and wanted him to pop by to have a look at that shed. He was indeed home and he was delighted that Peter was available so quickly. Although Marwick didn't have any animals, Peter knew his place well as it was on the same road as Tom's and Bill Chernov's farms. In fact he had driven by it on Tuesday morning when he went to Bill's after the barn blew up. Peter swung by the house to pick Pippin up on the way, as he hadn't been out much yet that day.

Elton Marwick was a widower and lived alone. He had worked as an engineer with Manitoba Hydro and used to come up to New Selfoss in the summer as a cottager, but after he retired, he sold his house in the city and converted the cottage into a year-round residence.

It was easy to see that Elton Marwick's place had once been a seasonal cottage and it was also easy to see, even in January, that he was a devoted gardener. The landscaping was extraordinary, and the yard was filled with all manner of whimsical statues of gnomes and forest creatures, arranged around an eclectic array of miniature buildings such as windmills, grain elevators, bridges, a train station and even a Mughal palace. It was like a mini-golf course without the mini-golf. At the far end was an enormous vegetable garden and orchard. Peter was able to identify it as such even though it was deepest winter because the garden was enclosed by deer-proof fencing and its entrance was marked by a wooden archway with images of vegetables and fruits carved into it and painted bright colours.

"Thank you so much for coming, Dr. Bannerman. And for bringing your friend." Even after 40 years in Canada, his voice betrayed the hint of an educated British accent, perhaps not quite Oxbridge or BBC, but close.

"You're welcome, and call me Peter, please."

"Certainly, Peter, and please call me Elton. I used to have a dog quite similar to this one. Reg was his name. I still miss him." He bent down to pat Pippin. "How old is this fine fellow? And what's his name?"

"This is Pippin and he turned three in November."

"What sort of a dog is he?"

"Well, we're not entirely sure, but Lab and husky and collie are definitely in there." Peter smiled at Pippin, who was enjoying Elton's attention. "He's a res dog from up at Dragonfly Lake."

"Ah, a rescue?"

"I wouldn't say that. The family who owned his mom were doing a good job looking after the pups, but there were just too many of them and not enough homes up there."

"Well, he's a lovely dog regardless." Elton straightened back up and asked, "Can I offer you tea or coffee, or shall we go directly to the shed? I don't want to waste your time."

"I'm fully caffeinated, thank you. Yes, let's see the shed."

The old man led Peter and Pippin around behind the house, past a clump of gnomes dressed as miners, and out to the edge of the garden, where it backed onto the pine forest. It was a relatively mild day, so it was not at all uncomfortable to stand outside and look at the shed while Elton explained what had happened. Peter let Pippin off his leash, and he proceeded to go and systematically sniff each and every gnome, structure and ornament, tail happily wagging like a metronome, while Marwick explained what had happened.

"On Monday I came back here to get an extension cord because I bought some new lights for the castle." Peter hadn't seen a castle yet, but he could imagine. "It all looked perfectly normal on the outside, but when I opened the shed, imagine my surprise when I saw that several items had been moved."

"Oh?" Peter raised an eyebrow.

"Yes, I have a system. Tools on the left and gardening supplies such as pots and soil and such on the right and my freezer overflow on the shelves straight ahead. That's only in the winter, of course. As you might guess, I have no need of the gardening supplies at this time of year, so I haven't touched the right side of the shed since October. Yet the pots were all jumbled up."

"Hmm, that is odd. Let's have a look."

Elton fiddled with the lock for a moment and then opened the double swinging doors. He reached around to the right and flicked on a light, revealing a hardware-store-catalogue-photo level of neatness and organization throughout the space. The tools on the left wall were hung with precision, sorted by size and type, and the shelves on the far wall were lined with neatly labelled Mason jars, evidently containing much of the bounty of his garden. Large Rubbermaid bins were stacked underneath these shelves, presumably containing more frozen produce. Even the gardening supplies on the right were in good order, except in the far corner where three stacks of pots were toppled over. *Not exactly 'all jumbled up,'* Peter thought, *but certainly not in keeping with the meticulous order manifest throughout the rest of the shed.*

"You don't think it was just an animal?" Peter ventured.

"Dr. Bann . . . Peter, as a veterinary surgeon, you should tell me what animal is tiny enough to sneak in here, yet also strong enough to knock these pots over? Or perhaps smart enough to foil the lock and then open and close the door behind them?" he said with a friendly chuckle.

Peter laughed. "Yes, I suppose you have me there!" Then he bent down and looked at the pots more carefully. They were the standard russet-coloured terracotta ones. They had been nested one in another and were quite heavy. No, no animal that would be able to get inside the shed could do this.

How curious.

"And absolutely nothing was taken?"

"Nothing."

"And the lock? Was it picked or broken?"

"Picked, I suppose, but it was cheap one, so I do not imagine that it was much of a challenge." Elton sounded mournful.

Peter stood up and crossed his arms, considering the scene carefully. Scenarios flashed across his mind like a slideshow at the highest speed setting. Each one was more absurd than the last. He examined every aspect of the shed thoroughly and then the area outside of it in a carefully paced, ever-expanding spiral. When he reached the edge of the yard he stopped. Nothing. There was nothing he could reasonably call a clue. No footprints, no dropped candy wrappers, no cigarette butts. Not even a stray thread or hair, goddamn it.

This was absurd.

What was he playing at? He should be lancing cat abscesses and curing dogs of mange, not marching in circles in some batty old Englishman's yard, pretending to be a "detective."

Elton had been watching quietly. When Peter stopped, he asked, "Do have any ideas?"

"No. I'm afraid not, but I'll take some pictures and I'll think about it."

"That's fine, thank you. I so appreciate you coming at all. It's just such an unsettling feeling to know that a stranger has been through your things, even if they are just garden things."

"I understand that. It would bother me too. It's an odd thing to have happen for sure."

Peter called Pippin back from his explorations and then took a few photos with his phone before the two of them drove back to town.

Friday and Saturday went by quickly. Peter did everything he could to stop thinking about Tom or Elton. He plainly didn't know what he was doing in either situation. This was an unfamiliar and entirely unpleasant feeling. Peter was used to being good at whatever he put his mind to, but then he hadn't strayed this far from his areas of expertise very often before. No, it was time to think about puppies and kittens and vaccines and x-rays and all that again, with room on the side for history, nature, geography, fantasy literature and a few other passions, of course. Leave the exploding barns and the toppling pots to their respective experts, whoever they might be.

Elton should have been easy to dismiss from his mind, but there was an aspect to the situation that troubled him in a vague way. He could sense the shape of this disquiet like something moving through the fog, but he couldn't put a name to it. The best he could do was park this in the corner of his mind and try to ignore it. And as for Tom, he really did want to help him, but how? There was no clear way he could see, but here also, truly forgetting about it would be difficult, as Kevin was coming over for Sunday dinner. Peter planned to make a serious effort to steer the conversation away from the barn fire. Perhaps they could talk about the weather, or vacation plans, or Kevin's breakup with his boyfriend, Tyler.

That effort was effective for two, maybe three minutes. Kevin had no sooner sat down and accepted his beer when he said, "Pete, you won't believe this, but guess what forensics found in that barn?"

Laura, who had just sat down in the living room with them and was pouring herself a beer, shot Kevin a sharp glance.

"It's OK, Sis, we've got a press conference scheduled at nine tomorrow morning. It'll all be out in public and I know you and Pete aren't going to sink my career by gossiping, right?" He winked and then gave a big belly laugh, before taking a long sip from his beer. "So . . . no guesses?"

Peter and Laura shook their heads.

"Wimps." Kevin laughed again. "Well as much as I hate to admit it, it turns out you were right, Pete. That partition was really solid and probably protected Jawbone from the blast. He didn't run to escape the fire because he was already dead before the explosion."

Kevin paused and waited for a reaction. Peter and Laura both just stared at him, expressionless, so he went on. "They found the rest of him. At least most of the rest of him. Extreme heat can really mess up bones and make them crack, break or even pop, but those forensics guys are jigsaw-puzzle ninjas. It took a while, but they got the skull put back together and it tells a story. The jawbone connects to the skull bone and the skull bone turns out to have a neat round bullet hole between the eyes and a big ol' jagged one in the back."

"What!?" Laura exclaimed. Peter looked ashen.

"Yup. Forensics figures a hunting rifle from close range. There's a scorched rifle barrel, a trigger and a few other harder metal bits nearby. That fire was incredibly hot. They figure the killer set a bomb after the murder to destroy the evidence. Body and weapon kaboom at the same time. Slick."

Peter and Laura continued to just stare at Kevin, their mouths partly open.

Kevin pursed his lips and pressed on. "Maybe it's a coincidence, but it reminds me of that John Doe that turned up in the lagoon at Grand Beach with a bullet hole in his head last spring. That case is still open. And we have had an uptick in missing persons in the region. We're starting to consider the possibility that we may be dealing with a serial killer."

Kevin looked at his lap briefly and ran his fingers through his hair before continuing, "You're not going to want to hear this, but Tom's back at the station now, being held for further questioning. I'm not sure yet, but there might be charges tomorrow." Seeing Peter's face, he added, "Sorry, Pete."

But Peter's very first thought wasn't about Tom. It was about the figure he'd seen in their own yard at dawn on Wednesday.

CHAPTER
Seven

A fter Kevin left, Peter watched Laura stoke the fire, add a log and sit back in the old leather club chair opposite Peter's favourite threadbare green brocade armchair. She reached into the cloth bag beside her and pulled out her knitting. She had gotten as far as the "p" in "captain." She double-checked the pattern, sorted the wool, straightened her needles and began.

"I'm going to take Pippin out. It'll help clear my head."

"OK, once 'captain' is done, I'm going to start on the logo," she said without looking up.

Peter could see that the sweater was almost half finished now. "I've Giv'n Her All She's Got Captain, An' I Canna Give Her No More" was one of her most popular *Star Trek* sweaters. Hogwarts house scarves and toques sold well too, as did Jedi capes. She also did a brisk trade in *Lord of the Rings*–themed garments, such as Aragorn's travelling cloak and sweaters that Galadriel would conceivably wear if it ever got cold in Lothlorien. Using beautiful local wool that had a story behind it, combined with the deep geek designs, had been the secret recipe to her success. Orders now came in from as far away as Florida and Finland, and one even from Japan the other day.

"I'll just be 15 minutes."

Laura looked up and smiled at her husband. They both knew that for Peter, 15 meant 15, not 14 or 16.

Sure enough, almost exactly 15 minutes later the back door opened, followed by the sounds of Peter rummaging for an old towel to wipe off Pippin's feet. While she would freely admit that her husband had a number of irritating quirks, the quirk of his spooky reliability and predictability was something she found comforting. She had told him once that in a world beset by chaos and turmoil, watching him was like watching a ship steaming on an arrow-straight course through an anarchic ocean. You wanted to be on that ship, she said. Its destination was secondary to the safety and comfort it represented.

"How was your walk?" she called to him, half over her shoulder.

"Good. It's pretty cold, but there's no wind, and the sky is beautiful." Peter was walking into the living room as he said this, rubbing his hands together vigorously in an exaggerated motion. "Should have worn the big mitts, though!" Peter sat down in his chair and then immediately got up again. "I'm going to make some tea. Do you want any?"

"Sure, please. Earl Grey decaf." Laura's voice was neutral and quiet, and he wondered if she were trying to defuse his obvious agitation. Peter was not normally this hyper. His unnatural calmness was another one of his quirks. Usually a positive one. The conversation with Kevin had unsettled him and unfortunately the walk hadn't helped much.

Peter returned with the mugs — hers the shape of an owl's head and his a plain black one, the CBC mug being only for mornings — and they sat and sipped in silence for a few minutes, looking at the fire. Laura resumed knitting and Peter rubbed Pippin's tummy with his foot.

"I still think Kevin's wrong, you know," Peter said quietly, still looking at the fire.

"I didn't think you'd change your mind," she answered, not looking up.

"Setting aside the absurdity of the serial killer suggestion for a moment, for this specific murder they'll never find any parts of that bomb timer they're looking for, because there wasn't one. It's too far-fetched. Tom's smart, but he's not technically sophisticated enough to figure out how to set up a proper timer and block up all the manure pit vents to let the gas build up. Too complicated and too risky. They're way out on a limb with this theory."

"You didn't give Kevin an alternative theory, though. Do you have one?" Laura said softly, setting her knitting on her lap.

"I don't know yet. There are a lot of variables to consider. Once we know who the victim is, then the range of possibilities will narrow considerably. For now, though, it's clear to me that the highest probability explanation is that this was a professional hit or a gang killing, and the killer or killers thought they'd be clever by disguising it as a hog barn manure pit explosion."

"But how clever is that? Wouldn't they realize that the body would still eventually be found? Wouldn't it be much easier to just burn it in a barrel, or something like that, if they wanted to eliminate the body?" Peter knew that Laura enjoyed being his foil and challenging his ideas, and over time he came to appreciate that as well. When they were first dating, he found it irritating, but now it was indispensable to him, much as every good writer needs a good editor.

Peter smiled. "Keep in mind that cleverness exists at many levels. The killer was clever enough to know that an explosion combined with a high-temperature fire would destroy more of the evidence than a simple gangland burning-barrel body disposal, but not clever enough to realize that forensics could still piece things together from the fragments left behind."

"And what about the weapon? They seem pretty confident that it was that wrecked rifle, and you know Tom has several similar rifles. Don't gangsters and hitmen use handguns?"

"In theory, most of the time, sure, but they'll use whatever they have access to and whatever works. It's possible that they were even a higher level of clever and knew enough about Tom that using a thirty-aught-six would throw suspicion on him and off them."

"Hmm, interesting. I hadn't thought about that." Laura took a long sip from her tea. "So, you think that after Tom left for Rita's early Tuesday morning someone drove onto the property, possibly with a kidnapped victim trussed up, and then shot him in the barn, blew the barn up and took off?"

"More or less, yes."

"Isn't that as much of a stretch as Kevin's theory? I mean, why Tom's barn specifically? And how would someone know to come exactly then? And be able to set off an explosion without being injured themselves? Wouldn't they need a timer too?"

"Tom keeps an extremely regular schedule. Almost more than me! He's at Rita's every morning when she opens at seven and he never leaves before eight-thirty. That gives someone an hour and a half, at least. And everyone around here knows that, so it wouldn't be difficult for someone to find that out."

Laura nodded while Peter was speaking. He watched as she stroked Merry, who had hopped up on top of the knitting on her lap.

"And as far as the timer goes," Peter went on, "they just would have needed a length of that pyrotechnic safety fuse cord that the fireworks shops sell. That'd give them enough time to get away. For Tom, on the other hand, to set off an explosion an hour and a half after he left the farm would require a real timer, not just a long fuse."

"Right, I see what you mean. But Peter, doesn't one of your favourite principles apply? Ockham's razor? According to that, isn't the simplest explanation usually the right one? And in this case, given that the murder was in Tom's barn using a type of weapon

Tom is known to have . . ." She trailed off when Peter glared at her. He knew that she didn't understand the type of person Tom was or, for that matter, his friendship with him.

Peter set his mug down on a side table and leaned slightly forward, which prompted Pippin to look up at him. "No, I disagree. Neither hypothesis is simple. The complexity in mine is merely different, more exotic-sounding perhaps, but no less probable. William of Ockham more specifically said that the explanation that involves making the fewest assumptions is probably the correct one. Think about how many assumptions Kevin is making. Tom has no known motive to kill anyone, no known history of violence or mental illness, no known method of triggering an explosion in his absence, no known reason to do any of this at the cost of his pigs and his barn. There are at least as many, if not more assumptions required to believe Kevin's version. In my proposed version, I'm just assuming that a professional wanted someone dead and saw a good, if admittedly unorthodox, disposal opportunity in Tom's barn." He sat back again and resumed scratching Pippin's belly with his foot.

"Hmm, I still don't know. It just doesn't feel right, but then I guess no explanation does. I can't picture Tom shooting someone in the face either. Mind you, I can picture a few people doing it to him . . . ha-ha!"

Peter laughed along with her. It was true, Tom may have had lots of friends, but he was also the kind of person who rubbed at least as many people the wrong way too. Being around him meant having to tolerate a lot of high-energy discussion about schemes and ideas and ambitions. Tom was a great talker and quite entertaining as one, but he was not a good listener and consequently perhaps not the most empathic of people. But this hardly seemed relevant to the matter at hand.

"And there are other theories that hold more water than Tom being a serial killer. The animal liberationist theory no longer works because of the murder — they may be wacko but they're not killers — but how about a missing person suicide? What if, for example, John Doe is a coincidence and Jawbone is the missing Leonard Alexander? Could be suicide or accident."

"Really?"

"OK, not super plausible, but regardless, I'm sure I can prove Tom's innocent," Peter said and then picked up a book that was on his armrest — *Alone on the Ice: The Greatest Survival Story in the History of Exploration* — and opened it in a way that indicated that he felt the conversation had run its course. At the edge of his consciousness was the uncomfortable thought that he was more motivated by loyalty than logic. They weren't even that close anymore, but Tom had been Peter's childhood defender against bullies. Loyalty was a powerful force in Peter's life. This thought hovered like an unwanted guest at the threshold of a room. Peter closed the door.

Laura took a deep breath as if weighing whether to speak or not before she finally said, "Peter, you're a veterinarian, not a detective, and definitely not a police officer. I know Tom's your friend and you want to help him, but to poke around a murder case? Are you serious? It's fine to speculate here over our tea, but to actually set out to prove something? Please leave it to Kevin and his crew. Please."

"Kevin and his crew?" Peter snorted. "He's your brother and he's a good guy and you know I like him as a person, but no, I can tell he's convinced it's Tom and I've seen that kind of tunnel vision before. I can help. Kevin might not appreciate it right away, but he will later."

Laura sighed and looked down at her lap for a long moment before looking up again. "You know what that sounds like . . ."

Peter cut her off. "No what? What does that sound like?" His face was flushed, and he had put the book down with unnecessary force, causing the back cover to bend.

Laura ignored the interruption. "It sounds like arrogance. I love you for many things including for how smart you are, but

I don't love how you think being smart provides the answer to everything."

"What does that even mean? Does being dumb provide better answers!?" Peter snorted again, gearing up for a full-on fight.

But Laura just shook her head, gently shooed Merry off her lap and resumed her knitting. Her eyes were moist, her hands were shaking and her breathing was rapid. Peter normally pressed every point to victory, but every now and then he understood when it was wiser to back off. This was one of those times.

Laura and Peter met for the first time when they were still in high school. In Grade 10 Peter joined the Gaming Club, which met Tuesdays at lunch in the science lab, expecting that it would be populated by other pimply, awkward teen nerds like himself. In this he was correct. However, he further assumed that they would all be boys, and in this he was not correct. Laura was not merely the only girl in the club, but she was the Dungeon Master (no, not Dungeon Mistress) for the subset of gamers who wanted to play Dungeons & Dragons. The other subset played WWII-themed board games like Squad Leader and Panzer Blitz, and then there was a tiny splinter group (i.e., two kids) trying to get the others interested in setting up battles with hand-painted miniatures of Napoleonic-era soldiers, but they were dismissed as the nerd's nerds. Peter had had a few crushes so far, but this was different. Laura was a girl who was not only beautiful, but deeply cool. She seemed to consider herself above the gawky, pubescent swarm around her, as if she had by some inexplicable act of munificence deigned to bless the Gaming Club with her DM prowess, despite having unspecified better things to do elsewhere. While friendly, she did not ever deviate from her professional DM persona. Peter's attempts at small talk, desperately fishing for some sort of rapport not linked to the club, were always met with conversation-ending answers.

Q: "What's your favourite *Star Wars*?" Peter's was *The Empire Strikes Back*.

A: "I don't know. I don't like ranking things."

Q: "Do you like Super Big Gulps?" Hoping that this would lead to an opportunity to go to 7-Eleven together.

A: "Nope."

Q: "Great weather out today, eh?" He knew that weather was a lame gambit, but he was becoming desperate.

A: "I suppose. I didn't really notice, though."

And so it went. The D&D sessions were great fun, and Peter continued to hope that this mysterious, magical, red-haired creature would, through some as yet unimaginable process, become his girlfriend.

He was right. She did become his girlfriend, and the process was indeed unimaginable. Laura did not return to the Gaming Club in Grade 11 or 12, and they had no classes together, so he only saw her in the hallways. She would say hello in return when he greeted her, and sometimes she would smile at him, but that was the extent of the interaction. Peter's hope for something more sputtered like a guttering candle and then was extinguished completely when he saw her in the park, walking hand in hand with Blaine Fast. Stupid Blaine Fast. Stupid cool, not-gangly, not-geeky Blaine Fast. Clearly, they were going to get married and have many unnaturally good-looking children together. Clearly. Peter was determined to work on not caring.

During the two years of pre-veterinary courses at the University of Manitoba, he did manage to care less and less until he almost, but not quite, forgot about Laura. Veterinary college was in Saskatoon, so in the fall of 2001 Peter packed up his rusted-out brown Toyota Corolla and drove west. He had only been on campus for two days when he saw her. She was walking across the Bowl, an oval expanse of grass between the science buildings and student services. The late August sun lit her red hair and drew his eye right away.

It couldn't be.

It couldn't be, but it was.

He ran up to her, waving his long arms, babbling something along the lines of, "Hey stranger, what brings you to these parts?" It turned out that the University of Saskatchewan was the only university in Canada offering paleobiology, which was an inter-disciplinary program straddling the intersection between biology, archeology and geology, and it further turned out that that was her particular passion, at least at the time. Who knew? Peter certainly didn't. Moreover, her parents had insisted that she study outside the province to become independent. She was still encouraged to spend her summers at home, and they hoped she would even-tually settle nearby, but it was otherwise time she explored life, had adventures — insomuch as that was feasible in Saskatoon — and fully became her own person. Kevin was already at RCMP college in Regina, two and a half hours south of Saskatoon, so that eased the transition a little. Wings were to be spread and tested, but not to any unreasonable extreme. And in the end her parents were right. There were no jobs for paleobiologists in or near New Selfoss, but she settled near home anyway because of Peter, and ended up loving knitting professionally more than she imagined she could love pollen fossils.

In 2001 Laura still didn't like Super Big Gulps, but she did like good coffee and she accepted Peter's offer to meet at a café on Broadway that he had been told about by his roommate. And on that coffee date they didn't speak about Dungeons & Dragons at all.

CHAPTER
Eight

The next few days passed in a far more routine fashion than the previous ones had. Tom had not been charged after all but was told that he may be brought back in for further questioning as the police investigation proceeded. Kevin made it clear that Tom was still the primary suspect, pending more detailed forensic analysis of the victim's remains and other unspecified clues and leads the RCMP were pursuing.

By the end of the week, it had become very cold. "Very cold" by Manitoba standards translates to a truly startling level of cold for anyone not from the region, or somewhere equivalent, such as Siberia or Antarctica. Daily highs settled in around −25°C and the wind, which blew unimpeded from icebound Hudson Bay, pushed the perceived temperature to −40°C. The radio was full of dramatic warnings about how quickly exposed flesh would freeze. But Peter's exposed flesh never froze. When he didn't have farm calls, he still walked to work. In fact, he did so with relish, only regretting the amount of time it took to put on the necessary layers. For this type of cold he broke out the Faroese wool sweater Laura had knit for him years ago. Faroese sheep must be equipped with a special super-wool to fend off the North Atlantic chill on the exposed slopes of those islands, as this was, by an order of magnitude, the warmest piece of clothing Peter owned. It was only sensible and comfortable to wear it on the very coldest days. Over this he wore the classic Frontenac parka from Mountain Equipment Co-op. His core was toasty and safe. But that was just his core. There were still seven more items of winter protective clothing to come. He pulled double-layered nylon snow pants over his work pants, wore heavy alpaca wool socks over his work socks and padded all-leather hiking boots over that. On his hands he had thick polar fleece mitts encased in a second windproof, waterproof mitt layer, and he had a bulky polar fleece tube over his neck and chin and finally, a quadruple-layer polar fleece toque on his head, under the fur-lined parka hood. This combination was so effective that, even at −40, Peter was grateful that the walk was only 20 minutes. Any longer and he would begin to sweat uncomfortably under all this armour. He was sure he was good to −60. In fact he still had a neoprene face mask he could deploy, but it had never been cold enough for that.

The best part of the walk was the silence. For a while he had listened to podcasts while walking, but found it was more enjoy-able not to do that and instead just to listen to the scrunch of his boots on the hard-packed snow, which somehow enhanced the silence rather than diminished it. If he was trying to work out a particular problem, such as an elusive medical diagnosis, then walking was the best way to generate new ideas. The trick was not to think about the problem directly, but rather to introduce it at the start of the walk, and then to let it go and encourage the mind to wander elsewhere at random. More often than not, something useful regarding the problem would suddenly present itself to his conscious mind in the midst of thoughts about a tree in his line of sight or the dance of snowflakes in the wind. It fascinated Peter that this indirect, crabwise approach could be so effective. He surmised that it meant that a lot of deep intelligence was subconscious and continually suppressed by shallow conscious brain chatter. Tapping into this made him more like an animal. He always believed that most animals were far smarter than they were given credit for. Their intelligence was just more specific and more focused on their needs, whereas ours was exceedingly broad and often wasted on enormous amounts of irrelevant trivia.

However, the walk did not always solve the problem at hand. A few times Peter submitted the problem of how to prove Tom's innocence to his walking and indirect thinking method, and nothing of note came of it. He would keep trying, though. He reasoned that the subconscious cannot be bullied or cajoled and, moreover, sometimes there is just not enough data to generate a solution. More time and more data were needed. Eventually there would be a solution. He made a mental note to pay Tom a visit over the weekend to see how he was doing and hopefully acquire more of that necessary data. He would tell Laura that he was visiting to cheer up his friend, nothing more.

In the meantime, he decided he would turn his thoughts to Emma Dinsdale's problem as he pulled on his overmitts and adjusted his toque. Emma was an older basset hound with an intermittent lethargy issue that had thus far eluded diagnosis. He had run all the standard tests and had come up with nothing. There must be an angle he was missing. Peggy was bringing her in again today for another recheck and he didn't know what he was going to tell her. He gave Pippin a pat and shouted goodbye to Laura as he stepped outside and smiled at the Arctic conditions.

Peggy Dinsdale was widely believed by the staff to be in love with Peter. Although he was gangly and awkward, some women were attracted to his height and to the aura of gentle but powerful authority he could give off. Being a successful and respected professional didn't hurt either. The fact that he was married, and by all accounts happily so, seemed to do little to discourage the most ardent of his fan base.

Theresa, the receptionist, winked at him when she told him that Peggy and Emma were set up in the exam room. "Wait until you see what she's wearing! Just for you, Peter . . ."

Peter blushed and groaned. He didn't openly admit to believing that Peggy felt that way but, if he was completely honest with himself, he was actually a little bit flattered. She was an attractive woman. Yes, he was happily married, but he supposed that Tom was right in saying that "it was good to have options."

"Hi! How's Peggy doing today?"

"Well, *I'm* doing fine, but Emma here was been through a rough week." Peggy laughed, tossing her long brown hair. Tom flushed crimson. He had done it again! This must be the tenth time he referred to the dog as Peggy or the owner as Emma. It was an easy mistake to make when owners and pets have similar names, but for some reason when Peter made this mistake once, he was far more likely to make it again. You'd think it would be the opposite, but no, once that neural pathway had been established, it became welded in place.

"Right, sorry! I don't know why I keep making that mistake!"

"It must be because I look like a dog again," Peggy smiled, her green eyes twinkling. She had shed her fashionable Canada Goose parka and was wearing a tight navy blue sweater over black Lululemon tights. She did not look like a dog, and she knew it.

"No, no! Ha! Of course not!" Peter was blushing again. "But poor *Emma* here," he said, quickly changing the subject and swivelling to look at the dog, "I'm sorry to hear things are still bad."

"Yes, she was really off for three days last week and barely ate anything during that time. She also seemed quite weak, wobbly even, and she had some diarrhea too." Peggy's expression had shifted from playful to concerned. She really loved this dog. Emma was, to the best of Peter's knowledge, Peggy's only companion.

"She looks perkier today, though," he observed.

"Yes, she always looks better when I bring her in. You must have some special powers." She had reverted to playful mode.

"Hmm, well, adrenaline probably helps too. She probably worries we're going to cut her nails and that gets her on alert and looking livelier!"

Peter bent down to examine Emma. She was always nervous on the table, so she was allowed to remain on the floor. Being a basset, Emma was low-slung, so it was not enough for Peter to crouch down, he had to actually sit on the floor. He folded his long legs under him and smiled at his patient. She wagged her tail. She did like him. Emma's ears smelled faintly of yeast, but that was par for the course for her, and she had a few minor chronic skin ailments, but as on the previous occasions, the exam yielded no clues to her episodic malaise. Peter straightened up and sat on his stool.

"Find anything new?" Peggy asked, back to worried mode. "What about that lump?"

"No, that's not related. It's just a benign wart. Yeah, I'm afraid she still seems normal on physical." He paused for a moment. A word had swum before his mind's eye during the walk to work, but it immediately darted away before he could bring it into focus. He could sense its shape and rhythm, but as was his experience with such things, the more he thought about it, the further it swam away, so he had dismissed it and allowed it to swim as far away as it wanted. Now — *bing* — suddenly it was back, and this time it stayed in place.

Addison's.

"But I have a hunch now. Let's run a new set of blood tests to test the function of her adrenal glands. She might have something called Addison's disease, in which those glands no longer produce enough of the hormones needed to keep her metabolism running properly. Rare and sometimes tricky to diagnose, but easy to fix."

"Oh, I hope you're right!" Peggy smiled at him and reached out to touch his forearm. Peter had to stop himself from recoiling.

She was a good client and a nice person, but all the talk about her being in love with him made him uncomfortable with gestures that wouldn't have bothered him coming from someone else.

"OK, let's set that up then with the front desk," Peter said as he stood up quickly and took a couple of brisk steps toward the exam room door.

"Sounds great! By the way, crazy thing about Tom's barn, wasn't it?" Peggy added as she stood up as well and gathered her things.

"Yeah, crazy for sure. Talk to you soon, Peggy." Peter stepped out of the room and, not for the first time, marvelled at the truth behind the clichés about small-town gossip. Tom's barn blowing up and a body being found in it was the biggest news in New Selfoss since Alice Richter was found to be running a BDSM dungeon under her craft shop, Krafts 'n' Things, on Linnaeus Street. Passersby had often wondered casually what the 'n' Things might be. Now they knew. Alice had been at the clinic a few times with Mr. Miller, her chihuahua, and Ms. Nin, her budgie. Peter tried to keep clear of gossip, but couldn't help but look at her differently after the news broke.

The rest of the day was quiet, with just a smattering of appointments and no farm calls. Fridays were usually one of the busiest days, but probably the extreme cold was keeping people away and keeping pets out of trouble. Even the phones weren't ringing. Then at 5 p.m., an hour before closing, the phone did ring and seconds later Theresa came running into the office. "Peter, Laura's on the phone! She sounds really upset!"

CHAPTER
Nine

"We've been broken into!" Laura told him before he could say more than hello.

"What? You mean the house? Someone broke into our house?" Peter's stomach clenched when he thought about the figure in the yard at dawn.

"Yes, someone broke into our house! I was doing my Canada Post run to ship that sweater and those mittens I've been working on. I was gone maybe 40 or 45 minutes. I knew right away. Pippin was barking like crazy, and the side door was open. I clearly remember closing it and locking it. Thank goodness the screen door was still closed, or Pippin and Merry could have gotten out."

"Oh no! Is there anything missing?"

"Yes, but it's weird. They tore the TV off the wall and took some jewellery from my top dresser drawer, but the weird part is that they cleared the deep freeze out too! I haven't looked everywhere yet. Maybe there's more."

"The deep freeze in the basement? Like, all that meat?" Peter and Laura had gradually and quietly become more and more vegetarian, limiting meat to Sundays when Kevin was over and when they were invited to someone else's house for dinner. But even with Kevin they were gradually slipping in more meatless meals, hoping he wouldn't probe them on the choice. They didn't want to start any arguments or be seen as holier than thou. However, Peter kept being given meat by his clients. Peter didn't have the heart to refuse his clients' gifts, nor did he want to start an awkward conversation about vegetarianism with someone whose livelihood depended on people eating meat.

"Yes, all the meat, including those monstrous pork shoulders." The pork had come from Tom and was at the bottom of the deep freeze. He knew that Peter and Laura didn't eat pork, but he asked them to keep the shoulders for him as he had run out of freezer space himself.

"That is weird. I guess meat has value too. There was just something in the news about kids in Winnipeg shoplifting steaks from meat shops and grocery stores. They can resell them easily to make cash. But to go for that and not the computer and stereo and stuff?"

"I know. And they didn't try too hard with the jewellery. They just took the cheap stuff in the top drawer. Most people would know to rifle through the underwear drawer to find the good stuff, but they didn't bother."

"Maybe Pippin freaked them out with his barking? Jorgensens next door were probably not home anyway, but they wouldn't necessarily know that. Any idea if it was one or more burglars?"

"I can't tell, but I'm guessing it was a group and they each hit a floor and grabbed something, although they would have had to make a few trips to haul out all the meat. Anyway, the cops will be here right away."

"I'm coming now too. It's dead here, so Theresa can just call me back if they need me."

Kevin and another officer named Kristine — an exceptionally tall, exceptionally blonde and exceptionally serious-looking woman

— were already at the house when Peter arrived. They were examining the side door, which was adjacent to the driveway, but not clearly visible from the street due to a bend in the drive and all the thick spruce trees planted alongside.

"Hey Pete, come and look at this," Kevin called to him as Peter came trotting up, puffing from having run in his parka. "This was a more professional job than we usually see around here. The standard m.o. of the local losers is to smash a window or jimmy the lock with a crowbar. This lock was picked. That's not something the average 15-year-old glue-sniffer knows how to do."

"But why?" Peter asked when he caught his breath. "Isn't smashing or prying faster? Why bother picking the lock?"

"Well, it's quieter for one when you don't want to attract attention, especially in broad daylight like this, and it can be just as fast for a pro."

Peter nodded. "OK, makes sense. I want to go inside now, though, so excuse me." The officers stepped aside to allow him to pass. As Peter shed his winter gear, he turned to Kristine, who had come in behind him, and asked, "And why broad daylight? Any theories about that?"

"It's not really that unusual. They're looking for times when people aren't home, so daytime and vacations are the peak break-in times, not night like you might think. Although if you've gone out for the evening, that's even better."

"Ha! No danger of that," Kevin, who was third in line to step into the foyer, shouted over Kristine's shoulder. "Pete and my sister never go out! Sitting and reading and knitting is their idea of a rocking good time!"

Kristine gave no sign of caring and stepped past Peter to look at the living room, where dangling wires and a chunk of missing plaster indicated the former home of a large-screen television.

"Well, you never invite us to join you at Fame or Club 200," Peter shot back, naming two gay bars in Winnipeg that Kevin had been visiting more frequently since breaking up with Tyler. He regretted his retort instantly.

"OK, next weekend, you and me, buddy, plus Sis. We're going dancing!"

"You're on!" Peter replied with forced enthusiasm. But both of them knew that Peter and Laura would find an excuse not to go. It had nothing to do with the gay scene and everything to do with their visceral dislike of noise and crowds and alcohol-fuelled bonhomie.

"You guys just relax while Kristine and I do what we need to do," Kevin said, indicating the couch. "You haven't touched anything, right, Laura?"

"No, I mean other than some door handles."

"That's OK. We're not going to be dusting everything for prints in a low-value B&E anyway." Kevin paused, seeing the looks on Peter's and Laura's faces. "Sorry, but it's not like the crown jewels were taken." He laughed. Peter and Laura did not join in. Kristine continued to ignore all three of them and was taking photos. "But it's better if nothing got moved around."

Peter and Laura sat on the couch as instructed and played anxiously with their phones, surfing news sites without really absorbing anything while the two RCMP officers took more photos and made notes. The whole process took the better part of an hour. When they were done Kevin came back into the living room.

"Kind of strange about the meat, isn't it?" Peter said. "What do you think? Why not the computer, or go through more drawers for cash or jewellery?"

"Meat is expensive, but yeah, I agree, it is a little wacky. The criminal mind, I guess, eh? Who ever said those doorknobs were clear thinkers?"

Peter nodded, and then changed the subject. "I should mention something else that might be relevant."

"Yeah?" Kevin struck a cautious tone and raised an eyebrow that all by itself seemed to say, "You're not going to start playing private eye again, are you?"

"The day after the barn fire, so Wednesday last week, early in the morning I saw someone out there." He gestured to the east. "Just at the edge . . ."

"You didn't tell me that!" Laura interrupted.

"Sorry, I didn't want to worry you. He, or she, I suppose, was gone right away. At that point there was nothing that could be done with that information anymore. It would serve no purpose to tell you. It would just make you needlessly anxious."

"Even with a possible serial killer on the loose?"

"Especially with a possible serial killer on the loose. If I told you, you'd just be freaked out with no practical consequence. If there's a killer, he's not targeting people like us anyway."

Laura still looked unimpressed, but Peter returned to his story. "He was at the edge of the yard, moving along the treeline. It was before sunrise, so I only saw a silhouette. I heard a truck go down the road right after and saw its tail lights. That's it."

"So, you think that could have been our burglar casing the place?" Kevin offered.

"You tell me. You're the detective." Peter tried to keep the snark from creeping into his voice but failed.

Kevin was unfazed. "Ha, yeah, but actually technically no. Corporal and investigator, but not detective. We don't have detectives on the force." He chuckled in a way that showed he considered this to be light-hearted banter. "But anyway, that seems like a reasonable theory. And I don't see our killer switching to doing B&Es so you don't need to worry about that, Sis, but Pete, for god's sake, call us when something like that happens!"

While they were talking, Kristine was on her phone at the door. She concluded the call and tucked the phone into her pocket before turning to the others.

"That was Derek at the station. Ken Finnbogason called there a few minutes ago. He found what sounds like your TV and a shopping bag with the jewellery dumped at that abandoned construction site at the end of Faraday Road. He was out walking his dog when he saw a black Ford-150 pull out of the site. He was curious because there hadn't been any activity there in years, so he went and had a look. Unfortunately, he couldn't make out a licence plate."

"No meat?" Kevin asked.

"No meat."

CHAPTER
Ten

P eter gave Tom a call the next day, on Saturday morning. He called the landline and listened to it ring and ring. Tom's answering machine seemed to be off, or perhaps the police had taken it for analysis and hadn't given it back yet. He was just about to give up when Tom picked up.

"Yeah?" Came the muffled greeting, as if the phone was not quite oriented to his mouth.

"Hey Tom, it's Peter!"

"What time is it?" Clearer, but still foggy and disoriented.

"Um, about quarter after eight. Did I call too early? I'm sorry."

"No, no, it's OK, man. I should be getting up anyway. We had band practice last night, so, you know . . . But anyway, what's up?"

"I'm free this morning and was just wondering if you were up for a coffee or something?"

"Yeah, sure. Do you want to come here? Say ten-ish?"

"Perfect. See you then."

Peter told Laura that he was going over to Tom's to check on how he was doing. She had planned a quiet morning with her knitting and the animals, so this was fine with her. In the afternoon, the Olsons were coming over to play Settlers of Catan, though, so she reminded him to be back by one.

As it would only take 20 minutes to drive to Tom's, Peter took a detour down Faraday Road. Kristine had already brought the TV — which was scuffed but functional — and the jewellery back to them, but Peter wanted to have a look at the site. It was a warmer day than it had been in weeks, but still below zero. With the warmer air came cloud and a stiff, southerly breeze. The dingy, late-winter snow under this low grey cloud made the old construction site even unlovelier than usual The wind knocking the bare stick branches of the trees together like rattling finger bones added to the grim atmosphere.

Peter stepped out of his truck and looked around. Somebody had planned to build a large home here at least ten years ago and then stopped after they finished just a portion of the foundation. Nobody seemed to know who owned the property as only a numbered company was listed at the land registry, and nobody knew why they stopped building. The popular guess was financial overreach, as the completed portion of the foundation hinted at something upwards of 5,000 square feet. The site had long since been stripped of anything of value and every flat surface had been decorated with unimaginative graffiti — penises, scribbles, hearts with initials in them.

Peter could see where the stolen items had been dumped as the tire tracks from the F-150 Ken had reported were clear, as were the subsequent tracks from the RCMP. Vehicles did not, as a rule, drive up onto this site. It seemed to Peter that the burglar had not made much of an effort to hide the goods. The burglar either didn't care or they weren't from the area. Anybody local would know that this quiet road was actually a popular walking route and part of the New Selfoss Heritage Trail. A better bet would have been to toss the stuff into the woods somewhere outside of town. After all, there were thousands and thousands of square kilometres of woods.

It didn't make any sense.

It wasn't the newest TV, but it was still worth something. And the jewellery wouldn't make anybody rich either, but nonetheless probably good for a couple hundred bucks at one of the pawn shops on Main Street in Winnipeg. It was like throwing money away. Weren't burglars interested in money? Wasn't that the point of the whole exercise? Were these some sort of alternative, postmodern burglars? And the biggest question — why toss this stuff but keep the meat? Maybe they panicked and thought that the TV and jewellery would be easier to trace, but the meat was OK because it was more generic and anonymous. That made a little bit of sense at least.

Peter stared absentmindedly at one anatomically improbable blue penis on the foundation wall while these questions flitted through his mind. He shook his head when he realized what he had been staring at, turned around and trudged back to the truck. As he did so, an amusing thought came to him. Maybe it was crazy old Art Blankenship reclaiming the three rib roasts he had given Peter before he decided that Peter had poisoned all his cows and should be stripped of his licence. Art was pretty wily, despite being bonkers, so he could probably figure out how to pick a lock. Taking the TV and jewellery would have been a ruse to conceal his true purpose and throw the police off the scent. But Peter was pretty sure Art's truck wasn't black, and it was a ridiculous idea anyway. He laughed out loud as he started the engine. Art Blankenship, the new Pink Panther, only in denim. Ha!

Tom was still in his housecoat, but he was obviously pleased to see Peter. He looked even more haggard than at the café the other day. Peter had to remind himself that they were the same age. Tom looked 61, not 41.

"Hey, big guy! How's it going!" Tom liked to clap people on the shoulder when he greeted them, but Peter was almost a foot taller than him, so he made do with a slap on the side of his arm.

"It's going pretty well, considering, I guess." Peter took his coat off and smiled weakly at Tom.

"Considering? Considering what? But get your boots off and come in first. Let's get settled and then we can shoot the shit. Black, right?" He called over his shoulder as he went into the kitchen to get the coffee. "Make yourself at home in the living room. Don't mind the crap all over the place. The guys are slobs." He laughed, signalling the inside joke. Tom knew very well that he had the reputation of being the biggest slob among their friends. Peter may have had a messy desk at work, but he and Laura kept a neat house and anything that smacked of hoarding set Peter's nerves on edge. His older brother, Sam, was a hoarder living a precarious existence in Toronto. They didn't see each other much. At least Tom was a jovial hoarder, whereas Sam was a cranky one. And to call Tom a hoarder was possibly misstating the situation. It looked more like Tom didn't throw anything out because he couldn't be bothered, whereas hoarders didn't throw anything out because they had an unhealthy attachment to their stuff.

Peter cleared magazines and paper plates and empty beer cans (Manipogo Pale Ale from the local microbrewery) from part of the couch and sat down gingerly. Gingerly because you never knew what was under the cushions and Peter was not about to check.

"Good band practice?" Peter shouted to the kitchen where he could hear the sound of coffee mugs being set on the counter.

"Yeah, great actually! We've nailed 'Relax' — you know, by Frankie Goes to Hollywood?"

"Sure!"

"And we got a good start on some Talking Heads," Tom said as he walked into the living room carrying two chipped mugs. One had "Bass Players Do It Deeper" printed on it and the other featured a cartoon moose. He handed the moose to Peter and then looked around for a clear spot to sit. Not finding anything, he shrugged and sat on what looked like a handful of crumpled The

Newer Waves T-shirts on the love seat opposite Peter. He glanced down at the shirts, pulled one out from under him, crumpled it into a ball and tossed it overhand to Peter like a football.

"New shirts came too. No charge for you, pal!"

"Thanks! Glad the practice went well. Must help take your mind off the fire." Peter was known for skimming briskly through the small talk. He knew he had to make some, but once he had asked one question not related to his primary purpose, he figured he had the green light to move along.

"Yeah, it helps for sure. But what about you, pal? What's up with 'pretty well, considering'?"

Peter shifted on the couch in a futile effort to get comfortable. It was low, and his legs were long, so his knees pointed up, making him look like a preying mantis, with his even longer arms folded, so that he could hold the coffee mug in both hands to warm his fingers. Tom was erratic at heating the house. Sometimes it was a sauna and sometimes it was a meat locker. Today was a meat locker day.

"We got broken into yesterday afternoon," he said after finishing a long sip of the coffee, which was exceptionally good. Tom had at least as many talents as he had ineptitudes.

"Really? That's crazy! Did they take anything?"

"The TV, a bit of jewellery and, bizarrely, all the meat in the deep freeze."

Tom visibly tensed. "All the meat? You mean including those pork shoulders?"

"Yes. Weird, eh?"

Tom sucked his breath in sharply. "You're sure the pork too? All of it? They didn't just dump it somewhere around your place?"

"Yeah, I'm sure. I'm sorry about that. Was it special? I mean, I feel bad for you, but how valuable could that be?"

"No, no, it's not that it . . . it's just that . . ." Tom appeared to be processing something and searching for the right words. "Just that I'm just shocked, that's all. Taken aback, you know."

"For sure. We're all shocked. And you know what's extra weird? They dumped the TV and jewellery right after at that old construction site on Faraday, but it looks like they kept the meat, unless they went to the trouble of dumping it separately somewhere else."

Tom didn't say anything and seemed lost in thought, so Peter went on. "My best guess is that the meat is easier to resell and harder to trace. Also, it was Ken Finnbogason who saw them pulling out of the construction site and called the Mounties. Maybe they noticed him coming from a distance before he saw them, and they got spooked or figured Ken's dog would find the meat right away."

"Yeah, I suppose," said Tom slowly, snapping out of his reverie, "but it's still frigging strange."

"I even wondered whether it was Art Blankenship's wacky revenge!"

Tom laughed. He knew the whole story with Art and his cows and his vow to take Peter down. "Ha! That's funny, but if old Art wanted to get you, he'd do something much more public and in your face, like fill your waiting room with manure or take out a full page ad in the *Trib* with 'Peter Bannerman Hates Cows' in giant red letters!" The *Trib* was the *New Selfoss Tribune*, the local weekly newspaper where Art Blankenship had in fact already written a rambling letter to the editor about Peter that flirted with actionable defamation. The truth was that Peter had tried his best to treat those cows, but Art didn't follow the directions and they got worse. It was one thing for Art to blame the medications for that, but quite another to accuse Peter of deliberately giving them "poison" because for some reason he hated cows, or at least Art's cows. Peter couldn't imagine any readers believing this and decided that involving lawyers would only make things worse, but he was aggrieved that Gail Boyko allowed the letter to be printed. They were starved for content, he supposed, so he let that go too.

"Yeah, you're right, and I don't think he drives a black Ford F-150. That's the vehicle Ken saw." He took another long sip from his coffee. Ethiopian Yirgacheffe, he guessed.

"No, I don't think he does. It is an F-150, though, but I don't think it's black. Maybe green?"

"So, anyway, that's our little drama. Thankfully, nobody was hurt, the animals are OK, and nothing was badly damaged. Just some plaster where the TV was mounted. They didn't even kick in the door. They actually picked the lock, if you can believe it."

Tom was quiet again and drank some of his coffee before responding. "Picked the lock? Really? So not just kids, I guess?"

"No. Kevin thinks it was pro job, which makes what they took even stranger."

"But these days with YouTube, maybe the sharper kids have figured out how to pick locks. Why not? Quieter and probably actually easier when you know what you're doing." Tom set down his coffee and shifted his weight so that he could reach into his pocket and pull put his phone. "Here, I'll type it in: 'YouTube how to pick door lock.' Bingo! There's piles of videos about this. The cops are clued out. These days you can learn how to do anything online."

"Ha! I'll mention that to Kevin. But I want to ask about you. How are you doing? You know, with losing the pigs and the barn, and with being taken in for questioning."

"Honestly, it's pretty rough. Thanks for asking. You're a good friend, Peter." Tom ran his hands through his unruly curls and looked down at his lap. "I loved those pigs, you know that, so I hope it was quick for them. And the financial loss is insane. Like I said before, I didn't have enough insurance and those assholes are going to drag their feet for as long as they possibly can. And then having everyone look at me funny because they know I'm still the No. 1 suspect." Tom paused for a moment and sucked his breath in. "Hell, man. I think I should just sell everything and start fresh in Costa Rica or Panama or somewhere. Seriously! I've looked at it."

"Geez, I'm really sorry, Tom. I know where the Mounties are coming from because it was on your property, but the case against you has got to be so weak. Who's the victim? Where's the motive? What about your alibi? It's Criminology 101: motive, means and opportunity. The only thing they have is means, because of your guns, but every second person around here has a hunting rifle."

Tom sighed and sat back, rubbing his head again. "They would have stopped investigating me by now if it weren't for Josh."

"Josh?"

"You remember — that young guy I had working here last summer, helping out around the place."

"Oh, him. Right. But he left in September. Planning to go find work in B.C., right?"

"Other direction, Ontario. But yes, him. He was kind of a drifter and it seems he drifted right off the map and his family eventually reported him as a missing person."

Peter set his mug down on the one clear corner of the cluttered coffee table to avoid dropping it. "The cops think Jawbone is Josh? That you killed him, hid the body until January and then decided to dispose of it by blowing it up?"

"Something like that, yes. I'm supposed to appear at the station to answer some more questions about him at three this afternoon."

"Really? That's pretty far-fetched. Again, where's the motive?"

"Exactly. But I guess ever since the Pickton thing they're looking at every pig farmer a bit differently. I bet they'll show up with a backhoe as soon as the ground thaws." Tom laughed at his own morbid joke. Robert Pickton was one of Canada's most notorious mass murderers. He killed dozens of women on his pig farm.

Peter didn't laugh. "But they'll be able to sort that out once they see that there isn't a dental match."

"Yeah, I hope so. Just so long as Josh had dental records somewhere. His teeth were pretty nasty."

"What's your theory? I know you thought animal rights people accidentally blowing themselves up, but that wouldn't explain the rifle and the bullet hole. Who do you think the victim is now?"

"I could have sworn it was those animal-army lunatics, but I guess now I'd have to say it was probably a biker hit. That was the original theory for the dude who was found floating arse-up at Grand. But then the missing persons list is starting to make them think serial killer." Tom shook his head.

"That's just Kevin watching too much Netflix. I figure biker hit too. Or possibly a suicide? Maybe that kid, Leonard Alexander, from the res?"

"Tricky to line up the rifle so that the barrel sits firm between your eyes and you can still reach the trigger. Most suicides put it in the mouth. But possible, I guess. Dental will tell them that one for sure."

They both drank their coffee in silence for a few moments. Peter thought about Frank, an old Czech vet who had done a locum for him once. Frank had tried to commit suicide with a rifle in his mouth, but it slipped so he shot out the back of his throat, severing his spine and paralyzing him. He was still alive, as far as Peter knew, and apparently had become quite a jovial quadriplegic, his near-death experience having performed a hard reset on his psyche.

Peter spoke again first. "The other thing I wanted to ask you about was your security camera. I'm confused, was it broken? It should have recorded other vehicles that came into your yard that morning." Peter knew that the police theory was that Tom had set a timer, so proving when he left wouldn't help clear him, but knowing who else might have been there would obviously be enormously helpful.

"Yeah, unfortunately it was busted. I'm not the most techie

guy, so I didn't notice it wasn't working. I put it up when I first started getting those email threats."

Peter nodded. "Very unfortunate. That would have really helped, although I suppose they could have parked out of view too if they were experienced biker hit men."

"For sure. I feel like a dope for not making sure it worked." Tom stretched and yawned. Then he peered into his cup. "More coffee, Peter?"

"Thanks no, I'm at my caffeine limit and I should be getting going anyway." He looked at his watch. "I'm going to do one more thing before going home, though."

"What's that?"

"This has been bugging me all along. That morning when the barn blew up, there were no cars coming the other way from your place."

"Maybe they did use a timer and left long before?"

"Maybe, but the easiest way to set off an explosion and not blow yourself up is to use pyrotechnic cord. It gives you enough time to clear out, but not so long that they'd be miles away. No, I think they left just before the explosion and since I didn't see them, that means they must have taken that little gravel road west to 59."

"OK, I guess that makes sense. It's not a school bus route, though, so it's a crappy road, especially in the winter."

"Agreed, but a better getaway plan than the main road to town." Peter paused and leaned forward, as he tended to do when he was about to make a decisive point. "Rod's place is at the corner to 59 and I bet he has at least one working security camera since he has all those classic cars. He probably has video, so long as it hasn't been written over already. I wonder if it takes in the road?"

"No idea, but I'm sure the Mounties have checked all that out already."

"Maybe, but maybe not."

CHAPTER
Eleven

P eter decided to drive by Rod's place on the way home. Rod's two massive German shepherds, Kurt and Fritz, were Peter's patients, but he'd never had a good look at the place. Tom was right, the road was horribly icy and rutted. It was also exposed so there was a lot of drifting snow that he had to punch through with his truck. It didn't look like anyone had driven this way in days. He slowed to a crawl as he approached Rod's property. Sure enough, there were two security cameras, one aimed at the yard and the front door and one aimed down the driveway to the road.

Peter smiled and turned onto 59, grateful to have smooth pavement again. As he drove home, he decided that he was going to use the "longest road" and "largest army" strategies for the board game with Laura and the Olsons. Nobody would expect him to do that. Peter was normally very predictable, so he knew he could use that to his advantage every now and again by being unpredictable and catching people by surprise.

Peter briefly debated whether to call Rod and ask about the security camera footage himself, but he thought better of it. He could, if he wanted, supplement and even aid the formal police investigation, but not replace it or interfere with it. No, this was the Mounties' job. Peter called Kevin and left him a message asking if they had looked at Rod's cameras. Ultimately this would both satisfy Peter's curiosity and help clear Tom. Win-win.

Sunday morning over oatmeal Peter had another idea. He put his spoon down and looked up at Laura, who was busy dissecting a grapefruit.

"You know, with Tom's situation, I still think the most likely explanation is a biker hit. Nothing else fits as well."

"Uh-huh." Laura didn't look up.

"So, do you remember me talking about a client named Darryl Parenteau?"

"I think so, maybe." She looked up now and cocked her head in the way that signalled that she was unsure where Peter was going with this.

"He's that ex-biker. You know, all tattoos and toughness, but he's got a little fluffy Havanese that's the love of his life?"

"Right, him." Laura chuckled. "Didn't he once tell you that he could use his bike gang affiliation to" — she used air quotes — "'help you' if you ever had a difficult client?"

"Yeah, that's Darryl." Peter smiled at the memory of the seriousness with which Darryl had made that offer a few years back when he was still walking. "He's in a wheelchair now, so I'm not sure whether the offer he had in mind is still valid, but that's not the help I'm looking for anyway. As it happens Princess Peach is due for a checkup and I said I'd do a house call, so I'll set that up for tomorrow afternoon and use the opportunity to ask him about the local biker scene."

"Do you really think he would know anything about what happened and that even if he did, he would tell you?" Laura furrowed her brows and crossed her arms in a teasing pantomime of skepticism.

Peter snorted. "Ha, well I really doubt he'd know anything about the hit itself, but he's probably still plugged into who's a player in the gangs and how bad the rivalries are right now. Just background data for me to think about. I could ask Kevin too, but I don't think he'd appreciate that level of interest."

Laura nodded. "OK, makes sense, but I'm not sure how I feel about this level of interest either."

"He's harmless and he loves his dog. I'm just curious about the gangs. Nothing more than that."

"If you say so. Isn't it still Loki's Krew and Brothers of Satan?"

"I think so. Darryl was in Loki's Krew." Although they were teens then, both of them remembered the biker wars of the '90s. Loki's Krew had divided up the drug trade with a couple of the Indigenous gangs, but then the Brothers of Satan came from Quebec. There were a rash of drive-by shootings and pipe bombs were set off at tow truck places. It ended when new anti-gang laws were passed and the police got serious. They infiltrated the gangs and also made good use of informants. Many were still locked up, spread out over the various federal pens.

"Wasn't one of their top guys a client of yours?"

"Yeah, Keith Blatt. Sort of a client. He was out of Stoney for a bit and got a dog, but it was always his stripper girlfriend who brought him in. Rottweiler named Cupcake." Peter chuckled at the memory.

"Right, I remember now. They had a summer cottage clubhouse up here. But changing the subject, what are your plans today?"

"I thought I'd take Pippin out onto the lake right after breakfast. It's nice out right now, but it's supposed to cloud over later. Do you want to come?"

"That's OK, thanks. I'm supposed to give Aunt Ingveldur a call right away. It's —" she glanced at the kitchen clock "— about 1 p.m. in Reykjavik now, so I'll catch her before her afternoon nap. And then I need to go to Rose's for coffee and to pick up some wool. But be careful, Peter. I'm not sure I like the idea of you being out there by yourself right now."

"Nothing will happen in broad daylight out on the lake, but of course I'll be careful." Peter pushed his chair back and called, "Pippin! Come! Do you want to go for a walk? To the lake? Of course you do!" And of course he did. Pippin ran over to Peter and looked up at him with a wide doggy smile, wagging his whole hind end.

Lake Winnipeg in early February looks like the Arctic Ocean. It looks so much like the Arctic Ocean that a number of movies have used it for that purpose. In Harrison Ford's *K-19: The Widowmaker*, a submarine coning tower was placed on the ice off Gimli to simulate a Soviet submarine breaking through the frozen-over polar seas. This greatly amused the locals. Stories of Harrison ordering vodka at the hotel lounge and graciously signing autographs were a beloved part of Gimli lore. The Canadian military also used the lake for Arctic drills and Arctic explorers did test runs out there.

Peter loved it because of the simple monochrome beauty — a vast, empty white surface to a sharp blue horizon, or, if cloudy, a vast, empty, white surface to a hazy grey horizon. He also loved it because it made the power of nature plain and it allowed him to thrill at his relative smallness. And it made him feel intrepid to face it and walk out onto it, especially after reading the harrowing account of Douglas Mawson's 1912 Antarctic expedition. Walking onto the ice here was a safe bit of role-playing for an exploration geek, much like running around with paintball guns might be for a military geek.

There were hills to the south of New Selfoss that offered the best vantage points to look out over the lake. Peter always made a point of going there in April, when it was fully spring on land, complete with butterflies and songbirds and crocuses, yet the lake was still completely frozen over. Standing there and looking down on the enormous white expanse made him feel like he was standing at the edge of the Pleistocene. A woolly mammoth would not be out of place. But it was far too early for that effect as the woods and hills were still as white and silent as the lake. Instead, he drove down to the nearest beach, which offered direct access to the ice.

Depending on the force and direction of the November winds at freeze-up, sometimes access to the lake was complicated by large ice shoals pushed onto the beach and freezing into place at inconvenient angles, but this year the margin was seamless. Flat and firm snow-covered beach became flat and firm snow-covered ice. Further out Peter could see vertical ice sheets in a jagged line to the southwest, and here and there patches of sastrugi, or wind-carved snow ridges, marred the smooth surface, but it was still easy to pick a level route and just march straight out.

Pippin loved it.

He raced ahead and then whipped around, tail wagging, barking, asking for Peter to throw him a snow chunk. The snow was too dry to form actual snowballs, but it was easy to break firm pieces out of the crust. Again and again Pippin would catch these and try to bring them back, only to have them crumble in his mouth before he could succeed. This did nothing to suppress his enthusiasm. *Oh, for the inexhaustible optimism of a dog*, Peter thought.

He also considered that the larger sastrugi and jumbled ice sheets would be a perfect place to hide a body. Drag it out here, tuck it behind one of those snow or ice barriers, fill its pockets with something heavy, cover it with snow and in the spring, it'll sink and not be found for a very long time. Simpler and cleaner than blowing up a hog barn. That's how Peter's brain had worked since the news about Jawbone. Everything now had a possible murder angle. But he quickly dismissed the notion and returned his focus to the walk.

They walked out in a perpendicular line to the shore. As always, Peter enjoyed the sound of his boots on the dense snow. It reminded him of walking on styrofoam. Not that he had ever done that. When he stopped, the silence was unearthly. It made it seem impossible that anybody else or anything else existed anywhere in the world.

There was only this.

Then his phone vibrated.

They were still in range of the cell towers. The middle of the lake was a different story, but they weren't nearly that far. Peter briefly considered ignoring it, but thought the better of it and fished it out of the inside breast pocket of his parka.

"Hello?"

"Hey Pete!" It was Kevin, and he sounded excited. "Where you at?"

"On the lake."

"Like out on the ice? Fishing? You don't fish."

"No, just walking."

"You know you're a freak, right?"

"Yup. What's up, Kev?"

"I'm just being a good guy and letting you know that we struck pay dirt with the video from Rod's place. Thank you. I owe you one. I can't say I enjoy you making us look sloppy, but fair's fair. I'll give you credit for thinking outside the box. But you're so far out of the box sometimes that I'm not sure you even see the box." He laughed at his own joke before quickly adding, "And I mean that in a good way. Just don't let it go to your head. You got lucky."

"Great, well, you're welcome. So, what did the security footage show?" Peter smiled down at Pippin, who was looking at him, plainly confused by the sudden stoppage of their walk.

"You know I can't tell you that, bro."

"Unknown vehicle at high speed just minutes before the explosion?"

"Really, I can't say. What I can say is that Rod Friesen's a strange dude."

"Oh? Another one?"

"Ha! Yeah, the place is full of them, eh? No, what's strange about Friesen was a real lucky thing. Normally these home security cameras don't store more than a couple days' footage, but he had a commercial grade system with 90-day backup and a whole little surveillance set-up in the corner of his basement with two dedicated monitors. He has motion sensors all over too. And those two shepherds, although they seemed pretty lazy. Normally all that security stuff's the sign of a grow op, but he was right proud of it all and more than happy to show us around."

"Expensive cars, I guess?"

"I suppose, but it seemed over the top for that. Guy lives alone, kind of like Tom. Probably bored a lot. Everyone needs a hobby, they say. Like walking on ice for no particular reason!"

"You bet. And with that said, I'll let you go. It's time to enjoy more of this hobby now. See you tonight."

"Later, Pete."

Peter tucked the phone back into his jacket pocket and then found a good-sized snow chunk to throw for Pippin.

They walked out for an hour, covering four kilometres. Under ideal conditions Peter's pace was as high as six kilometres an hour, but with the stopping to get snow chunks for Pippin and the fact that this was a leisurely Sunday stroll and not an athletic endeavour, four felt quite reasonable. The four back would make for a respectable total. Because of his long stride, the walking app on Peter's phone told him that he covered a kilometre with 1,150 steps, as opposed the average for most people of 1,300 to 1,500. This made today's walk 9,200 steps, give or take. The much-vaunted 10,000 steps was not his goal, as in his opinion it was a silly and arbitrary number based on the fact that the number 10,000 happens to sound good in Japanese. And in any case, he would easily exceed 10,000 steps over the course of the day with all the other walking around the house and so on.

The return was less pleasant as a wind had sprung up out of the east, driving cloud before the sun and blowing snow particles into Peter's face. Even Pippin squinted against the onslaught. It was manageable, though, so they trudged on while Peter's mind went back to the time he and Tom had crossed the lake three winters ago. Brian Palmer, Tom's dentist friend, was supposed to join them, but he backed out at the last minute when his sciatica acted up. Tom wanted to back out then too, saying, "Three's a crowd, but a crowd is a good time," but Peter talked him into sticking to the plan. Peter was all about sticking to plans. So, just the two of them set out to ski the 28 kilometres across to Gimli. This could be done in a single day, but they thought it would be more fun to camp on the ice in the middle of the lake. To give themselves even more of a sense of adventure they picked a route away from where most of the ice fishermen were. Brian was a worrier and had rented a satellite phone and suggested that the two of them still take it. It was hard to imagine the circumstance where they would use it, but they agreed, especially after Laura insisted. As it happened, it was so cold that night, despite their extreme Arctic sleeping bags, that it was comforting to know that the sat phone was there in case they became too hypothermic to carry on or go back. Peter hardly slept. By two in the morning, he had given up and decided to go outside and walk around to try to keep warm. He thought Tom was fast asleep and hated him for it, but later it turned out that he hadn't slept either. He crawled out of the tent into a moon-washed world. The full moon gave the snow a pearlescent glow. The whole visible world was luminous in the manner of a gorgeously shot black and white film. Peter was dumbstruck. And then, in the distance, he saw something moving. It steadily came closer, but at an angle that wouldn't take it directly through their camp. It was a wolf. A solitary wolf was crossing the lake. Peter had never seen a wolf in the wild before. It was like seeing a myth come to life. It paid no attention to Peter or the tent and just moved steadily across the lake until it vanished behind some far sastrugi.

Peter and Pippin returned home in time for lunch. Laura was back from the sheep farm and had made homemade tomato soup with sourdough croutons. This hit the spot.

The afternoon passed with newspaper reading and jigsaw puzzle-making (a 1,000-piece map of Middle Earth — easy because of the place names, but also difficult because it was mostly sepia monotone). At five Peter went into the kitchen and started preparing dinner while listening to a podcast of CBC's *Ideas* program. This particular one was on the spirituality of the saxophone. He found himself using it more as warm aural wallpaper and allowed his mind to drift along unrelated streams of thought as he chopped red bell peppers. This was interrupted by the sound of Laura's owl-hooting ringtone. He could hear her talking to someone but couldn't make out what she was saying. A moment later Laura was at the kitchen door. Peter glanced up. Her mouth was partly open and her eyes wide. Peter raised his eyebrows in a question.

"It's Kevin."

"He's going to be late?" Peter guessed and turned back to chopping peppers.

"He's not coming at all. He wants to talk to you. Tom's disappeared."

CHAPTER
Twelve

"**N**o, I have no idea where he might be!" Peter was having trouble containing his agitation.

"But you did see him yesterday morning?" Kevin's voice was matter-of-fact and businesslike.

"Yes, like I said, I went over for coffee to see how he was doing. He was definitely stressed, but otherwise in surprisingly good spirits. He did make a comment about starting over in Panama or Costa Rica, but there's no way he would just take off to do that without first selling his property and tying up loose ends here. And what makes you so sure he's taken off? Maybe he just went into Winnipeg for the night to see a friend or for a mental health break?"

"He did not show up for his scheduled interview on Saturday afternoon, he has not been back at the farm since and he has not been returning messages."

"Right, he mentioned you were planning on questioning him further."

"Let's assume that it's not Panama or Costa Rica for a moment, and let's just assume he was running away somewhere closer — where do you think he might go?"

"He's got that cabin up the east side of the lake he uses for some of his hunting trips."

"We've thought of that already and are sending a couple offi-cers up there by snowmobile tomorrow morning, with a dog from the specialty detection team." They both knew that Pippin was better than any of the dogs on the force, so the last statement hung in the air for a beat longer than it would have otherwise.

"OK," Peter finally said.

"Is there anywhere else? Anywhere else we should look?"

"Not that I can think of. Tom knows lots of people, though, and he knows the bush well."

"But you don't know anything?"

"Kevin, what is this? I told you already. I really have no clue. This is a total shock to me. I can only assume he's panicked. But that doesn't mean he did it. The murder, I mean."

Kevin just grunted.

"Come on, Kevin, why would someone who had, in your theory, so carefully planned a murder, or possibly even several murders, suddenly do something so careless and foolish as try to run away, especially when your case against him is clearly stalled and not going anywhere?"

"Maybe he's planned his escape just as carefully. Maybe he's somewhere where the odds of us finding him are low. You know, Pete, contrary to what you might have heard, the Mounties don't always get their man. Just keep your eyes and ears open and let us know if you notice anything, hear anything or think of anything. And if he contacts you, remind him that it will go better for him if he turns himself in rather than us having to drag him out of some hole somewhere. I've got to go now. Sorry about dinner."

Peter handed the phone back to Laura and shook his head. "I don't know what to say or think right now."

Laura hugged him and quietly said, "Do neither. Don't talk and don't think. Let's just have dinner, watch an old *Dr. Who* and go to bed early."

The next morning Peter's thoughts were no clearer. He sat in his usual chair with his usual tea watching the eastern sky lighten, which normally promoted calm and rational reflection, but he was only able to conjure a confused jumble of mental images and sounds.

Tom's anxious face.

The roof collapsing into the burning barn.

The skull with the hole in it.

Tom owing a lot of money.

The figure in the yard.

Rod's security cameras.

Kevin insinuating that Peter knew where Tom was.

The dumped TV and jewellery.

The empty freezer.

John Doe.

Leonard Alexander.

Laura telling him to stop trying to investigate this.

Elton Marwick's shed.

GADA.

Josh the drifter.

The black Ford F-150.

Tom's band.

Tom's guiding service.

Tom's three wives.

Peter shook his head as if it were a faulty mechanical toy, took a deep breath and stood up. The thing to do was write it out.

With Pippin padding along behind him, he walked over to his old rolltop desk, a fantastic yard sale find that Laura had restored many years ago, and switched on the green banker's lamp. He patted Pippin on the head absentmindedly with his left hand while he fished his big leather notebook out of a desk drawer with his right. It was a thing of absolute beauty, hand-stitched and bound in bison-hide leather. It had been a gift from a grateful client after Peter stayed in the clinic all night to perform a C-section on her bulldog. He called it Bella's book. For a few years he kept it blank because it was too lovely to write in at random. Then he tried to use it to write haikus, but they were terrible, so he stopped and even considered tearing those pages out. Now he used it for brain-storming. The right way to brainstorm was in a silent house, with this book and with his favourite fountain pen, purchased at that little shop in the Exchange District. Walking may be ideal for the unguided free flow of thought, but structure and discipline was needed for concentrated and focused thought.

He waited with his pen poised just over the cream-coloured page. How to begin? He continued to wait, knowing the answer would come. Yes, that was it. He would write out all the possible — not necessarily probable, but possible — theories for what happened in Tom's barn.

In estimated order of probability:

1. The Bikers
According to Michelle, Tom's first ex-wife, Tom owes a lot of money. He doesn't lead a flashy lifestyle that required borrowing money. Consequently, any large sums he'd spend would be on something not visible or obvious. Drugs? I wouldn't necessarily know. We're good friends, but that's mostly based on having grown up together and him protecting me back in high school. There's lots of ways our current lives no longer intersect. Moreover, drug addicts are often good at hiding their habits. And, if I'm honest with myself, Tom is "the type."
Around here, drugs mostly come from biker gangs. Tom would be in debt to them. This could have them

demand favours, such as using his farm for some of their
dirty work. Consequently, Tom ran away to escape the
bikers, not the police. Unfortunately, however, I have to
also consider that Tom did not run away but was killed
by these bikers.

Peter sucked his breath in as he finished the last line. Maybe
that was even the most likely possibility? The bikers killed Tom
because he knew too much? It didn't bear thinking too hard about.
He looked down at Pippin, who was now curled up on the small
rug beside the desk. Pippin must have sensed the slight movement
of Peter's head because he opened one eye to look at him. Peter
smiled and Pippin's tail began a slow wump-wump wag against
the floor.

"Soon, buddy. Let me finish this first."

In this scenario, the other pieces, like our break-in and
Elton's shed, belong to unrelated puzzles. But Kevin's
John Doe case may still relate.

2. Suicide
Jawbone is a suicide who accidentally blew up the
barn too. Maybe Leonard Alexander? Could the bullet
have triggered the explosion? Something to research.
As above, all of the other pieces would then be from
different individual puzzles. Tom just panicked and
made a foolish decision to run away because he was
worried that the police had it in for him.

3. Accident (Manslaughter)
Jawbone is Josh, but Tom killed him accidentally,
maybe while showing him how to hunt, or some other
gun-related activity. He hid the body until he figured

out how to dispose of it. *Although it broke his heart, he killed the pigs to take suspicion off him, not realizing that many people wouldn't understand how hard that was for him to do, so it didn't really work out as cover for him.*

Again, all the other pieces are from other puzzles and Tom panicked, but this time with better reason.

4. Serial Killer
Maybe the police are right, but they just have the wrong guy. John Doe, Jawbone, and maybe also the Alexander kid, and even Josh the drifter, are part of some sick plan to commit a series of murders and dispose the bodies in a pattern of "creative" ways. Jawbone by fire, John Doe by water . . . Maybe it's the elements? Earth disposal is easy. But air? Feed bits to eagles like the Tibetans do? This could use a lot of the puzzle pieces, although I hope not the burglar. Here also, Tom panicked, or possibly he had some kind of a sign or indication from the killer that he was next on the list.

5. Tom
If I am going to be completely rational, I cannot exclude the police theory. A crime of passion perhaps? But not serial killing. That's so improbable as to be the functional equivalent of impossible. Again, everything else would be coincidental.

N.B. There is no theory that connects everything strange that has happened in the last couple weeks, nor, rationally, should there be. The human mind that scanned for predators in the African savannah for thousands of generations is wired to automatically create patterns out

of any unusual events. Deep down it does not believe
in coincidence. Safer to assume that a pattern is threat-
ening than to be blasé about the grass rustling over
there, and that strange sound a few minutes ago, and
the fact the birds have all gone quiet . . .

Peter sat back and looked at his list. It was good and clean. His mind was much calmer and his thoughts not jumbled at all any longer. Perhaps he had items two and three in the wrong order? Hard to say, but it wasn't critical to get that right. The main thing was to address item one as best he could and then go from there. The biker connection shouldn't be too hard to rule in or rule out. The house call with his ex-biker client, Darryl Parenteau, was an excellent start. But first, Pippin's promised walk.

As the two of them stepped out of the house, he couldn't help but scan the east side of the yard for any unusual shadows. He knew this was ridiculous, as the odds were essentially zero that the presumed burglar would return, at least in that manner, but instinct was sometimes still a more powerful force than intellect, even for Peter Bannerman.

There was nothing. At least nothing he could see or hear.

CHAPTER
Thirteen

Darryl Parenteau lived in the centre of town now. He used to have a place in the country, but once his health declined, he decided it was better to be near his doctor and other services. His old rural property resembled Rod's, but with classic motorcycles instead of classic cars. Before meeting Darryl, Peter had assumed that the motorbikes were just window dressing for the bike gangs, something done to keep up an image and to honour a tradition, but not something they were actually personally enthusiastic about. Perhaps that was the case for some bikers, but Darryl was definitely a hardcore motorcycle geek. In fact, there were only two subjects Peter had ever heard Darryl talk about: Princess Peach and vintage bikes. Most clients made small talk when it was clear Peter had time (and sometimes when the opposite should have been clear) and Darryl's small talk was always about his motorcycles. Perhaps this was because Peter had become good at feigning interest, when in fact the subject bored him almost as much as golf or celebrity gossip.

Peter rang the bell. This prompted the expected shrill barking from Princess Peach, followed by, "Quiet, Princess! Let yourself in, Doc!"

Peter opened the door and stepped into a world of shining chrome. Had the room been more brightly lit, he would have needed sunglasses. Darryl probably had a dozen antique and new motorcycles at the old place, but now he only had room for three, all of which he kept in his house because they were too valuable to leave outside in the middle of town. "I know the criminal mind," he said at every opportunity. Also, he couldn't ride them anymore anyway, so he may as well enjoy polishing them and looking at them. The bikes were not only in his house, but all three were right in the living room. Two Harley-Davidsons — one newer and one antique — were against the walls, and his prized 1952 Vincent Black Lightning had pride of place dead centre in the room, where normally a coffee table would be. This was the exact model Richard Thompson sang about in Darryl's favourite song. Cliché bikers may favour heavy metal music, but Darryl was distinctly folky in his tastes. Peter suspected that he had been a hippie before he joined Loki's Krew, but that was not something he felt comfortable asking about.

The living room was otherwise sparsely furnished to allow Darryl to manoeuvre in his wheelchair, which also gleamed with chrome, so Peter sat on the only option, a small leather love seat facing the '52 Vincent. He wondered whether guests were permitted to sit on the bikes. Princess Peach regarded him warily from the entrance to the kitchen.

"Aw, come on now, Peachie. It's your doctor! He never hurts you." Darryl had rolled over to the little fluffy white dog. He used a high-pitched cooing voice that was wildly out of place with his Santa Claus physique, his leather jacket covered in violence-themed patches, the most prominent of which was a leering Loki, the Norse god of chaos, wielding a war-axe. He also had the word "Fuck" tattooed in elaborate Gothic script across the large bald patch on the top of his head.

"Take your time, Darryl, I'm in no hurry. I do have those special treats, though!" Peter rummaged in his jacket pocket and pulled out some of the freeze-dried liver that only the most skeptical or fussy dog refuses. Princess Peach was neither of those, so she was slowly lured, one treat at a time, over to him. Peter then let her sniff his hand and then very slowly moved it to begin stroking her on her side. She started to relax enough that he could slide the stroking hand under her belly and gently hoist her up onto his lap.

"See, he's a nice guy! He's your friend!" Darryl beamed, revealing an orthodontist's dream, or possibly nightmare, of a mouth.

Peter completed the examination, which was just a routine annual physical. No vaccinations were due this year, which was a blessing as Peter was not confident Darryl would be able to hold her well enough for that. He praised Princess Peach's health as well as Darryl's obvious stellar care of her and then waited for Darryl to relay the inevitable motorcycle anecdote. This one involved the trials and tribulations of getting some particular widget — Peter zoned out during this part — for the 1947 Harley-Davidson Knucklehead against the far wall.

"Knucklehead?" Peter snapped to. *What an oddly comical name for a motorcycle*, he thought. *Weren't they normally given fierce or powerful names?*

"Yeah, the valve covers look like someone's knuckles." Darryl nodded vigorously at Peter's interest. "See?" He rolled over and indicated what was apparently a valve cover on the old bike.

"Right, sure. That makes sense."

Darryl resumed his monologue while Peter mulled how he was going to pose his questions. When it sounded like Darryl was done, Peter said, "Remember how you once told me that I should ask you if I ever had trouble with a client?"

"Sure, Doc. What's up? You need to persuade somebody about something?" Darryl drew "persuade" out dramatically.

"Ha! Thanks, Darryl, but no, it's not that."

Darryl assumed a more serious facial expression and leaned forward slightly. "OK, Doc, anything. Just ask."

"Are you still in touch with Loki's Krew?"

"Yeah, a bit," Darryl said in a neutral but not unfriendly tone.

"Good. So, this is why I wanted to ask you. You know about Tom Pearson's barn, right? And the body they found in there?"

"Sure."

"What do you think the chance is that it was a hit, either by the Krew or somebody else? I don't want to incriminate anyone specific, and this won't go to the cops, of course. I just want to help Tom if I can because he's their main suspect right now."

"It's cool, Doc, don't worry. But I don't think it was a hit."

"How come?"

"Way too complicated set-up. If the Krew needs to take someone out, they shoot him, sure, but usually dump the body somewhere obvious, like Pipeline Road by the city, or along 59 up here. When you whack someone it's for two reasons." Darryl held up two fat fingers, each of which had at least three ornate, skull-themed silver rings on it. "One, to punish the fucker for whatever dumbass thing he did, and two, to send a message to all the other fuckers thinking of doing dumbass things. Destroying the body would only accomplish one."

"I see. I suppose that makes sense." Peter tried to keep the disappointment out of his voice. Darryl had punctured his favourite theory, simply and logically. While Peter hadn't been certain that was the solution, he had assigned it the highest probability. This was a setback. However, on the bright side, it was only because he was missing one key piece of data — the fact that bikers always wanted to send a message with their killings — not because his overall logic was flawed. Moreover, did they *always* want to send a message? Couldn't there be exceptions? He didn't want to quibble with Darryl, though, so he thanked him, gave Princess Peach the last of his treats and excused himself.

Peter had a spare half hour before he needed to be back at the clinic, so he detoured out of town to drive by Tom's farm. Not to stop there, but just to drive by in case that triggered any useful thoughts. Driving was not as good for thinking as walking or concentrating at his rolltop desk, but it beat sitting in the clinic working on files or returning phone messages about hairballs and smelly ears.

It was another clear and bright day and, being mid-morning on a Monday, there was no traffic. The road to Tom's was empty and the driving conditions were perfect, so Peter was almost there before he could begin to properly sort his thoughts regarding whether suicide or accidental manslaughter should be elevated to the top of the probability list now that he was forced to move bikers out of that position.

There just wasn't enough data.

Peter briefly debated about whether to turn around and return to town on the main road, or whether to carry on down the little gravel road and turn onto 59 at Rod's. He decided that while the former would be quicker, it would look more suspicious to any observer, so he drove on. He slowed down only slightly as he passed Tom's, noting with a flutter of alarm that there was an RCMP cruiser in the yard. He had made the right decision. Maybe an officer would have seen him and wondered if Peter had approached and then turned around.

He refocused his mind back on the theories as soon as he was out of sight of the farm.

Maybe he could call his friend Alvin Prince on Yellowgrass to chat about Leonard Alexander and try to get a sense about whether suicide was at all a possibility? But they had been over that ground before and it would seem weird — weird even for Peter — to bring that up again months later out of the blue. And besides, if it was a suicide, it didn't necessarily have to be Leonard. Now that he thought about this again, a significant problem with the suicide theory was that it required two different things to happen — the suicide and then the explosion. He would look into the likelihood of a bullet setting off a manure pit blast, but it struck him as improbable. Also, why commit suicide there specifically? The more he thought about it, the less likely the suicide theory was. Accidental manslaughter, possibly of Josh, was therefore theory number one now. That would explain Tom running from the police, even though it was a bad idea to do so. But Tom was volatile and could make bad decisions on impulse, like marriages one and three, or the infamous occasion when he challenged a heckler at a Newer Waves concert to a fight, which ended up sparking an all-out brawl, eventually involving the police.

It may be the best theory, but Peter knew that it was still not a good theory. This bothered him immensely. He wanted a good theory. His stomach was tight and his mind whirred. When it stopped whirring, he had one thought, like a roulette wheel settling on a number. The burglar. There was no rational way to connect the burglary and the murder, but Laura had instinctively done so, and Peter knew that he ignored her instincts at his peril.

CHAPTER
Fourteen

O n Tuesday morning Peter learned something new. They had run out of the Irish Breakfast loose leaf tea, so he brewed the East Frisian instead. He had misplaced his reading glasses, so he accidentally set the timer for two minutes, rather than the two minutes and thirty seconds that he had always believed was optimal for East Frisian. Once he noticed this error, he made an uncharacteristic decision: he decided to just go with it and see. To his astonishment it was even better at two minutes! The tea was softer and rounder, and faint floral notes that had been suppressed by the lingering tannins in the longer infusion were now detectable. He was pleased. This objectively trivial discovery cheered him because it reaffirmed that life still held unknown pleasures. Serendipity was still an active force in the world, and in his life. To be sure, so was "franklinity," so it was more accurate to say that surprise, irrespective of whether pleasant or unpleasant, was still an active force in the world. This was logical, as no person could possibly command enough knowledge to avoid ever being surprised.

Franklinity, as the opposite of serendipity, was a word of Peter's own coining. He was happy to have it cross his mind again as he enjoyed the improved East Frisian brew. He was fairly sure that he was the only person who used the word so far, but he still hoped for wider adoption as it filled an obvious gap in the language. If serendipity was the chance discovery of something good, named for the beautiful Isle of Serendip (now called Sri Lanka) that explorers had stumbled upon, then the chance discovery of something bad needed a word too. Sir John Franklin had sought fame and glory in being the first to navigate the Northwest Passage, but instead he had discovered hypothermia, cannibalism and abject failure. Franklinity. The adjective was franklinous. Peter smiled while he thought of the various ways one could use franklinous and franklinity in a sentence. "Joe made a franklinous discovery in the men's room." "Finding that four-month-old sandwich in the glove compartment was pure franklinity."

Meanwhile, dawn began to leak into the empty and silent yard while Pippin and Merry slept soundly and Peter's smile turned to a slight frown as he strained to see something that probably wasn't there.

Theresa met him at the back door of the clinic. She had obviously just arrived as she was still wearing her parka. Her face was flushed, and she didn't bother to say hi.

"Peter, did you come in last night and forget to set the alarm and lock the door?"

"No, how come?"

"The door wasn't locked when I got here, and I didn't have to disarm the alarm."

"That's weird," he said. "I was the last to leave and I'm sure I set the alarm and locked up. Does it look like anyone was in here?"

"I don't know, I just got here."

"OK, I'll go check the safe and you check the pharmacy. When does Kat get in?" Kat was the veterinary technologist, similar to a nurse in the human field.

"Not until nine-thirty today. We don't have any surgeries booked and she has to take Riley to the doctor."

Peter nodded and walked quickly to the office where the safe was kept in the back of the coat closet. He hung up his parka before kneeling down to look at the safe. It looked the same as always. Either nobody broke in, or they were very fastidious and closed the safe after cracking the combination, or they weren't able or interested in opening the safe. Peter twirled the dial to the right numbers and then opened it. The cash float and the narcotics were exactly as they had been yesterday.

He met Theresa in the hall connecting the office with the treatment area.

She smiled at him. "The pharmacy's fine. Nothing's been touched. Maybe nobody broke in? Maybe Kat came in for some reason and forgot to lock up properly? How would a thief know the alarm code anyway?"

"Safe's good too." Peter paused and rubbed his chin. Then he was struck by a thought. He turned around, stepped back into the office, and picked up a phone on one of the desks.

The line was dead.

Peter sucked his breath in and stared at the phone for a long moment, feeling his heart begin to pound.

"Phone line's been cut. That prevents the alarm from contacting the service. Somebody was here. They took a chance that we didn't have a loud, audible alarm."

Peter had shut off the siren feature years ago because it freaked out hospitalized patients when it accidentally went off, as it did far too often. And, being frugal, he had refused the alarm company's suggestion of adding a cellular phone connection to the service to prevent this exact scenario. The alarm was really just there to fulfil the insurance requirements. Peter was never actually worried about a break-in. It was New Selfoss after all. This burglar had gotten lucky with the primitive alarm set-up. Or they knew about it somehow.

"Well, that's super weird then," Theresa said, shaking her head in wonderment, making her long, magenta hair swish back and forth. Last week it was navy blue. "Someone goes to the trouble of cutting phone lines and picking a lock and then doesn't take anything?"

"Have you checked the freezer?" Peter's facial expression suddenly became stony.

"The freezer? Like the Ward F deep freeze? Not the one above the fridge?" Theresa furrowed her brow as she asked this, clearly unable to guess where this line of questioning was going to lead. The clinic had two small kennel areas for hospitalized patients named Ward A and Ward B. When they needed to be discreet about saying out loud where a deceased patient was, they referred to the freezer as Ward F.

"Yes, the deep freeze."

"Um, no, but why?"

Peter didn't answer. He ran to the little storage room between the washroom and Ward B. The chest freezer was closed, but there was blood streaked down one corner.

Franklinous.

"Theresa, look at this!" he shouted, but he needn't have been so loud, as she was right behind him.

Theresa gasped and held her hands to her mouth.

"Whoever was here cut themselves on that stupid edge." The freezer had a very sharp corner on the right side of the lid. Peter and the staff knew to keep clear of that corner. Peter carefully opened the lid and peered inside. Two euthanized pets were in there in thick plastic bags awaiting the weekly pickup from the cremation service. Both bags had been torn open and poor Digger and Whiskers were partially exposed.

"What the hell?" Theresa cried. "What kind of sicko breaks into a vet clinic to mess with dead pets?"

"They weren't looking for pets. They were looking for meat," Peter said very quietly.

"Meat?!"

"Yes. You know that break-in at my place last week? I didn't mention it, but that was one of the main things they took — meat from our deep freeze."

Theresa shook her head slowly, her mouth open and her eyes wide. "You think it's the same people? But why meat?"

"Too much coincidence for it not to be the same people. But I have no clue why they're after meat."

Kevin and Kristine were at the clinic ten minutes after Peter called.

"The meat bandit again, eh?" Kevin remarked after he checked out the freezer. "But you kept none of it here? The meat, I mean."

"No, of course not."

"Just checking."

"The blood might be useful, though, if we need to make a DNA match. And definitely prints this time."

"Look for someone with a big bandage on the back of his left hand."

Kevin raised an eyebrow. "Yeah? The back of the left?"

"In the summer it could be his left arm too, but nobody has short sleeves now. When you put the lid back down and then pivot to your right to leave the room, the only exposed part of your body that could come in contact with that corner would be the back of your left hand as you swing it. Given the amount of blood he must have hit it with force and even sliced a vein. There'll be a significant bandage, not just a little band-aid."

"Uh-huh. Don't you have a barfing chihuahua or an itchy cat or something to see now, Pete?" Kevin stretched and forced a stagey yawn.

Peter took the hint, nodded and headed back to the office. There were no barfing chihuahuas or itchy cats, not yet anyway, but he had to call Peggy Dinsdale. Emma's results had come in and she did have Addison's disease. Peter was relieved when he saw that. Although he would never wish a disease on a patient, this was the best kind of result — a conclusive diagnosis of a treatable disease. Emma would be on pills for the rest of her life, but the success rate was high. Peggy would also be relieved to hear this. Uncertainty is often the worst part of any medical process. This effectively took his attention off the freezer for ten minutes, until Kevin appeared at the open door of the office, doing a pretend knock in the air where the door would be if it had been closed. Peter was still talking to Peggy on the phone and waved to Kevin to take a seat at the second desk where his ex-partner used to sit.

"Find anything else?" Peter asked once he had hung up.

"No. Kristine's collecting samples and she is dusting for prints this time because of the possible pattern, but this looks like a pretty clean and focused in-and-out job, except the blood of course."

"Same guy as at our house, right?"

"That's reasonable to assume. Picked lock. Pro job. Freezer fetish. Yeah, I'd say it's the same customer or customers." Kevin stroked his thick red beard before leaning slightly forward. "Pete, I've got to ask you something else. Mind if we close the door?"

"No, of course not." Peter stood up, went to the door and called out to Theresa, "Hey! I'm going to be tied up with Kevin here for a few minutes, OK?"

"Yeah, no problem. You're clear for at least 20 until Mr. Wiggles comes for his anal gland expression."

Kevin widened his eyes for a moment, but otherwise looked more businesslike and serious than he had so far that day.

Peter closed the door and sat down again.

"Thanks, Pete. So, here's the thing. That security footage from Rod's showed a dark grey Honda CRV driving away from Tom's at high speed just five minutes before the explosion."

"OK . . ."

"So, that's when Tom was at Rita's and that's not Tom's vehicle."

"Like I've been telling you. It can't be Tom."

Kevin sighed and shook his head. "Look, Pete, even if Tom didn't pull the trigger or light the fuse, he's involved. Why else would he disappear?"

"Because he got scared, of course. A lot of innocent people end up in jail."

Kevin guffawed. "I won't take offence at that, bro, but 'a lot' is a big overstatement. There's been a handful and they've all been in the news. Anyway, I'm not here to debate you on that. I'm here to ask you about Tom's friends and possible accomplices."

"Accomplices?"

"Yeah, the CRV guy." Kevin sounded slightly impatient. "It ties up a lot of loose ends. A two-person job makes more sense."

"Do serial killers ever work in teams?"

"Not often, but, A, sometimes they do — Bianchi and Buono, Lake and Ng, there are a few more — and, B, serial killer is just one theory."

"Well, Tom had —" Peter caught himself "— sorry, *has* lots of friends, including lots I wouldn't even necessarily know about."

"Any that drive a grey CRV?"

"No idea, Kevin. You know I don't pay attention to cars."

"OK, well, be a pal and just write out for me all the friends and contacts you know of. Add anyone at all who comes to mind. Email it to me by lunch, OK? Can you do that?"

"Sure, I'll try."

"Thanks. Catch ya later." And with that Kevin stood up and let himself out of the office. Peter was conscious of the fact that Kevin had dialled back his normally jovial style by several notches. He wasn't sure whether that was just the way he was with him now or whether that had become his new default mode for this investigation.

Mr. Wiggles lived up to his name and the next three patients were equally uncooperative, so it was a trying morning. Peter found that his mood depended far more on the personality and behaviour of his patients and his clients than it did on the nature of the cases themselves. He always said that he'd rather have a difficult case in an easy pet with an easy owner than an easy case in a difficult pet or with a difficult owner. As long as the difficult case wasn't heartbreaking. He didn't like those either. By lunch he was grumpy and tired. Theresa noticed and suggested that he could go home as there were no more appointments until mid-afternoon and no farm calls were scheduled either. It was definitely still the slow season. "I'll give you a shout if anything comes up!" she called after him as he left.

Peter rarely napped. He knew it was a generally accepted recommendation for optimal health and that it was natural, in that his Neolithic ancestors surely napped, but it conflicted with his deeply ingrained drive to be productive. He was even able to construe reading or playing a game as "productive" (learning and cementing relationships, respectively). But he was trying to nap more, reasoning that it could improve his productivity afterwards. Quality over quantity, or something like that. So, feeling too tired to talk to Laura about what happened, he snuck into the spare room where he lay down, fully clothed, on the old couch, and set an alarm for 20 minutes. He was so tired that he quickly tumbled into a dream. Later, the only thing he'd remember about it is the smell of blood.

CHAPTER
Fifteen

Peter slept through his nap alarm, but fortunately Laura heard it and roused him. She suggested a quick coffee before heading back to the clinic, but he was still trying to reduce his caffeine intake, so he said no, feeling absurdly heroic in doing so. But once he had brought his muddled senses back online, he agreed to a small decaf, which Laura cheerfully made for him while he called into work to check on things. Apparently his one appointment, a check lump on Marvin, an elderly cocker spaniel, had cancelled when Mrs. Irving's son pointed out to her that it was the same benign cyst Peter had already checked twice. Theresa told him that he may as well stay home if he wanted. She and Kat could look after phone calls as well as food and drug sales and would of course call him if he were needed. A completely free afternoon like this was rare, even in the slow season, so Peter, still feeling a little befuddled from his nap, readily agreed.

As he sipped his decaf, he admired Laura's toques, which she was just putting the finishing touches on. She had knit them in Slytherin green and grey, with a series of subtle snakes in the shape of the letter S around the brim. She was especially adept at knitting designs that would make fans smile but would manage to walk just ever so slightly on the near side of the copyright infringement line.

In an amusing, and entirely self-conscious twist, the law firm in Toronto that ordered them, Sinclair & Sniderman, specialized in copyright and trademark law. The world was a weird place if you knew where to look. Laura knew where to look and loved it.

Slowly Peter's neurons sparked back to life. This afternoon had confirmed once again that, contrary to the widely accepted wisdom, napping was not for him. Was there really any advice that applied to absolutely everyone? No. That would not be sensible. Clearly there were nappers who sprung up from their naps, vigorous and sharp, and there were non-nappers who staggered out of their ill-advised naps, befuddled and dull. Peter was the latter. He was feeling much more like himself now, but that dream memory of the smell of blood clung to his mind, refusing to dissipate and allow him to fully restart the day. Laura had left the room to do something in the kitchen. Peter was about to stand up and follow her to tell her what happened at the clinic when he looked down at Pippin, who was lying on his side, sprawled, all four legs straight out, deep asleep.

That was it.

Pippin.

The smell of blood.

Of course.

Peter got up so fast that he felt woozy from the head rush and then, once steady, walked quickly into the kitchen, where he described the break-in at the clinic while he rummaged about in the fridge for liverwurst.

"What? Why didn't you tell me right away?"

"I don't know. The morning got busy and then I was so tired and . . ." His voice trailed off from inside the fridge.

"So obviously not a random break-in then. Jesus, Peter. What does Kevin think?"

Peter stood up, having found the liverwurst. "He thinks it's the same person, or people, too, but he doesn't have a clue either why they're after frozen meat."

"Specifically, after frozen meat that has something to do with you."

"Yes, it's bizarre."

"Does Kevin think we should be worried? Like, for our safety?" Laura had her arms folded across her chest. Her facial expression could be interpreted as either fear or anger. Or possibly both.

"He didn't say, but I take that to mean that it didn't cross his mind for us to be worried. If you think about it, a burglar who is careful and meticulous is less likely to be violent. Why would he be? Nothing to gain." He hadn't told her about the blood, lest that muddy the picture of the sophisticated high-class freezer bandit he was trying to paint for her.

"I don't know. When the situation is this strange, I think anything is possible. I think we need to be careful."

"You're right. We will be careful. I will be careful. And Kevin's only minutes away. We've both got him on speed dial. If we see anything suspicious at all we'll call him."

Laura relaxed her posture slightly and nodded. There was nothing else to be done. They weren't going to move or hire 24-hour guards. Then she noticed the liverwurst in Peter's hand for the first time since the conversation began. "Hungry?" She smiled, knowing that Peter couldn't stand liverwurst and that it was for Pippin.

"Ha. Theresa said my only appointment cancelled, so I've got the afternoon off and am going to do some scent training with Pippin."

"Oh? Any particular reason?"

"No. Just haven't done it in a while."

Laura gave him an appraising look and then shrugged and smiled. "OK, have fun then."

This almost always worked, unless Pippin was really deeply asleep. And often, when he seemed to be deeply asleep, he was actually dozing. So, when Peter stood at the door and quietly said, "Walk?" even though Pippin had been sleeping two rooms away, he came running, tail wagging, mouth wide in a big doggie smile.

"You heard that, eh?"

Wag, wag. Smile, smile.

"So how about it? Do you want to go for a walk?"

Wag, wag, wag. Smile, smile, smile.

"Of course you do. You always do." Peter smiled back and clipped the leather leash on.

"First, we're going to the clinic, OK?" Pippin cocked his head at this. As far as Peter had been able to figure out, Pippin knew maybe a dozen words. He hadn't thought that clinic was one of them, so possibly he was just responding to the rising inflection he put on the word, which usually signified something pleasant, like "park" or "forest" or "lake."

It was a relatively mild February day with high cloud and little wind. Pippin trotted happily along beside Peter, stealing frequent glances up at the right side of his parka. Peter had put the liverwurst in a Ziploc bag deep in a pocket there. Pippin hadn't seen this happen, but he knew. When they arrived at the clinic, Peter shouted a cheery, "Hey guys, I just stopped by to check something in the storage room on our way to our walk!"

"Is Pippin here?" Kat called from the reception area.

"You bet!" Peter let Pippin go so he could race up front to see Kat and Theresa, who he knew would spoil him with pats, scratches and treats. Peter went quickly into the storage room, picking up a pair of small forceps from the magnetic strip above the treatment room counter on the way. The freezer had been cleaned up since the police finished collecting samples and taking photos this morning, but Peter had a hunch. He looked in the big garbage can in the corner of the room.

He was right.

Among all the other nasty detritus were five or six wadded-up paper towels stained pink. Wearing his gloves, he delicately plucked them out and placed them in a large Ziploc he had brought along for this purpose. Then, working as fast as he could because he didn't want to be found and have to explain what he was up to, he peered carefully at the inside of the loose metal corner of the freezer. Just as he had hoped: there was some blood there that the staff hadn't noticed when they were cleaning, and he was confident there'd be a bit of skin with it, although he couldn't see that clearly. He scraped and plucked at this with the tip of the forceps.

Footsteps were approaching.

Then he heard Kat say, "Where's your dad, Pippin? Find your dad!" Peter quickly stuffed the forceps into another Ziploc and began to straighten up just as Kat and Pippin walked in.

"Just seeing how we can fix that corner! One of these days one of us is going to get a nasty cut."

Kat nodded and smiled. "Where you guys walking? It's a nice day."

"Just down the heritage trail and then into the Jarvinen Forest. Not too far in case you need me."

"Don't worry about it — have fun."

"We will. Bye, Kat!" And he shouted another, louder "Bye, Theresa!" as he and Pippin walked out the back door.

"OK boy, let's do some nosework!" This was another word Peter wasn't entirely sure Pippin specifically knew, but the tone was the same upbeat and emphatic one that he used for "play," "walk," and "run," so Pippin got the message that something fun was afoot.

CHAPTER
Sixteen

T he New Selfoss Heritage Trail was started in 1973 as the community's ParticipACTION project. The federal government of the time had become alarmed by declining fitness standards, citing a comparison that the average 30-year-old Canadian was only as fit as the average 60-year-old Swede. The pleasures of television, automobiles and modern convenience foods were taking their toll. Parliamentary debates ensued, monies were allocated and ParticipACTION was founded to fund local fitness initiatives. New Selfoss took to this concept with enthusiasm, in large part because being shown up by Swedes was particularly galling to Icelanders and Finns. So, a 20-kilometre trail was carved out of the woods in a large, wonky circle around the outside of town, dipping into town at various intervals to provide access and to highlight a particular landmark, such as the first fish smokehouse, now a preserved historic landmark, or the first sawmill, also now a preserved historic landmark. Occasionally it ran along little-used roads, but for the most part it was a pleasant nature trail, beloved by walkers, joggers, cyclists and cross-country skiers. From the clinic the easiest way to get onto the trail was from the pioneer cemetery, overlooking the lake on the west side of town.

Peter was pleased that they were the only ones at the cemetery. Nosework often attracted curious questions from passersby, and he wasn't in the mood to field those. Pippin sat quietly and attentively as Peter pulled the most blood-stained of the paper towels out of the Ziploc. Then he fished the forceps out of the other bag and scraped a little reddish chunk off the tip of it onto the paper towel. Pippin stared at this but was very still. Peter rolled up the paper towel into a tight tube with the chunk on the inside. He wrapped this tube in a clean piece of paper towel and then sealed the ends with some surgical tape he had brought along. Pippin tensed because he knew what was next. He had seen versions of this process many times before. Peter got the liverwurst and his Swiss army knife out. He carved off a piece of liverwurst the size of the end of his small finger. He kept this on the tip of the knife in his right hand while he lowered the paper towel to Pippin's nose with his left hand. Pippin sniffed at it deeply, his upper lips flaring slightly. Then Pippin stopped and looked up at Peter. Peter said, "Good seek!" and let him take the liverwurst off the end of the knife. Liverwurst was Pippin's favourite food in the known universe, and he only got it for successful nosework, not for any other tricks or good deeds. To say he was motivated to earn this reward would be an understatement of the highest order.

The next step was for Peter to hide the bloody paper towel roll, as well as several dummy ones he had made up, throughout the cemetery and then give the command, "Seek!" Pippin set off immediately, nose to the ground, tail in the air. He was fast and he was accurate. He stopped briefly at two of the dummy rolls before finding the target. Once he found it, he sat at attention and looked at Peter. If Peter was out of sight, he was trained to bark. He was not otherwise much of a barker and he was always hyper-focused on the job, so there was no chance that he would confuse matters by barking at a squirrel or some other distraction.

"Good seek!" Another piece of liverwurst was proffered. Now they were ready to head down the Heritage Trail and then veer into the connected Jarvinen Forest, just to the south, where there was a maze of smaller trails and less chance of interruption. Once they arrived at the Jarvinen Forest, Peter made Pippin sit while he walked ahead into the trail network, well out of sight, to hide the target and the dummies. After two tries, Pippin went directly to the target without stopping at any dummies first. It would have been easy for him to simply follow Peter's tracks instead, but Peter had stomped back and forth to make it more difficult to cheat.

Dog and owner looked at each other and smiled. This was going really well, and both of them knew it. Peter now took one of the other pieces of blood-stained paper towel, tore off a small piece about the size of his thumbnail, and then went deeper into the forest to hide it in the knot of a tree, again zigzagging and criss-crossing his own path.

"Seek!"

Pippin took off, nose down and tail up as always, moving up the branching paths systematically, almost as if he had a map in his mind's eye that he was shading in as he eliminated areas.

Exactly six minutes later Peter heard Pippin's signature bark.

It had taken Peter three times as long to hide it and to cover his tracks. His boy was a star, although he had to admit that the species as a whole was remarkable in this regard. He always enjoyed explaining to clients how far beyond our imagining a dog's sense of smell was. There are dogs who know that there is a trace of narcotics sealed in a Ziploc on a different floor of a building. There are dogs who can detect the presence of lung cancer on a person's breath with a higher degree of accuracy than a radiologist looking at that person's chest x-ray. And there are dogs who can smell that some-one's blood sugar has dropped too low. Dogs have been trained to sniff out buried cadavers, smuggled currency, illicit cellphones, invasive mussels, termites, mould, bedbugs, firearms and truffles. The list is only limited by the human imagination for what might emanate a few odour molecules and be of interest to locate. Some dogs were specialists in particular odours, but Pippin was a generalist. A Renaissance dog, if you will.

"What a good boy you are! Now let's go try this out for real." Pippin wagged his whole hind end at the praise and at the tone suggesting more fun, and liverwurst, was to come. It was two kilometres back to the house via the shortcut down Virtanen Street and through the schoolyard to Pasteur. Pippin's enthusiasm flagged as he noticed they were headed home.

"Don't worry! We're just getting the truck!"

Pippin took note of the enthusiastic tone and began to wag his tail as they went right by the door of the house, into the garage and up to Peter's work truck. The cargo area was occupied by a custom-built system of cabinets and storage areas for all his large animal supplies, so Pippin hopped into the passenger seat. Laura noticed them backing out and waved. Peter smiled and waved back.

"She probably thinks I've been called out to an emergency. That's fine," he said to Pippin. "But we're going to Tom's!"

Before driving out there, Peter tried Tom's phone again. He had been trying regularly since Tom disappeared. It felt both futile and necessary to do so. Each time the result was the same: "The customer you are attempting to reach is unavailable. Please try again later." *Don't worry*, Peter thought, *I will.*

Peter was concerned that the Mounties could be out at Tom's farm again right now, conducting further investigations, or possibly have it staked out in case Tom came back, so he approached it slowly and had his story ready — that he had been at Ed Baldurson's and decided to take the short-cut to 59. But nobody was there. He had also feared he might see the black Ford F-150 at Tom's. It was a ridiculous fear, especially in the still-bright late afternoon, but he couldn't shake it. And in a sense, that's why he was there.

Tom's yard was open, empty and silent. The destroyed barn was an eerie sight. He hadn't really looked at it closely on Saturday when he visited Tom. Now he and Pippin walked up to the heap of blackened beams, which protruded at every angle, festooned with enormous icicles. Charcoal and ice. It had a strange, abstract beauty, like an ambitious modernist sculpture symbolizing the end of civilization. Pippin strained to go into the ruin, but Peter didn't let him. They skirted the edge until they came to the aspen bluff on the east side. Peter reached into his pocket and showed Pippin the paper towel tube.

"Seek!"

Without the clue of seeing Peter go ahead in a particular direction to set the game up, Pippin began more slowly, sniffing in an ever-expanding arc around where they were standing. Peter put his hands in his pockets and narrowed his eyes, scanning around, although the chance of him seeing something before Pippin smelled it was exceedingly low, especially since the Mounties had presumably already done a thorough visual sweep. He knew this was a long shot. The frozen-pork connection to Tom could well be a coincidence, but perhaps not.

Pippin was taking his time. He was mostly out of sight now, working through the aspens to the east, and a little to the north. Peter shivered. He was rarely cold, but the wind had picked up and the cloud had thickened and lowered. Crows were gathering on the ruins and looking at Peter.

Black crows perched on black wood.

White aspens standing in white snow.

The crows had been silent, but then one of them suddenly cawed and flew by so low and so close that he could hear the soft rustle of feathers and feel the air move against his cheek. He found himself wondering what the crows knew.

He snapped out of this reverie when he heard the sound of a vehicle approaching.

Shit.

Then Pippin barked.

CHAPTER
Seventeen

T he vehicle sounded like it was still ten or twenty seconds away. The side of the ruined barn where Peter was standing was not clearly visible from the drive or the parking area, although his truck was obvious in the yard. The truck had New Selfoss Veterinary Services written across both sides in big letters. There was no mistaking that Peter was there. So he made a snap decision to run toward where Pippin had barked and then address the question of who was coming and how to deal with them afterwards.

Pippin was sitting beside one the few burr oaks in this patch of forest, on the far side of the ruined barn from Tom's yard and house. Aspen poplars are clones of an individual, connected through the roots, so they grow in tight clumps, initially excluding all other trees. As the clump expands and the oldest aspens at the centre die, space opens up, creating a doughnut. It was in the middle of the doughnut hole that a handful of small burr oaks were growing.

He saw right away why Pippin had barked. A wadded-up piece of paper was stuck under a fallen branch at the base of the tree, right beside Pippin's right forepaw. Peter quickly praised Pippin and gave him an extra-large piece of liverwurst.

The engine noise suddenly stopped. Whoever was coming had arrived.

Peter stuffed the piece of paper into his inside parka pocket without looking at it. Then he and Pippin stood there as quietly as they could, straining to hear what the visitor might be up to.

"Peter!? Where are you?" came a shout.

It was Kevin.

"I'm over here!" Peter shouted back and began walking toward the yard.

Kevin met him at the edge of the aspen bluff. His often red-tinged face was crimson, and his brows were set low over his narrowed eyes.

"What. The. Fuck. Pete?!" He spat out each word as if it were an entire sentence on its own. "What the fuck's sake are you doing out here?!"

Peter tried to smile, although he knew it looked fake. "I'm sorry, Kevin, I know I shouldn't have. I just had a hunch about maybe some of the pigs having escaped and thought I'd bring Pippin out to help me look."

Kevin stared at him, not showing any change in the level of anger on his face.

"I didn't touch any evidence or any part of the barn," Peter added hastily. He would ask himself afterwards why he didn't simply explain about the scent training and the piece of paper, but somehow it was easier to lie in the moment.

"Escaped pigs? Like, from two weeks ago? In the middle of winter? With nobody having reported seeing any frozen hogs anywhere? What the actual fuck are you talking about, Pete?"

"I guess when you put it like that it sounds pretty stupid, but I just thought there might be a small chance . . ."

Kevin cut him off. "And so what if? What if this lame-ass theory is right? So the fuck what? One fucking pig gets out and fucking freezes in the woods here. How does that fucking help anyone or justify fucking coming onto a fucking crime scene that is still under active investigation?" He was screaming at Peter now.

Pippin moved quietly to stand between the brothers-in-law and looked up warily at Kevin.

"Sorry. It was dumb. I'm really sorry." Peter tried to sound as contrite as he could. Contrition was not his natural state. His instinct was to doggedly argue each and every point until the other person either conceded or changed the subject in exasperation. But sometimes he managed to recognize in time that that was a bad idea. This was one of those times.

"Dumb is a big frigging understatement." Kevin's tone had softened ever so slightly. "I should charge you, I really should. This Sherlock crap has got to stop. One more time and I swear I will. And I bet Laura would back me up."

"It won't happen again."

"Just get out of here." Kevin had stopped screaming and now sounded more tired than angry. This was not the first time Peter had been chewed out by Kevin like that. Kevin was quick to anger, but also quick to calm down. Nonetheless, with each such encounter Peter felt that the ice was growing thinner beneath him.

Peter desperately wanted to ask Kevin what he was doing back at the farm, how the investigation was going and what the current thinking about Tom's fate or whereabouts was, but again, the voice of prudence overcame the voice of curiosity, prudence pointing out that he wouldn't get an answer anyway. It took an enormous amount of willpower not to pull the piece of paper out and examine it as soon as he got back to his truck, but obviously the best plan was to just drive away without any suspicious pauses. Once he was far enough down the road to be out of sight of the farm, he pulled over and, his fingers clumsy with haste, fished the paper out of his pocket and smoothed it out as best as he could.

It was lined paper that looked like it had been torn out of a notebook, and it was covered with writing in an unfamiliar alphabet. Perhaps Japanese? Peter wasn't sure. It was all in smudgy, dull pencil and had apparently gotten wet at some point, so even if it had been in English, the legibility would have been marginal. He sat for a moment, thinking, but then realized that Kevin could easily be on his way back down the road any time if he had just gone to the farm to do one quick thing. He shoved the paper back into his pocket, shrugged at Pippin and drove home. The sun was setting somewhere in the west, but it was one of those mono-chrome days where it only felt like the gradual turning down of a cosmic dimmer switch.

"How was your afternoon off?" Laura called to him from the kitchen. Peter could smell ratatouille. He loved ratatouille, although there were several years where he couldn't face it because they had made it far too often. Absence makes both the heart and the stomach grow fonder.

"Good! Pippin did really well. I'm sure he'll qualify for the Worlds this year."

Laura made a positive non-verbal noise.

"And I found something peculiar in the Jarvinen Forest." More lies. He couldn't stomach two people yelling at him today. Kevin might tell her about their encounter at Tom's, but there was no possible upside to explaining everything about the paper to her.

"Oh?"

"It's nothing, just a scrap of paper, so I picked it up to get rid of litter and then saw an unfamiliar script and was curious. Any idea?"

Laura dried her hands, took the paper from Peter and held it directly under one of the spotlights that illuminated the countertops.

"Hangul," she said immediately.

"Hangul?"

"Korean alphabet. I think it has 24 letters. It's supposed to be very logical."

"Huh. No idea what it says, though, eh?" Peter chuckled.

"Not the foggiest." She handed it back to him. "If you're dying of curiosity you could check with Anne Shin. Her parents are from Korea and I'm sure she still speaks it."

"Anne Shin?"

"You know, the principal of the elementary school."

"Right, married to Bill Nurmi. They used to bring a pair of cats to the clinic, but they were under his name."

"Yup, that's the one." Laura turned back to her cooking and said, over her shoulder, "Dinner will be another half hour."

Peter made a mug of rooibos tea and went to the rolltop desk, where he took his leather notebook out of the drawer and flipped to the page where he had listed his theories. Now none of these made sense anymore.

Suicide. Accident. Serial killer. Tom the murderer. None of these squared with what he had learned today.

He sat back and took a long sip of his tea. Merry wandered over, purring like an idling outboard motor, and rubbed up against Peter's right leg.

"Hi, Meriadoc," Peter quietly said, using the cat's formal name, and scratched him behind the ears. After a good long scratch Merry was satisfied and lay down near Peter's feet, still purring extravagantly.

Peter leaned forward again and stared at the paper flattened out on the desk beside the open notebook and tried to concentrate. His lips moved as he silently articulated his thoughts. *So, first of all, the burglar is Korean, or at least knows how to write or read Korean. Secondly, as I feared, the break-in at the clinic, and probably the house, has a connection to what happened at Tom's farm. Could the Korean be the killer? Possibly. Are there Korean bikers? Maybe, but probably not. Maybe in Korea, but not here. Would a serial killer also steal meat? No. Seems too unlikely. Now that I've linked the two crimes, serial killer no longer makes sense. Ditto for suicide, and accident, and Tom as theories.*

Peter took another long sip of tea and thought about any way to explain the presence of the meat thief at the exploded barn. *Could it just be a wild coincidence? Say all five theories are still valid, but we* also *have a Korean pork bandit on the loose who happened to wander through Tom's farm, maybe looking for meat?* Peter smiled to himself at the absurdity of this idea, but then began to reconsider. *I don't know how old that note is, though. And Tom's not around to ask whether any Koreans came by asking maybe about meat or pigs or bears. Maybe they did and this paper fell out of a pocket and blew into the trees. In fact, didn't he once have some wealthy Korean hunting clients? But why would they want to steal meat from my freezer?* Peter groaned lightly. He was more confused than ever.

"What do you think, Pippin?" The dog had just padded into the room and looked up quizzically at Peter.

"No idea either, eh? Thought so."

CHAPTER
Eighteen

The next day at work Peter looked up the Nurmi file. Fred and Ralph, their two fat black cats, were listed as alive, but hadn't been to the clinic in four years. Strictly indoor cats didn't always visit the vet regularly, although the advice was to continue with annual checkups. A year was five biological years for the cat, after all. There were two work numbers listed and when Peter checked, one was the same as the school's administrative office, so that must be Anne's.

After two rings Anne Shin herself picked up. *It must be the secretary's coffee break*, Peter thought.

"New Selfoss Primary, Principal Shin speaking." Her voice was cheerful and bright.

"Hi, Mrs. Shin, it's Peter Bannerman from the vet clinic."

"Dr. Bannerman! It's great to hear from you. I know we're way overdue for the boys. I feel really guilty."

"No, no, don't worry about it. That's not what I'm calling about."

"Oh, that's a relief. But Bill and I will bring them in soon, I promise. What can I help you with then?"

"This might be a strange request, but I found a piece of paper with Korean writing on it and wonder if you could translate it for me?"

"Sure, that's no problem at all. Where did you find it?"

"Just out on a walk." Peter decided to add a white lie to make the story more plausible. "But it was in an envelope with a bunch of money, and I'd like to see whether the writing gives any clue to the owner."

"Of course, that makes sense. It's worth a try, isn't it? I'm done here at four and I come right by the clinic on my way home. It's easy for me to stop in if that works for you?"

"That would be wonderful, thank you. See you then!"

The day passed in a blur of spays and neuters Peter was doing for the Dragonfly Lake First Nation, who had flown down six puppies destined for a shelter in Winnipeg and, hopefully, good homes. Peter wondered whether any of Pippin's relations were in the group, as some looked reasonably similar. He also idly wondered whether Pippin would appreciate a friend, but then quickly swatted the thought away. Puppies were cute, but they were a lot of work. Also, Merry had only recently come to terms with Pippin's presence after three years of low-intensity warfare.

No, a puppy was a bad idea.

He was just putting in the last stitches in the last surgery when Theresa popped her head into the OR.

"A Mrs. Shin is here to see you. She doesn't have an animal with her, and she didn't say what it was regarding, only that you were expecting her. Is this another case?" She smiled and raised her eyebrows.

"Oh no. I just need help translating some Korean." Theresa and Kat, who was assisting Peter, glanced at each other. They both knew enough not to ask for clarification, as it was likely something strange and boring.

Anne Shin was a short, round woman with bobbed black hair, dressed in a dark blue pantsuit accented by a red and white scarf. She had a warm, friendly smile and shook Peter's hand enthusiastically.

"Nice to see you! I'm very curious about this mystery Korean visitor to New Selfoss!"

"I am too!"

Peter ushered her into his office and handed her the paper once they had both sat down.

Mrs. Shin put her reading glasses on, which had been hanging around her neck on a beaded chain.

"Hmm . . . Well, it's just numbers and a few letters, Dr. Bannerman. Let's see, the first line says, '3.5 geom-eun 52,500, 4.1 hayan 123,000.' The second is '2.7 hayan 81,000, 6.4 geom-eun 96,000.' Geom-eun means black and hayan is white."

"No name or identifying information anywhere on there?"

"No, I don't think so. It is hard to read, but what I can make out is more numbers and letters. Always a short number with a decimal, followed by the word for black or white, followed by a longer number. It's interesting that the writer uses Hangul numerals rather than the Western ones. Most people use Western numerals now when it's not part of formal writing."

"And most people make notes on their phone, not on paper," Peter observed, although in saying so he had to think about the story he had just read about the Russian secret service dusting off old typewriters for more secure, unhackable communication after seeing how much damage WikiLeaks did to the fully digital Americans.

"Especially Koreans!" Mrs. Shin agreed. "Do you want me to translate the rest? It doesn't look like it will provide any clues to the poor person who lost the money."

Peter would have loved to have asked her to write out the full translation, but this would have seemed odd as he was supposedly just interested in returning the lost cash, so he satisfied himself with committing the first two lines to memory.

"No, that's fine if it's not going to help. Those numbers aren't some way of expressing Korean phone numbers or IP addresses or something like that, though, are they? Can you read the first two lines again?"

Mrs. Shin agreed and then commented, "The longer numbers sound more like money to me, with the multiple zeros at the end each time. How much was in that envelope!?" She laughed as she said that, but her eyes betrayed genuine curiosity.

"Ha! You might be right. That does sound like dollar figures. But no, there was about a hundred bucks in the envelope. Enough to make it worth trying to find the owner, but not enough to make me suspect that they are an eccentric millionaire!"

"Well, in that case, maybe you and Laura should have a nice dinner with this."

"Good idea."

"And Bill and I will bring the boys in next week, I promise!"

The moment Mrs. Shin left, Peter quickly wrote out what he had memorized:

3.5 black 52,500, 4.1 white 123,000
2.7 white 81,000, 6.4 black 96,000

He was confident that he was right. He had learned a few different memory tricks over the years, with his favourite being a memory palace for a complex series of nouns and images, such as a grocery list or a to-do list, but this didn't work for numbers. Here the consonant system was better, wherein each number was assigned a specific consonant — 3 is W, for example (because it takes three downstrokes to write), and 5 is L (from the Roman numeral for 50; the more obvious V is less versatile). Then you fill in vowels to make a memorable word or phrase. So, 3.5 becomes "wall"! The decimals made this note a bit trickier, but they were easy enough to remember as well.

He had no more appointments for the afternoon, so he was able to mull this over to the quiet sounds of the staff cleaning the clinic in the background. He made himself a cup of tea — non-caffeinated peppermint, as it was getting late — and closed his eyes to visualize the numbers floating in his mind's eye. This was sometimes more effective than staring at paper.

Mrs. Shin was clever — those longer numbers probably did represent money. He mentally swapped the second and fourth cluster so that the two blacks were side by side, as well as the two whites. On a hunch, he opened his phone's calculator. Yes, there was a relationship between the first short decimal number and the second long number was consistent within its colour group. The 52,500 and 96,000 with black were exactly 15,000 times 3.5 and 6.4, respectively. And white's 81,000 and 123,000 were exactly 30,000 times 2.7 and 4.1. Now he wished he had swallowed his pride and asked her to read out all the numbers. He still had the note, so he could always find another way to translate it.

Regardless, though, he had no idea what any of this meant.

CHAPTER
Nineteen

P eter stayed at work later than usual, catching up on paperwork and thinking about the Korean note. He texted Laura to alert her that she should just go ahead and eat without him, and then, after Kat left, he enjoyed the deep silence of the clinic for another hour. He managed to tie up every obvious work-related loose end on his desk, but he made no further progress with the note, or any other aspect of the strange events of the last few weeks.

It was already dark when he started walking home and rush hour, such as it is in New Selfoss, was over. The street was empty as he moved from one streetlamp's pool of light to another, occasionally looking into people's brightly lit living room windows, mostly seeing large screen televisions playing a Winnipeg Jets game. Peter had no idea who they were playing or how they were doing this season, but he always knew when a game was on, because the town became even quieter than normal and the window glow down the street was eerily synchronized, dimming and brightening to the broadcast's rhythm.

He had only gone a block when he heard a car behind him and saw headlight beams sweep up, causing him to cast a long shadow on the snow ahead. The car slowed down, so Peter, feeling a quick surge of anxiety in his chest, turned around to look.

It was an RCMP cruiser.

Kevin pulled up beside him and rolled down the window. "Let me give you a ride. I tried to call you, but you didn't pick up."

True, after texting Laura and receiving her reply, Peter had put his phone in his backpack and forgotten about it.

"Is this the part where you drive me ten miles past the edge of town and tell me to keep walking?"

"Hilarious. Just get in the car."

Given the fight they had had the day before, he didn't want to do anything else to aggravate Kevin. He climbed into the passenger seat, struggling to get his backpack off.

"Kevin, I'm really sorry about . . ."

Kevin cut him off, holding out his right palm in a stop-talking signal. "Whatever, Pete, you already apologized. I didn't pick you up to listen to another one. Maybe someday you'll tell me what you were really doing there in the woods by Tom's place, but it's water under the bridge now." Kevin looked at Peter out of the corner of his eye as he said this, and then he put the cruiser back into drive.

"But really, Kev. . ."

"Stow it," Kevin cut him off again, but his tone was neutral or even slightly amiable. "As long as you stick to your promise to stay away from the case, we're cool. This is why I wanted to talk to you, though. I know you well enough to know that your effing curiosity will push you to do dumb things, even when you promise not to. It's like there's another tiny, sociopathic version of you deep inside who sometimes gets his hands on the controls. He's not bad or evil, just unconcerned about the rules or what other people think."

Peter made a noise like he was about to try to speak, but Kevin immediately held up his right hand again and said in a sharper tone, "Let me finish. Anyway, I'm not judging, I'm just saying. So, my thought is that I will tell you whatever I can about the case to satisfy that curiosity and make it easier for you to keep the tiny sociopath away from the controls. Sound good?"

"Sure." Peter wanted to say more, but he kept it at that.

"So, for starters, a team went up to Tom's hunting cabin and there was no sign anybody had been there for a couple months at least. We've now also spoken to all of his contacts and nobody has anything for us. But this morning we found Tom's burnt-out truck on a logging road on the other side of the river."

"Really? But no sign of Tom?"

"Absolutely squat. Nothing. To be honest, Pete —" Kevin glanced quickly over at his passenger "— I'm starting to wonder whether you're right that he's not the killer but is somehow mixed up in something and is missing because he was the next victim. Sorry, but the longer there's no sign of him, the more likely it is because he's dead."

"Yeah, that's what I've been thinking too. Poor Tom. That would be so terrible. But we're not sure of that yet. He could still be frightened and hiding."

They pulled into Peter's drive. The only light on inside was the faint yellow glow from a reading lamp in the living room.

"Yeah, he could be. But with no truck and with his skidoos accounted for . . . He wasn't much of a long-distance snowshoe guy, was he?"

"No, Tom liked his loud engines and his padded seats. Likes, not liked." Peter corrected himself.

"There's another thing. We got the dental back."

"Oh? So, do we have a name for Jawbone now?"

"Afraid not. But we can take one name off the list. It's definitely not Leonard Alexander. Also, it's none of the missing members, associates, dealers or known contacts or enemies of Loki's Krew or the Brothers of Satan. At least not any of the missing that we have dental records on file for."

"What about Josh? Tom's hand from last summer."

"We can't completely rule him out because we don't have any dental records for him. But I really doubt it. Jawbone had some unique and expensive dental work. There were a half dozen gaps, including both upper incisors, so we started thinking homeless guy with missing teeth, but then the x-rays showed implants in the jawbone. The remains of little metal anchor screws, but nothing attached to them."

"Really? That's strange. Crowns should survive the fire."

"Porcelain crowns, yes, but gold crowns, no."

"Gold? Six gold teeth?"

"That's what it looks like. The fire was intense enough that the gold crowns melted away, as well as the tops of the screws. After we got the dental forensic report we went back, and sure enough — little gold bits in the ash and debris under him."

"I've got one gold bicuspid because Brian said it was more durable and barely any more expensive, but I've never seen anyone with a gold incisor, let alone two!"

"Yeah, this guy had a lot of bling in his mouth, which you would think would make it easier to ID him, but there's nobody in the national database who matches."

"Huh, that's interesting. Thanks for telling me." Peter paused before adding, "And I'm glad you're coming around on Tom not being a murderer."

"We're definitely keeping an open mind on this one. Anyway, have a good night and we'll talk again soon." Kevin unlocked the passenger door. As Peter began to climb out, Kevin added, "I'm not going to tell Laura about yesterday. Not unless you mess up again."

"Thanks, I appreciate it."

After a dinner of leftover ratatouille, Peter settled into the living room, where Laura was reading and both pets were sleeping. Laura had started a fire in their big, open stone fireplace. Merry slept as close as possible to the fire and Pippin as far away as possible because of his heavy winter coat. He usually picked a spot of bare floor under the draughtiest of the windows. Peter tried to settle into his book, but he could not absorb anything he was reading. The words just flowed by like a river of type, the meanings no more distinct than ripples and eddies of water. He normally had excellent powers of concentration, but it was hopeless tonight, so he closed the book and looked up at Laura. She noticed this and smiled at him.

"Rough day?"

"Not especially, but I'm tired."

"Did you talk to Anne?"

"Yeah, she actually stopped by the clinic to translate the note for me, but it was just a bunch of numbers."

"Oh well." Laura shrugged and returned to her book.

"I think I'm going to take Pippin out into the yard and just walk around the property a bit. Maybe that'll clear my head."

"Sounds good," Laura said without looking back up from her reading.

Pippin was already at Peter's side, head cocked, one ear up, one ear down.

It was a clear, moonless night with a spectacular starscape. Peter had hoped there would be northern lights, as solar flare activity was up, but the Milky Way was a wonder in its own right. Space was mostly a void, but this was far more star than void. Stars stacked upon stars for millions of light years, like seeing a forest where there are no open gaps between the trees, only more trees behind. He never tired of looking at it.

Sociopath, Peter thought to himself. *Is that what Kevin really thinks of me? And is it true, even a little bit?* He thought that sociopaths were generally aware of their condition and didn't care, whereas Peter would care if he were one and would hate it. No, that wasn't it. Kevin was wrong, or just used the term off the cuff without really thinking it through properly or understanding the diagnostic criteria. He did wonder, though, what made him lie to everyone about that silly piece of paper, and about being on Tom's farm. Stubborn intellectual pride was probably a more accurate diagnosis. He just had a compulsion to solve a problem himself and reaffirm to the world that Peter Bannerman was indeed the cleverest boy in the class.

"Is that it, Pippin? Am I just vain and attention-seeking?"

Pippin looked at him. Peter was using a soft voice that generally didn't prelude anything interesting, but he had learned that it was always worth listening carefully for a change in tone, in case a treat, or a run, or a scent hunt was proposed.

"I think it's more like an addiction. I just can't help myself when it comes to something like this. Free will is a myth. At least it's not booze or drugs or gambling. Or," and now his inflection went up, "freeze-dried liver, eh boy?"

They walked the perimeter of their ten acres where Peter and Laura had cut a meandering nature path of sorts. When they reached the portion of fencing on the east side where the presumed intruder had been seen lurking that morning, Peter slowed down, wondering whether Pippin might pick up a scent after so long, but Pippin didn't stop to sniff at anything other than his own old pee marks.

Back in the house, the fire was burning well, its amber light dancing on the walls. Merry was still lying beside the fire and Laura had put her book aside and was knitting mittens. Peter smiled at this picture of wintertime domestic bliss.

"What are those?" Peter asked, tempted to sit down again, even though he was very tired and should really go to bed.

"Pokémon mittens," Laura said, without looking up.

"That's new, isn't it? Special order?"

"No, it's just something I'm trying out. I'll put them on Etsy and Artfire and see what happens."

"Pikachu?"

Laura smiled, "Eevee. Pikachu is too obvious. And besides, Eevee is cuter."

"If you say so." Peter was not a Pokémon fan. "I'm exhausted. I'm going to bed now, good night."

"Good night, Peter."

Peter gave her a peck on the forehead and headed upstairs to their bedroom.

Years ago, Peter had taught himself to have lucid dreams. Dreams had always interested him, but the science was unclear on what, if any, purpose they might serve. Freud was clearly wrong with his rigid, symbolic, usually sexual interpretations, yet Peter felt that there must be something of value to be gleaned from them. The conscious mind was so highly developed in humans compared to animals that it often drowned out what the subconscious had to say. And unfortunately, while asleep, the conscious mind was fully offline, so it had no opportunity to examine the subconscious ramblings of the dream state. Consciousness was either over-whelming or absent. Scattered, foggy memories of dreams after waking were useless. The solution was to bring a small amount of consciousness to bear by training himself to have lucid dreams. Then he could explore this state and perhaps learn something. Or at the very least, escape the nightmares that had plagued him when he was younger. So, he bought a couple of books on the process and found it was easier to learn than he had expected. Soon he could just walk out of his nightmares into an Arcadian meadow, or, if the monsters pursued him there, just wake himself up.

Tonight, he decided that once he started dreaming, he would look in everyone's mouth for gold teeth and he would ask everyone whether they spoke Korean. Who knew? Maybe his subconscious, his more intuitive animal mind, had a helpful perspective.

As it happened, in his dream, he was in a canoe drifting down a river. It wasn't anywhere familiar. The water was almost unnaturally blue, and the riverbank was very green with a series of neat white wooden houses on it, one after another. People smiled and waved at him. He looked at their smiles for gold, but there was none, and he called up to them, "Do you speak Korean?" They all laughed and said, "No!" He half-recognized some of the people, but most were strangers. At the last house was a familiar person, though. Michelle Nyquist was hanging white T-shirts on a clothesline on the bright green grass between her house and the river. They snapped and fluttered in the stiffening breeze and he caught the scent of fresh laundry. This distracted him long enough that he didn't notice that the river was freezing. Soon he was trying to paddle his canoe across solid ice. The world turned white. Michelle was gone. The laundry was gone. All the houses were gone. The ice made cracking noises, at first quiet, then very loud. Peter began to panic. He knew that when the ice broke there would only be space below. An infinite, starless void.

He woke himself up.

CHAPTER
Twenty

Obviously, his subconscious mind had no better grip on the matter than his conscious mind did. It had been worth a try. Michelle Nyquist's appearance in the dream was banal and predictable because Peter had known that she was booked as his first appointment Thursday morning. Paisley, another one of her Russian wolfhounds, had been gagging on and off for a couple of days. Michelle would have come right away at the first little gag, but she had been out of town. The dog sitter wasn't concerned because Paisley was fine otherwise, and she didn't want to bother Michelle. It was only when Michelle called her Wednesday to check on the dogs that the information came out. Michelle would be getting a new dog sitter.

Theresa had recounted the ensuing phone call to Peter, doing a remarkably good job of mimicking Michelle's high, screechy voice: "I can't believe it! I just can't believe it! And after I gave her explicit instructions to text me with anything, anything at all about the dogs. Millennials! Present company excepted of course, Theresa. Anyway, I'm coming back late tonight, and I need to see Peter first thing. Double-book me if you need to!"

Double-booking was unnecessary as the previous 9 a.m. appointment, an elderly cat who hadn't eaten in days, had passed away at home overnight. This was likely a blessing for the cat, and it was definitely a blessing for Peter, who became frazzled whenever he was double-booked, especially when it was a demanding client booked on top of an emotional end-of-life consultation.

Michelle was impeccably turned out, as always, with a dress, hair, handbag, jewellery, makeup and nails that even Peter, who was profoundly unschooled and uninterested in such matters, recognized to be top of the line. Even Michelle didn't normally dress like this for the vet, though, so she must have had another appointment afterwards.

"How was your trip?" Peter inquired once they had settled into the exam room.

"Oh, fine. I always love New York, but the weather was even more miserable than here, and then of course I couldn't enjoy the last day, after finding out that that airhead had ignored Paisley's cough."

"It's a cough, not a gag?"

"Well, kind of both and kind of neither. I tried to catch it on video on my phone, but it's always over so quick. Here, I'll try to demonstrate."

Peter was treated to the spectacle of New Selfoss's wealthiest citizen, dressed in haute couture, stretching her neck forwards, pearl necklace dangling, and making the harsh, strangled sound a cat makes when it is trying to bring up a hairball.

"I see. You're right, that is both a cough and a gag. He's doing OK otherwise? Appetite? Energy?"

"He's eating well, but then Paisley is just a stomach disguised as a dog. Eating is all he ever thinks about. But I think he's got a little less energy. Brittany thought it was just because I was away, but it's not."

"Well, Mr. Hairy-Stomach-On-Four-Legs, shall we have a look at you then?" Peter addressed the tall, slender dog, who had been watching him intently. Out of well-worn habit he moved through the examination methodically so he wouldn't forget anything, but it was difficult not to jump directly to listening to the heart, which was normally the last thing he did. He had a hunch regarding what he would hear, and his mind was already racing ahead to how he would break the news to Michelle.

His hunch was correct. Paisley's heart rhythm was erratic, akin to the sound of sneakers in the dryer.

Shit.

Peter straightened up and looked at Michelle, trying to keep his face neutral. "Paisley has an arrythmia, an irregular heartbeat."

"Oh, is that serious?"

"It can be. It depends on what's causing it. What are you feeding your boys these days?" Peter had a dark suspicion.

"Always the best, most expensive dog food you can buy! Why, do you think it's the food?"

"I'm sure you buy the best, but what brand? What are the main ingredients?"

"It's Black Wolf Ultra-Premium. The groomer recommended it. Pure, natural, holistic, all-Canadian ingredients. I think it's Yukon elk and Quebec split pea. Grain-free, of course."

Peter had to stop himself from groaning audibly. "Oh, I thought we talked about diet during his annual checkup?"

"Yes, but this has such great reviews online!"

"Right, well there may be an issue with the grain-free aspect, especially since peas are a major ingredient in this food. We're seeing quite a few dogs develop heart problems on diets where grains have been replaced by legumes such as peas and lentils."

"Is that what Paisley has? Is it really bad?"

"I don't know yet, but if he does, we can stop it from getting worse by changing the diet and we can treat the problem with meds in most cases."

"Not all cases?"

"Not all, but Paisley will be fine. You caught it early." Peter mentally crossed his fingers as he said this. "I can confirm what's going on and how bad it is right away with a quick ultrasound. Let me just check with Theresa first and make sure that the next patient isn't waiting already."

"OK. But I'm so shocked, Peter. Tell me again that Paisley will be fine."

"He will. But let's make sure with the ultrasound." Peter's mental fingers were still crossed. He popped his head out the exam room door and confirmed that the waiting room was empty. He would have given Paisley an ultrasound right away regardless, but for some reason he felt compelled to demonstrate to Michelle that his time was in demand.

"We're good, follow me to the back, please," Peter instructed Michelle.

Peter's ultrasound machine was a portable one that looked more like a laptop than a $40,000 piece of medical equipment, although it did come in a padded aluminum briefcase that resembled something nuclear launch codes would be kept in. He primarily used ultrasound for pregnancy checks in cows and other large animal work, but he was able to diagnose some of the more common small animal conditions with it too. Complicated cases with more subtle changes required referral to a colleague in Winnipeg. Unfortunately, what he suspected was wrong with Paisley was all too common.

Peter called Kat over and asked her to hold Paisley while he shaved a small square in the dog's right armpit. Peter then asked Michelle to turn the lights off. The ultrasound keyboard glowed pale green. Peter tapped a few keys and twiddled a knob with his left hand as his right hand guided the ultrasound probe across the shaved patch of skin. Paisley stood very still. The screen showed a series of flickering, fuzzy grey and white patches on an otherwise black background.

"It looks like bad TV reception from the 1950s." Michelle gave a nervous laugh.

"Hang on a sec," Peter said as he adjusted a few more knobs. Suddenly something resembling a pulsating doughnut sprang into view. "That's his heart. It's his left ventricle, to be more specific. It's the biggest and most important of his four heart chambers, because it is responsible for pumping blood out to the body. Just like in a human."

"Wow, that's amazing," Michelle said, leaning forward. "That's your heart, my love," she murmured, patting Paisley on the head. "Is it OK, Peter?"

Peter manipulated a cursor on the screen before replying, "Well, you see what I just measured here? It's how strong the left ventricle's contractions are. Normally the number is in the 30s or low 40s, but he's at 22."

"What does that mean?"

"It's not as bad as it could be. I had a dog in last month at 12. Anything below 25 is a worry, though. I'm going to prescribe something to strengthen his heartbeat and you absolutely have to change the diet back to something more traditional with grains."

"Whatever I need to do. I'm just so glad he's going to be OK, right?"

"He will." Peter mentally crossed his fingers one more time.

Later, as they stood at the reception desk after having gone through all the instructions for the medication and plans for follow-up, Michelle shook her head and said, "I still can't believe it. First Tom's truck being found and now this. Not that I give a rat's ass about what happened to Tom, but still, it's a shock too."

"You think he's dead then?"

"I'm sure he is. Whoever he owed those gambling debts to finally got fed up with him."

"Gambling? I know you said before that he was in debt, but I didn't know why."

"That's the word anyway. Sports betting, mostly hockey. High-roller stuff outside of the regulated system."

"Really? Wow. But what about the body in the barn? How does that fit in?"

"I don't know," Michelle replied, as she put the pills in her purse. "But once you start owing money to that kind of people, a lot of bad stuff can happen. Maybe they shot some other poor loser in front of Tom to show him that they're serious? Who knows? Who really cares? Lowlifes taking out other lowlifes."

"Isn't that a bit harsh?"

"You're sweet and naïve, Dr. Bannerman." Michelle glanced at her glittery watch. "I've got to run now. I've just got enough time to drop Paisley at home before heading into the city to see my lawyers. Will he be OK by himself for three hours?"

"Yes, he'll be OK, don't worry."

The next two appointments were routine cat vaccinations and then Peter had an obese Rottweiler spay to tackle. Sheba belonged to a buddy of Darryl Parenteau's, another old ex-biker named Phil Mackenzie. She was a sweet dog and the procedure really needed to be done, but she was also the size and shape of an Oktoberfest beer keg, so it was going to be time-consuming and exhausting. The public tended to think that a spay was a spay, but comparing spaying Sheba to spaying a little cat, like Tigs, his last appointment, was like comparing a ten-kilometre hike in the Amazon rainforest to a two-kilometre stroll in Assiniboine Park. Both involved walking, but the comparison ended there.

As he slowly worked his way through the surgery, his mind kept replaying Michelle's comments about Tom's gambling habit. He had had no idea. He knew Tom was a big sports fan, but that was another area where their lives didn't intersect. If this information was correct, though, it represented a new way to be confused about what was going on. Peter hated being confused. His brain kept sorting and resorting the puzzle pieces. He'd have to write out a new list in his notebook tonight and work the gambling in, assuming again that all the pieces belonged to the same puzzle. He remembered hearing about a jigsaw puzzle manufacturer who, to increase the level of challenge, put in a few extra pieces with the same design that didn't fit. Drug debts fit better for a guy who dabbled in the rock-and-roll lifestyle than gambling debts, but maybe there was a Korean sports betting racket? Maybe that was a thing? He had no idea.

"Does Ethan bet on sports?" Peter asked Kat, who was monitoring the anesthetic. Ethan was Kat's boyfriend and was a serious sports fan, usually appearing at clinic functions in team jerseys. Peter always struggled to make small talk with him. The feeling was presumably mutual.

Kat was used to these out-of-left-field questions from Peter after long stretches of silence during surgery. "A little. Mostly Bomber games, sometimes Jets."

Peter didn't say anything for a minute while he struggled to ligate a vein. "But not big money? And nothing to do with Asia?"

Kat glanced up at Peter from her chart. "Asia? Uh, no. I mean, he likes watching martial arts, especially tae kwon do, but I'm sure he doesn't bet on it. And when he does bet on, say, the Grey Cup, it's just one of those pools with his buddies. Fifty bucks is a big bet for him."

Peter nodded and lapsed back into silence, mopping out a bit of blood with a gauze sponge and beginning to prepare for the closing sutures.

"Why do you ask?" Kat finally said, as it looked like Peter had dropped the subject and she wouldn't find out otherwise.

"Oh, Michelle Nyquist was in . . ."

Kat snorted. She never made any attempt to hide her dislike of Michelle.

Peter smiled under his surgical mask. ". . . and she was saying that Tom had big sports gambling debts. Plus, I know that he had a developed an interest in Korean culture," Peter added, making up another of his white lies on the spot, "so I wondered if there might be a connection?"

"Beats me." Kat shrugged. "Sounds like a stretch, though."

"Yeah, it does."

CHAPTER
Twenty-One

That afternoon Peter had three farm calls, which made it the busiest day in a week. It was the peak of the winter calving season, so in theory it could be extremely busy every day, but the New Selfoss district only had a handful of cattle operations, and those producers, such as Bill Chernov and Ed Baldurson, were sophisticated and experienced enough to handle a lot of the minor obstetrical problems themselves. He shared after-hours calls, alternating weeks with his colleague Sheila Thiessen in Lac du Bonnet. The two on-call weeks in February were usually the worst, as it was the season of the dreaded 3:00 a.m. phone call. Typical was, "Peter, I think I've got a breach . . ." as the farmer described a calf stuck in the birth canal and requiring an emergency C-section. So far this year, however, he hadn't been called out once yet, which was a record.

Nonetheless, Sheba's spay that morning and the farm visits, which included a very upsetting euthanasia of an old horse belonging to a friend of Laura's, made for a draining day. Consequently once Peter was home for the evening, he glanced at his phone with loathing every time it vibrated. He had originally planned to write out a new set of theories in his notebook, but Laura persuaded him to watch *The Big Lebowski* again with her. Peter's phone sat on the armrest of the chesterfield, screen down, but being on call, he had to check every time it vibrated or that glow emanated from the edges of the screen. This happened twice and it was nothing each time, and then the third time, just as Walter and The Dude were about to scatter Donny's ashes, it was a text from Elton Marwick. Peter wondered whether something else had happened with the garden shed.

peter, can you come?
i have something to show you

The movie was almost over, and it didn't sound urgent, so he didn't reply right away. Then as the credits rolled, he texted back.

Sure. I can come first thing tomorrow, say 8:30?
I don't have an appointment until 10.

He stared at his phone for a minute, expecting a reply, but it was late, so possibly Elton had gone to bed after sending the request, or possibly no reply was needed. But Elton was always very polite, so Peter did expect some sort of response eventually.

"Who was that?" Laura asked, yawning and stretching.

"Elton Marwick. He says he has something to show me."

"Oh. Any idea?"

"I presume something to do with the shed break-in a couple weeks ago. At least it's not a calving!"

"Right. You're in no shape to handle a middle-of-the-night surgery. But be careful if you go to Marwick's tomorrow."

"Careful?"

"I know you think I'm being silly, but anything criminal around here has me on edge now."

"It's just a garden shed."

"It doesn't matter. Nobody knows what's going on, so nobody can be sure what's connected and what isn't."

"I think Elton's gnomes are safe, but I'll be careful, of course."

The next morning was Valentine's Day. Peter and Laura exchanged chocolates and joke cards — Peter's to Laura said, "I love you so much, I'd give you a kidney. Maybe even my own." And Laura's to Peter had a picture of Donald Trump with the caption, "I want you on my side of the wall." They agreed that Peter's was funnier.

"Keep an eye on the weather while you're at Marwick's," Laura said. "Looks like there's a big system moving in pretty quickly." She held up a weather radar image on her phone for Peter to see.

"Yeah, good point. That's a low-priority road for the ploughs. Fortunately, Elton's not much of a talker, so he won't keep me long."

"If you got stuck out there you'd be late for work, which would make you late for that fireside fondue I have planned for us tonight." Laura grinned broadly.

"Don't want to be late for that!" Peter said in a happy sing-song before giving Laura a hug and a kiss.

Peter kept glancing at his phone through his breakfast of oatmeal, a slightly underripe banana — which is the way he preferred them — and East Frisian tea. He continued to expect a follow-up message from Elton, but there still wasn't one by the time he was ready to leave, so he quickly texted before heading out.

I'm on my way. Be there in 20.

There was no reply to this either, but Peter thought, *Oh well, Marwick's probably not that tech-savvy. In fact, it's surprising he texted instead of telephoning.*

The sun had been up almost an hour, but at this time of year it was still low in the southeast and it was a grey day, so the light was milky and diffuse. A steady southerly wind was blowing snow across the road, causing small, irregular drifts to form. There had apparently been no other traffic in the last hour or two, so Peter's truck was the first to punch through the drifts. As he approached it, Elton's normally bright blue house looked pale through the veil of whirling snow, and the rainbow-hued garden decorations were also muted and dull. Elton's car was parked out front, but the walk hadn't been shovelled and the steps hadn't been swept, as if he weren't expecting Peter after all.

Curious, Peter thought, *perhaps he's unwell?*

Peter stomped through the snow that had blown onto the walk and the steps and rang the doorbell. It echoed in the house. Then there was silence except for the wind, which was picking up and making a whistling noise as it rounded the corner of the house. From the step Peter could see into the living room through the front window. It was dark and appeared empty. He rang the doorbell again and then knocked loudly.

Still nothing.

Peter tried the doorknob. It was locked.

He waited a long minute, pondering what to do. *I'll try calling him*, he thought. He tried both Elton's cell and his landline. The former went directly to voicemail and he could hear the latter ringing in the house and then an answering machine came on.

But Elton's car was here. Peter felt very uneasy.

He went back down the front steps and walked around to the rear of the house. The snow had drifted even deeper here. Peter tripped on a buried gnome, cursing lightly as he did so. He had to use his hands and feet to clear the snow away from the back step so that the door would be able to swing open. But before trying the door he tried to look in the adjacent kitchen window. The kitchen was dark, and from his angle he could only see the upper cabinets and ceiling.

Peter was about to grab the door latch when out of the corner of his eye he noticed that across the yard to the far left, the garden shed door was wide open.

He felt his heart clench. The backdoor was unlocked, so he pulled it open and shouted, "Hello! Elton! It's Peter! Dr. Bannerman! You texted me to come!"

Silence.

There was nothing that his objective conscious mind could identify as objectively frightening, but wordless fear flooded him from his subconscious.

"Hello! Are you OK? I'm going to come in!"

Peter stepped into the back landing. He was immediately confronted by a strong odour. It was extremely familiar, yet he couldn't put his finger on it.

Basement stairs led off to the left, and ahead two steps went up to the kitchen. From the landing he could only see what appeared to be a small breakfast nook. He went up the two steps and turned to his right to look into the kitchen, dimly lit from the window over the sink.

Blood.

So much blood.

The white tiled floor was flooded with it. The first thing that came to his mind was that it looked like a slaughterhouse floor. That had been the smell. Blood.

"Jesus!"

Then he saw Elton. The old man was slumped, half-sitting, in the far dark corner of the kitchen, legs spread before him, knees slightly bent, shoulders against the corner cabinet, chin down on his chest.

His chest.

"Oh my god! Oh no, oh no, oh no."

Blood wasn't flowing now, but a gash in his chest, directly over his heart, made it obvious where it had come from. The gash formed the apex of a sticky red triangle whose base was the entire kitchen floor.

CHAPTER
Twenty-Two

P eter felt faint. He leaned forward and put his hands on his knees to steady himself. His breathing came in rapid gasps. Then he sat down on the floor and squeezed his eyes shut.

The house was utterly silent. No ticking clocks, no electronic hum, only the sound of his pulse thrumming in his ears.

He opened his eyes again but avoided looking directly at Elton. The countertops were in disorder. A bin of flour had been knocked over. The toaster lay on its side. There was a large kitchen knife out, but it did not have any visible blood on it.

Peter stood up slowly, still breathing hard and fast. He was able to walk just far enough to get to the landing. Then he sat down hard again on the steps, almost falling over as he did so.

Death was a weekly visitor to the veterinary clinic, and while it was the death of animals, the grief it provoked in their loved ones was as intense as a lot of the grief Peter had seen for human deaths. But it was never violent and bloody. It was always peaceful. Over the years he had seen a handful of dead humans, including his and Laura's parents, but they also looked peaceful. This was different. It was different in a way that defied comparison to anything at all. A door had opened to a completely new realm of human experience that he had previously only had abstract theoretical knowledge of.

He made a conscious effort to steady his breathing before he pulled out his phone and dialed 911.

His memory of the subsequent minutes was hazy, but when Kevin and Kristine arrived, they found Peter standing in the yard, in the gathering blizzard, his jacket open, shaking.

Peter's next clear memory was of sitting in the passenger seat of Kevin's squad car. The grey white of the blizzard was punctuated by flashing blue and red lights scattered at random around Elton Marwick's drive. Kevin had given Peter his thermos of coffee. Despite what had just happened, Peter's thoughts were only that the coffee would be terrible and surprise that Kevin had had time to grab coffee. But then he supposed that Kevin might have already been in the car on patrol. These banal thoughts having run their course, Peter stared blankly out the window at the lights.

Then Kevin returned to the car and motioned for Peter to roll down the window. "How are you doing, buddy?"

"Better, I guess."

"Are you ready for some questions?"

"Sure." Peter was relieved that Kevin's tone was gentle. There was no way this could be construed as meddling. It was just a classic wrong-place-at-the-wrong-time scenario.

Peter described the whole sequence of events, beginning with the break-in of Elton's shed, and him asking Peter for his thoughts, through to the text message and then finally the discovery of the body.

Kevin listened quietly to the whole story, staring into the middle distance over his steering wheel.

"OK, thanks, Pete. You'll have to give a formal statement at the station, but this is enough to start with. Can you show me the text message?"

Peter swiped to the appropriate screen and handed him the phone.

"Sent at 10:03 last night. He's pretty much in maximum rigour now, so he's probably been dead since at least eight or nine last night."

"What? How's that possible?"

"His phone is missing, or at least we haven't found it yet." Kevin paused and took a deep breath before going on. "I'm pretty sure they used his dead finger to unlock his phone. It was the killer who texted you."

"Jesus," Peter said softly. "No caps or punctuation . . . I thought that was strange."

Kevin made a quizzical facial expression.

"Elton was an educated 60-something. I was surprised that he didn't capitalize or punctuate properly in his text message."

Kevin nodded. "Right. But now the big question: Do you have any idea, any idea at all, why the killer would want you to see the body?"

"Was it a trap? Were they trying to lure me out to kill me too?"

"Maybe. But similar question then: Do you have any idea why someone would want to kill you, especially right after killing Elton?"

"God no, Kev, none. Marwick and I barely knew each other. The only thing I can think of is something to do with that shed and that whoever it is knows that I looked at it too, although as I said, there was sweet bugger-all to see." In spite of himself, Peter took a swig from the vile, now lukewarm coffee. He couldn't stop himself from adding, "You guys didn't want to look at the shed when he called you about the break-in."

"Fair point," Kevin replied, not rising to the bait.

"Do you think there's a connection to the murder in Tom's barn?"

"I don't know. The two are totally different in terms of weapon and style, if you can call it that. There was a struggle here and there was no attempt to blow Elton's house up. But having said that, two murders within a month already doubles our previous annual record, so if they're not related, then it's one heck of a coincidence."

"Have you found the weapon?"

"No. A kitchen knife was out, but I think Elton may have tried to use it for self-defence. It was not the blade that killed him."

Peter nodded. He could feel the energy draining from him like water from a bathtub after the plug is pulled.

Kevin noticed the change. "Hey, why don't I get Kristine to drive you home. She can bring Laura back for your truck. Let work know you can't make it in today, then relax for a bit and meet me at the station at one for the statement. OK, pal?"

"OK." Peter couldn't think of a better plan.

Laura was so shocked she could hardly speak. Once she found her words, she insisted Peter have a hot bath, which always relaxed him. Peter agreed and ran the bath as hot as it would go and used a eucalyptus scented bubble bath, which always connoted purity to him. It was relaxing, but as much as he tried to drag his mind away, it would always return to the picture of Elton Marwick in a pool of congealed blood, with a knife wound in his heart.

He did not stay in the bath long. Afterwards he sat down in the living room with a mug of perfectly brewed tea, hoping to press some sort of hidden restart button on the day. His eyes moved across the various souvenirs they had on display from their travels, trying to conjure distracting memories. A batik wall hanging from Indonesia. Carved wooden figures from Malawi. Ceramics from Portugal. But still his mind was filled with Elton and blood.

Laura had returned in the meantime, and, after checking in on Peter, wisely left him alone. Conversation was not what he needed now. He needed the silence and the space to mentally process what he had seen and experienced. Rational thought was his friend.

Emotion was not his friend. What he was coping with now was emotion. Shock. Fear. Grief. Anger. He knew that these emotions would subside soon, and then he could begin to examine what had happened with clarity and logic. But not now. For now, emotion still had the tiller and was setting his mind's course.

The formal statement at the station went smoothly. Peter was already feeling a little better by then and more in control of his emotions. When he had finished describing everything, Kevin leaned back in his office chair, stroked his beard for a moment and asked, "So, do you have a theory about the garden shed?"

Peter had begun to think about this on the short drive over. "I assume the killer hid in there."

Kevin nodded. "OK, but why?"

"He probably came intending to break in, so he waited there for the house to become quiet, or for Elton to leave. It has a little window."

"Wouldn't his vehicle be obvious? Most of the road is visible from Elton's place."

"I thought about that. I think he walked, at least a little way. A spur of the Heritage Trail runs through the woods behind the shed. Probably the same person was there a few weeks back, casing the place, when he knocked over those pots."

Kevin looked unpersuaded. "Hmm, OK." He stroked his beard some more. "That's one theory, anyway."

"Is anything missing from the house?" Peter asked.

"Not that we can determine."

"How about his freezer?"

"Packed full, so nothing missing."

"Really?"

"Yeah, really. I was surprised too. I figured that that was the connection between you and Elton. Elton resisted our mysterious meat bandit and got killed in the scuffle, is what I assumed."

"Me too."

Peter was positive that that was what had happened and was going to explain his reasoning, regardless of the countervailing evidence, when Kevin continued, "I'm really concerned about that text message luring you out there. However, if they wanted to attack you, they probably would have done so, because they knew exactly when you were coming. They wanted you to find the body. And that makes me think some sort of psycho is out there."

"We're back to the serial killer idea?"

"Not exactly. Two killings don't make it a serial crime."

"What about John Doe and Tom?"

"We don't know for sure that Tom is dead, and we can't connect John Doe. Also, the crimes are different. No pattern like we see with serial killers. Anyway, it doesn't matter what we call him, he's dangerous and you need to be careful."

"I know. Laura and I talked about this."

"Well, we're going to run more patrols by your place, and I want you to get an emergency locksmith to come and swap out your locks for the keyless digital ones. Nothing is foolproof, but they can't be picked the same way." Kevin paused and took a swallow of coffee.

"OK, makes sense." Peter had an instinctive preference for analog over digital whenever there was a choice, but Kevin was right, and Laura would overrule him anyway if he resisted.

"Thanks, Pete. Don't take this the wrong way, but this is more about protecting my sister than it is about protecting you."

They grinned at each other.

CHAPTER
Twenty-Three

Peter felt much more like himself the next day, Saturday. That's not to say that he wasn't still horrified by what had happened to Elton, or that he didn't still have some level of fear regarding the murderer's apparent interest in him. It was more that those emotions no longer drowned out his thought processes. He was now able to quiet them whenever they began to make too much noise, like settling unruly children. He liked this metaphor. As far as he had been able to observe, children were mostly governed by emotion, jumping freely from sad to happy to angry back to sad again. Even dogs were more emotionally stable, although, interestingly, puppies less so. The process of becoming an adult was largely a process of developing mastery over these emotions. But the child within never went away entirely. This was possibly a good thing as it allowed access to useful and pleasant emotions, but more often it was just a nuisance. Like children.

As Valentine's Day yesterday had been a bust, he and Laura decided to go cross-country skiing together today, have coffee at Rita's, go home and change and then go to The Flying Beaver for dinner. Peter had an ulterior motive for wanting to visit the Beaver. Elton's darts club normally met there Saturday evenings and they were likely having an informal wake for him. He didn't mention this to Laura, but she loved the food and the cozy faux-English pub vibe, so it was an easy sell.

The Flying Beaver was a New Selfoss institution, having been there in one form or another since the early 1960s. Visitors often assumed that the name would refer to something like a cartoon beaver as a World War One flying ace, or possibly piloting a bush plane in the north, so they were usually surprised and amused to be confronted by a taxidermy beaver sprouting goose wings above the bar.

"Ah, that's Castoropteryx," Lloyd, the barman and owner, would explain in a stagey deadpan. "The local Indigenous people have a legend that on the first full moon after the autumn equinox, the winged beaver will take flight from his lodge. You see, the rest of the time he keeps his wings hidden. The fur is very thick. They say that anyone who sees him will have good fortune through the coming winter."

The visitors would laugh and take photos and sometimes comment on the similarity to the jackalope. If Lloyd heard this he would interrupt, "Oh no, it's not the same thing at all. Jackalopes were invented by a couple white guys in Wyoming in the '30s. The flying beaver is not only part of ancient local legend, but there are people here who swear they've seen him. More like Nessie, or the Sasquatch, or Manipogo than like a jackalope. I'm not saying I believe it, but as I told you, he even has a Latin name — Castoropteryx, meaning beaver with wings."

At this point the visitors would usually nod, smile politely and turn their attention to the beer tap handles.

By the time Peter and Laura arrived at the Beaver it was busy, but fortunately their favourite table was one of the few remaining free ones. The place was done in dark wood, with exposed beams along the ceiling and a large fireplace in the far corner. Various posters, old signs and bric-a-brac from the UK and Ireland lined the walls. On either side of the hearth were nooks with a rough-hewn table for two in each. The nooks were set off by archways that had dried hops hanging from them. Lloyd kept the music, which tended to folk and classic rock, quiet, although there was often live music on Saturday nights. Tonight, a band called The Plague Doctors was advertised, but they wouldn't start playing until nine. The place was filled with locals this time of year, so there were lots of nods and hi-how-are-yas and slaps on the shoulder as they made their way over to their table.

Peter ordered the house Castoropteryx Bitter, brewed down the road by the New Selfoss Brewing Company, while Laura went for their Raven's Eye Stout. Rural Manitoba was dominated by a meat and potatoes culinary aesthetic, but the Beaver was one of the few places with good vegetarian options. Lloyd had worked in a pub in London for a few years and brought some modern, big-city sensibilities back with him when he took over the place from the previous owner. Out with the Bud Lite and Labatt Blue, in with the microbrews and B.C. wines. Out with the chicken nuggets and previously frozen curly fries, in with portobello mushroom burgers and hand-cut chips. To be sure, there was still plenty for the meat lover, but the quality had gone up and, to everyone's pleasant surprise, it turned out people didn't mind paying a little more for that.

Peter and Laura chatted a bit about the people they had bumped into on the way in, and when that conversation lapsed, Peter let his eyes wander over toward the darts area, on the far side of the bar.

"Hey, that's Chris and Ken. I had better go over and say hi."

"Of course, sure," Laura said. "They were friends with Elton, right?"

"And Tom too. They all played in a darts league together."

"Wow, what a weird coincidence."

"Yeah, really weird."

Laura smiled and appeared to weigh what she wanted to say next before she laughed and said, "Well, good thing you don't play darts!"

"That's not funny." But Peter smiled too. He was glad to see Laura make a joke. She had been tense all day, even after the vigorous ski.

"I thought it was!"

Peter made his way over to Chris and Ken and shook their hands, saying how terrible what happened was. He knew that a hug might have been called for, but he was not a hugger. Not at all. Thankfully neither of the other men made a move to hug him either.

Chris Olson, a short, thin, balding man with frameless, round glasses, replied first. "Yes, terrible, just terrible. And unbelievable. Murder? Elton? Here in New Selfoss?"

Ken Finnbogason, also balding and thin, but with a moustache and much taller — almost as tall as Peter — joined in. "Really unbelievable. Really, really unbelievable." Both were wearing forest green Flying Beaver Pointsmen Darts Club T-shirts.

"And you found him, Peter? My god, I can't imagine!" Chris said.

"Yes, just my bad luck, I guess." Kevin had told Peter not to let anyone know that he had received that text message.

Chris and Ken both shook their heads in sympathy.

"And so soon after Tom's disappearance too," Ken said. "You've got to wonder whether it's got something to do with the Pointsmen!"

Nervous laughter.

"Maybe it's the Gimli Bullseye Gliders! We're the biggest threat to their defence of the Golden Dartboard this year," Chris said.

More nervous laughter.

"Did Tom and Elton hang out outside of the club?" Peter asked.

"Not that I know of," Ken answered.

The three of them were quiet for a moment, and each took a sip from their pints. Then Chris spoke up, "There was just the thing about the frozen hams."

Peter sputtered and was afraid that he was going to spew Castoropteryx Bitter out of his nose. "Frozen hams?" he said once he recovered.

"Yeah, remember, Ken? It was the Saturday before the barn fire and Tom was asking if anyone had temporary freezer space. He had these huge hams that he needed to keep somewhere because his freezer had died or something."

"You're right, I do remember that," Ken said, nodding.

"Huge frozen hams, you're sure?" Peter tried to keep his tone neutral and even.

"Yeah, like really huge. There was something a bit comical about it. Almost Python!" Chris laughed.

"Makes sense," Peter said. "He asked me to temporarily store some big pork shoulders for him too. Same reason." He was tempted to tell them that they had subsequently been stolen in the break-in, but decided not to. He wasn't entirely sure why. He had told Theresa, after all, and the story was probably starting to trickle through the rumour mill anyway, but somehow it didn't feel right to tell them now.

"Really? You too? Kind of weird. But anyway, Elton offered and the two of them made some kind of arrangement to meet."

"Did Tom go to his place to deliver the meat?" Peter asked.

"I don't know. That would make sense, but they were just going to text each other to figure out the details. Just then the Selkirk Steeltips showed up for the tournament, so we dropped the subject." Chris took a long pull from his beer, draining it.

"More beers?" Ken asked them both. Peter's glass was empty too.

"Sure."

"Your bet!"

Ken took their empty glasses and headed to the bar, which was now quite crowded.

"You didn't have freezer space?" Peter asked Chris.

"I did, but Elton gives off a more honourable and trustworthy vibe, so I think Tom felt safer taking his offer! Not that I would 'accidentally'" — Chris used air quotes — "eat one of those hams, but that's probably not the reason. He just needed to pick someone, and he picked Elton."

"I think he picked me because I'm a flexitarian."

"Forgive me, but I always have to laugh when I hear that word, 'flexitarian'! Sounds like you're a yoga cult member," Chris teased him.

Peter nodded. "I agree, there should be a better label for someone who is not a complete vegetarian, but keeps meat eating to a minimum, and then only ethically sourced. Meat minimalist? Ethivore?"

"Flexi, mini, ethi, whatever. Not a full patch member of the Church of Bacon anyway!"

"Did anyone say bacon?" Ken said loudly as he walked back with three full beer glasses carefully gripped in a cluster between his hands.

"Just bugging the vegetarian." Chris smiled.

"Flexitarian." Peter smiled back at him.

Peter laughed along with them and then excused himself with his fresh glass, pointing to Laura in the booth across the room. On his way back to her he stopped at the bar and waited until he caught Lloyd's eye.

"Pulled pork sandwich to go, please!"

Lloyd raised his eyebrows. "Really? Now all of a sudden you're crossing over to the pork side?"

"No, no. It's for Pippin."

CHAPTER
Twenty-Four

C uriosity killed the cat. That's what everyone says. It's one of those sticky aphorisms, like "a penny saved is a penny earned" or "absence makes the heart grow fonder" or "you can't fight city hall" that Peter felt were taken to be truer than they actually were simply because of the memorable phrasing. Effective advertising works on the same principle. But with respect to curious cats, Peter could only think of two cats in his whole career who were actually killed by their curiosity. More often curious cats came in with minor injuries, and Peter was sure that they were unrepentant. In fact, most of them went right back to the same curiosity-driven adventures that led to the injury. These were lean, happy cats with glints in their eyes and tails held high. The incurious specimens on the other hand were often sloppy, dull couch-dwellers, domesticated to within an inch of being reduced to the status of animated furniture. These were, of course, gross generalizations, but nonetheless Peter was a devotee of the power of curiosity. And he was not worried that it would kill him.

Consequently Sunday morning found Peter and Pippin scent training with bits of pulled pork. Laura had questioned Peter about this, clearly suspicious that it somehow had something to do with Tom's pigs, but Peter explained that he had heard that the World

Scent Dog Championship would, among other things, involve detecting smuggled pork, which was important because of the African swine fever outbreak. Another lie. But a white one again. Nonetheless, he made a mental note to start writing these down somewhere so that he didn't stumble over them later and get caught out in a contradiction.

On the positive side of the honesty ledger, Peter had texted Kevin after they got home from The Flying Beaver to let him know that Tom had apparently given hams to Elton for safekeeping, thus cementing the connection to their own break-in.

But where did Elton keep these hams, if not in his freezer? It was, to be sure, a minor detail, but one that nagged at Peter. He had a theory however, and he wasn't ready to share it with Kevin just yet because he wanted to prove it for himself first. And thanks to Pippin he was in a better position to do so than Kevin was.

They drove down Faraday Road, past the construction site where the TV and jewellery had been dumped, all the way to where it ended at a T-intersection. There they turned right, down a small gravel road that was the back way to Elton's and ultimately Tom's place too. Peter slowed down when they reached a stand of jack pines. Here there was a small parking area on the left, beside the trees. This was an access point to the spur hiking trail that connected the New Selfoss Heritage Trail to the Trans Canada Trail further to the south. Elton's property was not far away as the crow flies on a parallel road to the south of the one they had just driven on. The north-south road connecting these parallel roads was a long way farther east, but this spur trail swung by the back of Elton's only a kilometre or so from the parking area.

Pippin was excited. His eyes followed Peter's every movement as he checked his phone, checked his pockets, checked the contents of his backpack and then locked the truck.

"Are you ready?" Peter asked in the upbeat voice he knew would get Pippin's whole hind end wagging.

"I guess you are, so let's go!"

The trail wound through the jack pines, which were on a bit of a rise, and then down into the mixed aspen and spruce forest that dominated the Yellow Grass Creek Valley. It was a bright morning and only about –10, which was warm for February. It always amused Peter to think how "warm" and "cold" were such relative concepts. Upon returning from a mid-winter tropical vacation, as they did last year when they went to Belize, –10 feels absurdly, intolerably cold, but after a stretch of –30s, it feels balmy. Peter didn't even wear his toque. Pippin bounded along a few paces ahead of him, glancing back frequently, waiting for the scent game to begin. Chickadees flitted back and forth over the trail, singing their eponymous chick-a-dee-dee-dee melody, and nearby somewhere a woodpecker was drumming his staccato beat. Otherwise, the forest was silent.

Soon Elton's yard came into view between the trees. The various gnomes and structures looked different from this perspective, but Peter knew that his recent experience at the house coloured his view. Despite the bright sun, even the gnomes with the broadest smiles looked forlorn.

Peter stopped and signalled Pippin to sit and stay. He quietly pulled his binoculars out of his backpack and scanned the yard, the house and visible portions of the drive for any sign that the police were still there or had set up surveillance. He did not want a repeat of the confrontation at Tom's.

There was police tape across the back door and across the drive, but otherwise everything was quiet and empty. In fact, with Elton's recent violent death, it felt like a state beyond empty, like not only an absence, but a subtraction from the neutral state that mere emptiness represented.

Peter examined his feelings. He was still sad for what had happened to Elton, even though he hadn't known him well, but he no longer felt afraid or angry. Neither of these were rational emotions. There was nothing to be afraid of in this place at this time. Anger might still be appropriate, but he no longer felt that either. He had no target for any anger other than the vague notion of a murderous burglar who appeared to have a pork fetish and who may drive a black Ford F-150. You needed a face to be angry at, and even then, anger fogged judgment and reduced effectiveness. He was glad not to feel anger anymore. No, what he felt was sadness and, more than anything, curiosity.

Peter and Pippin left the trail and made their way through the trees into Elton's yard, beside the shed. The shed was not locked, and the padlock was missing. Peter opened the door and then stepped back as he got a Ziploc with a bit of pulled pork out of his pocket and opened it for Pippin to sniff.

"Seek!"

Pippin went to work, his sniffing audible when the chickadees and the woodpecker were quiet. He first circled the outside of the shed, sniffing all along the perimeter, and then, having completed one circuit, he went in through the open door.

Peter had already seen that two of the large Rubbermaid tubs were open and were no longer arranged with that trademark Marwick precision, but rather lay slightly askew, so he knew before Pippin confirmed it: the hams had been stored in the bins. An unheated shed was as good as a deep freeze in Manitoba from November through March, and Tom had only asked for short-term storage. It did raise the question of why Tom didn't just store the hams and pork shoulders outside at his place, but possibly it was because he didn't have a bear-proof, unheated structure. Elton had made his shed very sturdy and secure because of all the food he kept in here in the winter.

Peter obviously couldn't let Kevin know how he found this out, but he could call him and say that he had a hunch about the plastic bins based on his first visit to Elton's when he'd been called out to look at the shed. He could fib and say that he just remembered that Pippin was interested in the bins during that visit, but he had thought nothing of it then. The Mounties could test them for swine DNA if they wanted, although it wouldn't really change anything with respect to the investigation. Yes, that's what he would tell Kevin. He smiled to himself at the neatness with which at least this problem was solved.

CHAPTER
Twenty-Five

A s they climbed the gradual slope toward the jack pines, Peter caught sight of something glinting in the sun at or near the parking area. It could have been his own truck, except for the fact that he had parked on the shady side of the lot, and they had not been gone long enough for the sun to have moved so much.

There must be someone else there.

It wasn't an unknown trail access point, and it was a lovely Sunday morning, so this really shouldn't be a surprise, but something made Peter take out his binoculars.

It was a black Ford F-150 truck.

This was a common make, model and colour, but nonetheless Peter felt the hair stand up on the back of his neck. Pippin looked at him curiously but remained still and quiet.

Then Peter saw him.

A figure dressed in what looked like a black Canada Goose parka and black snow pants stepped into view. The figure was moving slowly around Peter's truck and seemed to be looking in the windows.

This was no hiker.

It was the killer. No doubt about it.

Peter's heart began to thump hard against his ribs, and all of his muscles tensed.

The sun was over his shoulder in the east, so the binocular lenses would not catch it and give them away, but still, they were very close. Too close. Probably only 50 metres away.

Peter strained his eyes and adjusted the focus, but he couldn't make out the face with the parka hood up. *Probably not from around here*, he thought, *having the hood up on a sunny, windless –10° day.*

The figure then went back to the F-150. *Whew, he's leaving*, Peter thought, feeling both relieved and a little disappointed. *It would be impossible to see the licence plate from this angle.* But the man only opened the passenger door to reach in and retrieve something before closing it again. Peter couldn't quite make it out.

Was it a pistol?

Maybe. Possibly. Right size.

Could be a camera though.

But he put it in his handwarmer pocket, whatever it was. And who carries an actual camera anymore?

The figure stood still for a moment, as if considering something, and then began walking toward the start of the trail.

Shit.

He was walking quickly, probably around six kilometres an hour, Peter estimated, so he'd cover the 50 metres to where they were hidden in about 30 seconds.

In an instant, two options flashed across his mind.

The first option was to stow the paranoia and just walk ahead and meet whoever this was and then play dumb. Peter's truck had New Selfoss Veterinary Services emblazoned on it, but as far as he knew, the burglar had never seen Peter up close in good light, so he could plausibly pretend to be someone else. "Hey, nice day, eh? We've walked all the way from town and are heading back now!" Just a man and his dog out for a Sunday morning hike.

The second option was to turn around and walk the other way, as quickly and quietly as possible, and be prepared to break into a sprint at any moment.

Peter chose the second option.

Pippin needed no signals or commands to begin trotting quickly back in the direction they had just come from. Fortunately, both of them knew how to walk quietly, and the forest concealed them well with dense underbrush at this point, but it would thin out soon. They would be visible to the man in the black parka within a few minutes.

Peter needed another plan.

As they walked quickly, really more of a half-jog than a walk, Peter reasoned that even if the man had a pistol, he would not just shoot at him. It wouldn't make any sense. As Kevin had said, if the alleged burglar and murderer had wanted to kill Peter, he would have done so by now. No, he wanted something else, but whatever that was wouldn't be resolved by gunshots from a distance, so as long as he and Pippin could stay ahead of him, they were fine.

Should he try to dial 911? No time, and the sound of his voice would give him away. No, keep moving rapidly was the best plan right now.

But moving rapidly where?

There was no point in going into Elton's yard. What was after Elton's place on the trail? A long stretch of aspens and then . . .

Suddenly there was the unmistakable sound of someone running — boots pounding on snow, nylon swishing on nylon.

Shit.

Peter glanced over his shoulder. The man was closing in on them quickly.

Shit.

Acting without any conscious thought, Peter plunged into the trees off the trail to the right.

It was a mix of black spruce and birch, and the snow was not too deep, so it was passable, although slower than on the trail. Their pursuer was hopefully less experienced in winter bushwacking, so this should work in their favour. The trail had been angling south and they were now some distance from the road, but Peter had a good sense of direction and was confident he could pick the most efficient route.

Get to the road.

Run to the truck.

Get the licence plate of the Ford.

Drive off as fast as possible.

Call Kevin.

That was the plan.

He could hear grunting and crashing sounds behind them as the man tried to plow directly through snow-laden branches. Peter and Pippin had been zigzagging more, avoiding those branches while generally following deer tracks, which indicated where the snow was the least deep or the most solid.

Nonetheless, the man was not falling behind. The gap between them remained roughly the same.

Peter could see the trees finally thin out up ahead, indicating that they were nearing the road. *Just a little further*, he thought. He glanced at Pippin, who was bounding along beside him, fur sleek, ears back, eyes intent.

Then they broke through the last trees and were at the ditch. In the spring it would be impassable with melt water, and even now it could be tricky because the snow had blown in and was very deep.

The deer trail veered off at an angle to the left to reach the road, and the parking lot was to the right, but without hesitation Peter and Pippin followed the tracks left and raced down into the ditch. At the bottom the snow was halfway up Peter's shins, but there was firm footing under that, and in seconds they were up the other side and on the road, where they spun right and began sprinting.

The man smashed through the trees just as they reached the point on the road directly opposite. Peter saw this from his peripheral vision but didn't turn to look.

Just go. Just run.

Then there was a loud groan followed by more of the laboured grunting sounds they had heard in the forest. Peter knew what had happened. The man had tried to run straight across the ditch and was now floundering in deep soft snow.

This might buy them enough time.

It might.

Time became meaningless and untrackable. Peter had no idea if it was seconds or minutes or hours, but the parking area came into view and the man had not caught up to them.

Nor had he fired his pistol. If he had one.

Nor had he shouted at them or made any sounds other than grunting and groaning.

But he was not that far behind.

Peter was not an athlete, but he was dressed more appropriately for running, so even if the pursuer was more athletic, there seemed to be a rough approximation in speeds.

They would make it.

From ten metres away Peter pressed the key fob to unlock the truck and for the first time in his life regretted that he did not have remote command start.

He yanked the door open, Pippin leapt in and Peter followed, slamming the door behind him, and starting the truck as quickly as he could.

He jammed it into reverse and stomped on the gas, glancing up in the rear-view mirror to see their pursuer leaping aside. Peter still could not get a good look at his face. Black hair maybe? Darker complexion? Not pale anyway. This brief thought reminded him to look at the licence plate as he stopped and shifted into drive.

It was hard to see because they were not that close anymore and the pause between reverse and drive was only a split second.

MXV556, or MXW555, or some permutation of that.

He committed it to memory as he accelerated up the road toward the intersection with Faraday. In his rear-view mirror he could see the black truck pulling out of the lot and then turning onto the road in the opposite direction.

Peter glanced at Pippin in the passenger seat beside him. He was looking straight ahead, ears up, tongue hanging out, tail wagging, delighted.

CHAPTER
Twenty-Six

"**O**K, we'll run all the permutations of that plate through the system. You're sure you're OK, though?" Despite the professed concern, Kevin's tone on the phone was neutral, even slightly distant. Peter slowed down on Faraday as he spoke to him. He kept glancing in the mirror.

"Yes, I'm fine. A bit shaken for sure, but fine."

"And you think he had a gun?"

"I think so, but I can't be certain. Through the binoculars I just saw him put something dark about the size of a pistol in his pocket. Could just be my imagination running away with me."

"But he didn't pull it out again or say or shout anything at any time?"

"He might have pulled it out at some point, but never in those brief glimpses I got of him. And no, he didn't say anything."

"He just walked toward you, and then started running after you? Did he start running before or after you started running?"

"Like I said, before."

"OK. It's good just to repeat to verify. For example, explain to me again what you were doing so close to Elton's place." Kevin's tone hadn't changed; it was still very professional and neutral.

"It's a beautiful day for a walk, and that's one of our favourite trails. Just a coincidence."

"You didn't feel weird going so close to where just two days ago you saw a blood-soaked murder victim?"

"You know me, Kevin, I base my decisions on reason, not emotion. And 'feeling weird,' as you put it, is an emotion I can dissipate with logical thoughts."

This broke the tension that had been building. Kevin laughed. "Yeah, you've got me there, Spock! But whatever, at least we're a couple big steps closer to catching this nutjob. I've got Selkirk and Beausejour RCMP blocking the roads south, we've got east and north covered, and he can't go west!" Kevin laughed again. West was the lake.

"Kevin, do you think he was following me, or was headed back to Elton's for some reason and happened to run into me?"

"Probably following you. Seems like too much of a coincidence otherwise."

"Right. I wonder what he wants from me." Peter still had the metallic taste of adrenaline in his mouth, but his breathing was beginning to slow down, so he allowed himself a mild joke. "More pork products?"

"Ha. Maybe. It's all way messed up no matter which way you slice it."

"Slice it. Pork. Good one, Kevin. I'm going to go home now. Can you keep me in the loop?"

"Yes, I will. Stay in and keep your doors locked. One unit is staying in town and they'll be at the end of your road."

One thing other people sometimes remarked on was how Peter and Laura never seemed to fight or argue. They were not demonstratively affectionate either, but they always appeared to be so calm and agreeable around each other without the sly digs, passive-aggressive sniping and subtle undermining that occasionally cropped up in other marriages. This was of course not true. They did fight and argue, but not very often and never in front of others. They were very private people, guarded even, one might say. Consequently, if a friend could have heard what went on the Bannerman living room late that Sunday morning, they would have been taken aback.

"Are you out of your freaking mind?!" Laura was yelling at Peter, who was sitting in his armchair, beginning to sip a mug of lapsang souchong after he finished telling her about his encounter with the probable murderer. "What the hell were you doing rambling around near Elton Marwick's house two days after the murder?"

Peter took a deep breath and then answered in the slow, exceedingly calm tone that he was unable to stop himself from using, even though he knew that Laura found it condescending and incredibly irritating. "Be reasonable, Laura. We like that trail and there was no reason at all to believe that the murderer would be so close to the scene of the crime. That old trope is a myth. The great majority stay as far away from the scene of the crime as possible. Therefore, one could make an argument that that should have been one of the safest places to be. Do you see?"

This enraged Laura further. "I do not see! First our house, then the clinic, then the text message from the killer and now this!" She paused and took a deep breath. "Peter, do you not *see* that you're in danger? I thought you were just walking around town where there'd be other people . . ." Laura was crying now, but it was angry crying.

"I'm sorry. I honestly didn't think there was any risk." Peter stood up and went over to Laura and hugged her. He knew that strictly speaking this wasn't true. Nothing anyone does has no risk. It's just a question of assessing the level of risk and the level of benefit. Occasionally these assessments were off, due to a lack of accurate data. But that, apparently, was life and sadly unavoidable.

"OK, but you're still an asshole for being so bloody oblivious."

"I know I am."

"Let's just stay home the rest of today until they catch him."

"Of course."

Just after two o'clock, as Peter and Laura were preparing to play a round of Pandemic, reasoning that an intense co-operative board game would be an ideal distraction, Peter's phone buzzed twice in rapid succession. First it was Kevin, and as he was picking up his phone to answer that call another one came in from Michelle Nyquist. He let Michelle go through to voicemail.

"Hi, Kevin?"

"Hey, how's it going?"

"All right, I guess. Any news?"

"No sign of that truck anywhere. The area's sealed tight, so I don't think he could have slipped away. We might get aerial surveillance out tomorrow."

"He could easily hide it in an abandoned barn or down some logging road and then cover it with branches. He was dressed for winter and who knows what gear he had in the back of the truck. I didn't get a chance to look."

"I'm not sure it's that easy to quickly hide a half-ton truck, but yeah, we're considering that angle."

"And the plates?"

"Stolen. Taken off some guy's Honda Civic in Transcona a month ago."

"Dead end."

"Dead end. But we're tracing the all the F-150s in the province and we'll see where that takes us. There's a shitload of them though. Look, Pete, you and Laura are going to sit tight, right? I still don't think this guy is out to kill you, at least not immediately, but he does want something from you and wanting something can make shit go sideways in a hurry."

"We're not going anywhere today."

"OK. I'm not going to make it to supper tonight again, but I'll check in on you guys later tonight. In the meantime . . ."

"Yeah, I know. Thanks, Kevin. You be safe too, eh?"

"Always."

Peter hung up and then connected to voicemail, while Laura went to get game time snacks from the kitchen. Peter assumed something was up with one of Michelle's wolfhounds.

"Hi, Peter," came Michelle's high-pitched voice. "Call me back please when you get a chance. Bye. Talk soon."

Peter hated it when people didn't say what they were calling about, even though his voicemail specifically instructed, "Leave a detailed message." People didn't listen anymore. People didn't read anymore. Soon all communication would have to be through short, animated videos, or possibly finger puppets.

"Laura! Michelle Nyquist just left a message. It's probably about Paisley. I'm just going to call her back right now, OK?"

"OK!" came the shout back from the kitchen.

Michelle picked up on the first ring. "Hi, Peter, thanks for calling me back."

"No trouble. What's up? Is Paisley OK?"

"He seems fine. I've only heard him gag twice this weekend, but you told me to monitor his breathing rate and let you know if it went over 30 breaths per minute. It was 32 when I called you."

Peter made a mental note to be more literal and specific in his instructions next time. By "let me know" he meant "let me know next time we speak," not "let me know the second it happens and call me on my cellphone." Oh well. She was an old friend, a good client and she took excellent care of her dogs.

"OK, and what was it before?"

"Let me grab my chart, hang on."

Chart? Sigh.

"At seven this morning it was 26 and then at eight it was 29, so I checked again at eight-thirty and it had dropped to 25, but by nine it was back up to 27, and then at ten . . ."

Peter interrupted her. "So pretty steady, really. Those are not big fluctuations. I'm more concerned if it suddenly doubles or jumps by ten points and is accompanied by more gagging or coughing. It is a judgment call. Thank you for the information, though." He made another mental note to be more explicit about only checking once a day, or if there was a visible change.

"Oh, that's a relief. Thank you. But can you come see him, just to be sure?"

"I'm afraid I'm not supposed to leave the house today!" He kept his tone light, half-laughing as he said it.

"Why, are you ill?"

"No, it's a bizarre story, but you know Elton Marwick's murder? Well, I may have accidentally encountered the murderer this morning while out walking Pippin, and then he chased us!"

"What?"

"Crazy, isn't it? The police are looking for him now. They've set up roadblocks. They think it may be the same person who broke into our house."

"Oh no, that's terrible, Peter! The police think you're in danger, so they want you to stay inside while he's on the loose?"

"Yes, that's more or less it."

"Do you have any idea why he's after you?"

"That's the $64,000 question. I really don't know, but it probably doesn't hurt to tell you that both Elton and I had been given pork from Tom for safe keeping. Somehow, bizarrely, that seems to be the thread connecting us."

The line was silent for what felt like a full minute. Peter wondered whether they had been disconnected. Then Michelle spoke, her voice quieter, slower. "And that also connects you and Elton to Tom."

"Yes, it seems that way."

"Did you get a good look at whoever was chasing you? You're sure it wasn't Tom?"

Now it was Peter's turn to let the line go dead. He was floored by the suggestion. "No way! Absolutely no way! How could you think that, Michelle? I mean with all due respect and whatnot, but no. Not only was the size and build of this guy completely different, but if Tom wanted the pork shoulders and hams back, he could have just asked!"

"Not if he's supposed to be dead, he couldn't."

"But our break-in was before he disappeared, and he genuinely looked shocked when I told him about it. No, that theory makes no sense."

"Look, Peter, there are more things I haven't told you about Tom beyond just the gambling. He's not been in his right mind the last couple years. I wouldn't expect what he does to make sense, so don't use your doctor logic on this. I assumed he was dead, but now I'm not so sure."

"He always seemed like his regular self when I saw him."

"But how often has that been lately?"

Peter had to admit to himself that their friendship had been going through a long fallow patch.

"A little less, sure, but unless he is actually mentally ill, I don't believe such a radical personality change could happen."

Michelle sighed audibly over the phone. "I don't even know the half of it, but here's something that will change your opinion of him. Tom and Brian Palmer were investigated up in Nunavut on suspicion of poaching polar bears."

"Poaching polar bears?"

Laura was back in the living room now and looked up at Peter with a "WTF?" facial expression.

"Yes, poaching polar bears. It didn't make the news because they weren't able to prove anything, but I know it's true and I know they did it."

"How do you know that?"

"Liz, Brian's ex, told me."

"But even if that's the case, it's quite the leap from poaching polar bears to murdering English garden gnome collectors."

"Is it?"

"Come on, Michelle, you know it is."

"There's more, but I'm being inconsiderate. You've had a terrible day, Peter, I'm sorry. I'll let you rest now."

"Thanks, it's OK. I know we have different views of Tom. Nothing really makes sense, so it's hard to know what to think."

"Agreed. And could you possibly see Paisley tomorrow? I know it's a holiday, but it would put my mind at ease."

"Right, Riel Day. Let me see what Kevin says." Peter had forgotten that it was Louis Riel Day on Monday.

"OK, I'll wait for your call either way."

They said their goodbyes and Peter put his phone down on the armrest, lost in thought.

"What was that all about?" Laura asked. She had finished setting up the game and had been waiting for Peter. "Who's poaching polar bears?"

"Tom, and Brian Palmer, according to Michelle." Peter stared blankly at the far wall, past Laura.

Laura snorted. "Well, that's not such a long shot."

"You don't think so either?"

"No. I mean, maybe they're not the first guys I would think of if I heard that someone around here was involved in that, but I could see it. I could definitely see it."

Peter said nothing, but just kept staring, looking somewhat vacant.

Laura smiled. "Your naïveté is one of the things I love about you. But does this relate to everything that's going on?"

"I don't know. I wish I did, but I don't know." But as Peter said this, he could feel something shifting in his mind, as if a marble that had been travelling through a vast Rube Goldberg machine had now tripped a lever, making a clicking sound and changing everything.

Polar bears.

Laura went to bed early. The emotional intensity of the day had drained her. Peter felt drained as well, but only physically. Mentally he felt paradoxically hyper-alert and knew that he would have trouble falling asleep, so he said good night to Laura in the living room and told her he'd be up for a while still.

Pippin stayed with him. Sometimes in these situations the dog would follow the person who was going to bed earlier upstairs, but more often he would stay with the night owl, presumably in the hope that something interesting might still happen in the waning hours of the day. Merry was a comfort-seeker though and always oriented to any available warm human body under thick goose down covers, at least until such time in the morning when breakfast seemed plausible.

Peter stretched and paced the living room, occasionally glancing out at the black night. He had all the lights off, so there were no distracting reflections. He could see the RCMP patrol car still at the bottom of the street. It was a moonless night, and many stars were visible. It felt odd to be looking at them from inside the living room. Nothing was moving out there, nothing at all. It was as if time had stopped in the outer world, and everything and everyone in it had been fixed in place. Only inside this house did time continue. This illusion was powerful.

Then the Mountie turned another light on in his car and time restarted in the world.

Peter went to his desk and lit a candle. He sometimes found that the small pool of wavering, warm candlelight helped him to banish distractions and think more clearly. Writing with a high-quality fountain pen helped as well. Perhaps it was the feeling of kinship with millennia of pre-electric scholarship. Regardless of the quality of the resulting output, he enjoyed writing and thinking this way, and that was worth something too.

He opened his bison-hide notebook and flipped to a fresh page. Then he began to write a list of everything that could be considered a clue, starting from the explosion through to the alleged polar bear poaching. He had 34 items on the list when he was done. Then beside each he noted the relevant date, even if approximate, and the associated location. It felt good to write this all out. The ink flowed beautifully. It was of the highest quality and had been purchased on holiday at a stationer in Oxford no less. Then he leaned back and folded his arms behind his head. Pippin looked up at him, having been woken from a light slumber by Peter's sudden movement.

"Eh, Pippin? What do you think? How many of these are red herrings?"

Pippin went back to sleep.

Some had to be. Vague outlines of the answer were forming, and that answer meant that some things that seemed liked clues would have to be discarded as coincidence. Peter kind of hated that, but he craved neatness and symmetry. In the service of that, as well as in the service of the truth, some cherished notions would have to be sacrificed. He was ready. That Rube Goldberg marble only had to travel a little further.

CHAPTER
Twenty-Seven

The next morning was bright and clear again. Louis Riel Day had the reputation of being one of the coldest days of the year, but this year it was only moderately cold, with highs of -18 °C expected. Peter liked the fact that Manitoba had foregone the more anodyne "Family Day" favoured by most of the other provinces for their February holiday, and had named the day after a quirky, messianic defender of Métis rights who had been hanged for his troubles.

After his sunrise tea and a quick jaunt around the yard with Pippin, Peter texted Kevin.

> How's the search going? Michelle Nyquist needs
> me to look at one of her dogs today. Do you think
> it's OK for me to head over there?

He didn't expect an immediate reply, as Kevin wasn't an early riser unless he had to be, but either Kevin was on duty already or was up for some other reason, as the reply came immediately:

> It's OK. Looks like he slipped through somehow
> because the truck was spotted heading west
> of Winnipeg. We're trying to track it down now.

Uh-oh. Peter thought for a brief moment before replying.

> Maybe took one of the logging roads through
> the Belair Provincial Forest that link up to 304?

That's what we're thinking too. They're pretty
rough in Feb, but who knows? Anyway, go see
the dog. Be careful anyway.

> I will, thanks.

Michelle Nyquist and her three Russian wolfhounds lived in an
old timber mansion on the top of the highest hill at the south-
western edge of town, affording it a glorious, sweeping view of
Lake Winnipeg beyond. It was a prominent New Selfoss landmark — built by the town's first millionaire, a Finnish-Canadian
lumber baron named Paavo Jarvinen. As a local history enthusiast,
Peter was familiar with the story of how Paavo was the first non-
Icelander to settle in New Selfoss when he arrived in 1890. Paavo
immediately felt ostracized, although not in a hostile way, but
rather in a polite and cold way. Being a non-Icelander himself,
Peter empathized, although the divide had become more subtle.
The existing New Selfossians spoke Icelandic, and Paavo did not.
They fished, and he did not. They were scientific atheists, and he
was not. Paavo was nominally a Lutheran, but his real religion was
Paavo. His vivid self-confidence was unseemly to his neighbours.
This reaction only served to buttress his ambition to show New
Selfoss who he was and what he was capable of.

Paavo's first house was a hand-built hut on the east side of town,
backing onto the forest. The Icelanders were focused on fishing the

lake, but Paavo could see that with Winnipeg booming, the real money was in the trees. The 1882 real estate bubble, during which property at Portage and Main was more valuable than in Manhattan, may have burst, but the population of the city still tripled in the 1880s. There was no end in sight to the growth. "Chicago North" was on everyone's lips. All these new Winnipeggers needed houses. And all these houses needed wood. Paavo saw gold in the green behind his hut, and he saw that the river was his ally. Its power would be used to drive the largest sawmill in the west.

By 1902 he was ready to trumpet his success by building Voitto Talo, or "Victory House" in Finnish, although everyone else just called it The Big House. It was on the highest point of land on the west side of town, where he could figuratively and literally look down on the Icelandic New Selfossians both as they slept, when he looked east, and as they worked out on the lake, when he looked west. It was a massive log cabin–style timber frame construction, reputed to be the largest in Canada, if not the world. It was as if Louis XIV had decided to build a rustic summer home in Canada — rustic, but large enough to accommodate his entire court.

Soon after Paavo arrived, New Selfoss began to receive other Finnish settlers, as well as ultimately Germans and Scots and Ukrainians and so on; but still, Paavo did not feel accepted. He brooded over this for years and then, quite suddenly, without no forewarning or hints, declared that he would return to Finland, where he knew he would be greeted with the admiration and respect he deserved. Unfortunately, the First World War had broken out and normal travel was not possible, so in the spring of 1915 he set off north in a canoe, stating his intention to reach the Arctic coast by freeze-up, from where he would travel across the Arctic Ocean to Finland by dog sled team, a distance of 4,500 kilometres. He estimated that he could cover that in six months if the dogs were good enough. He was never heard from again, although for a long time there were rumoured sightings of him in Finland, much along the lines of the Elvis Lives phenomenon later in the century.

Before leaving New Selfoss he sold his business assets and, according to another rumour, converted the proceeds to gold bullion, which he carried with him north, spawning many fruitless searches over the ensuing decades. Peter knew some people who were fervent believers in the lost bullion tale. He could only shake his head at their naiveté. Voitto Talo remained in Paavo's name and was boarded up until he was declared presumed dead, at which point it was sold on auction by the town. It first became an unsuccessful hotel and then a slightly less unsuccessful retreat for recovering alcoholics. It had been empty for 30 years by the time Michelle Nyquist bought it. One wing had collapsed and become home to an array of woodland creatures, but she not only salvaged the rest of the mansion but restored it to a state beyond what it had been in its heyday. Paavo had had a quirky design sensibility, whereas Michelle's taste was unassailable. She planned to eventually run a high-end bed and breakfast out of it, but for now was content to enjoy the space alone with her wolfhounds, punctuated by the occasional elaborate dinner party.

Peter was greeted by curious sniffing from the three wolfhounds. He often wondered what went through a dog's head during a house call. If they were regular patients, they certainly recognized the veterinarian, but it was presumably confusing to have him appear at their doorstep. No matter how much he tried to adopt a jolly playful tone, most dogs, and all cats, remained on guard. Friendly, but wary. Parker, Paisley and Pavlov concluded their sniff and then withdrew to a safe distance to watch Peter as he was ushered into their house by their mistress.

"Have you been up here in daytime before, Peter?" Michelle asked as she showed him into the great room, an enormous, vaulted space at least three stories high with panoramic windows to the west looking out over the lake. The logs had been varnished to a honey colour and glowed in the bright sunshine. Massive, black wrought-iron chandeliers hung from long chains and a stone hearth the size of a small garage dominated the wall opposite the windows. The floor was also of the same golden wood, but was accented by expensive-looking, brightly coloured Persian rugs. The furniture managed to look both stylish and comfortable, which was a rare combination in Peter's experience. Scandinavian probably.

"No, just that one time for the dinner party. The Venetian carnival–themed one." He stepped forward toward the windows as the dogs backed away further. "Wow, that is some view you have!"

"Isn't it? Old Paavo knew what he was doing when he chose this site. There aren't many places in a flat province where you can get views like this. Although I think he had surveillance and security more in mind than beauty."

"Ha, yes. Hey, speaking of surveillance, that's a nice-looking telescope." Peter pointed to a white tube the size of a cannon mounted on the railing at the far end of the deck, just beyond the windows.

"Yes, I have ambitions to take up astronomy, but never seem to find the time."

"You can probably see everything that's going on in the south basin of the lake with that. Mind if I have a peek?"

"By all means. The door is over here." Michelle walked to the corner of the room and opened a glass door for Peter.

The view from the deck, unobstructed by any aspect of the house, was even more spectacular. Peter really could see the whole south basin. He took the cap off the telescope and fiddled with the focus for a moment before training it on what to the naked eye looked like black specks halfway out onto the lake. They were ice fishing huts. The more he looked, the more he saw. There had to be at least 30, some in clusters and some by themselves. This was normal, of course, but it was interesting to see from this perspective. Most of the huts were directly west of New Selfoss, in the direction of Gimli, but he noticed one far off to the south, sitting by itself behind a particularly large jumble of ice ridges.

Michelle grabbed a jacket and came out to join Peter. "What are you looking at?"

"There's an ice fishing hut way to the south. Kind of weird because the ice is usually much less stable down there."

"Huh, let me have a look."

Peter lowered the ocular for Michelle, who was a good foot and a half shorter than him, and stepped aside.

"That's a rental," she said after a brief look.

"So, tourists?"

"I guess, or people just trying out the sport. Someone should tell them that that's not a great spot."

"Doesn't the rental company set them up?"

"Not necessarily. You can haul it out yourself behind a truck to wherever you want."

"Interesting."

"Really? Why?"

"No reason. I guess you're right, maybe it's not that interesting!" Peter laughed and changed the subject. "So, where's my patient?"

After determining that Paisley's heart condition was stable and that no immediate change in his medical plan was required, Peter accepted the offer of a cup of coffee from Michelle. He was eager to leave and test out a theory, but he had a feeling that Michelle had something more to say. He often misread people, but it was still early, so even if he was wrong, it didn't matter if he wasted a little time.

They settled into a couple chairs that were made of black leather stretched over chrome tubes, creating a kind of sling that was slightly bouncy. This pleased Peter. He fidgeted sometimes, and this was an excellent outlet for that.

Michelle smiled at him as he tried a couple of tentative bounces.

"They're from a designer in Reykjavik," she said.

"I didn't know they made furniture in Iceland." Bounce, bounce.

"Not much, but I like to support those who do. Plus Finnish and Norwegian designers. The Swedes and Danes can look after themselves." She chuckled as she poured the coffee from a metal cannister into small navy-blue cups set on the round glass table between them.

"What about the Faroese?" Bounce, bounce, bounce.

"Ha! Yes, I hadn't thought about them! It's all sheep and fish there though, isn't it?"

"I expect so. I was joking!"

They sipped their coffee quietly for a moment. It was the polar opposite of Kevin's Mountie coffee. This was the kind of coffee that enthusiasts would insist had pomegranate and roasted persimmon notes, or something like that. Regardless, it was fantastic. Peter was glad he had stayed, if only for this coffee.

"I had to think of Tom when we were looking at those fishing huts," Michelle said quietly.

"Oh?" Peter had read that sometimes it was best not to say much in order to get the other person to say more. This seemed like a good time to try this out.

"Yeah, you know it wasn't all bad times. He may have been a prick, but he could be a fun prick. But you know that."

"Sure."

Michelle smiled. Peter waited, but the technique didn't seem to be working as she didn't say anything further.

"So, you were saying about the huts and thinking of Tom. Did you guys go out there a lot?"

"In the first while. I had never been ice fishing before. My family wasn't into any outdoor stuff. My dad always said that we should leave wilderness to the wild and civilization to the civilized. That's one of the things that attracted me to Tom. He was so different. So yeah, we went out to his hut regularly and even spent a couple nights out there when we were first dating."

"Romantic!"

"Sort of, and sort of not. He knew how to set up with a heater and furs and big sleeping bags, but the lack of plumbing became a deal-breaker for me. I tried to be the roughing-it-back-to-nature type for him, but you can't keep denying who you are forever. I'm this." Michelle swept her arm to indicate the luxurious surroundings.

"Cognitive dissonance is what the psychiatrists call it."

"Exactly! That's what my shrink said too. But anyway, there were some good times, even without the plumbing." She laughed. "More coffee, Peter?"

"Sure, just a splash."

"Did you ever go out to his hut?" she asked.

"One time. As you know, I'm not the fishing type either, but I did spend a nice afternoon out there drinking with him and the two Brians."

Michelle wrinkled her nose. "If it's anyone I can't stand more than Tom, it's Brian Palmer. But it was a nice hut, wasn't it? As far as those things go."

"Yes, really surprisingly comfortable. The smaller ones look like repurposed outhouses, but Tom's was decent."

There was a long pause as they both drank their fresh coffee and looked out at the lake.

"I suppose the police have checked for him out there, haven't they?" Michelle asked quietly, not looking at Peter.

"I'm sure they have. You think he could be hiding out there this whole time?"

"Maybe, but he could also be dead out there. I look at his hut through the telescope sometimes and think about it. But if they've checked . . ."

They lapsed into silence again. The dogs had quietly and cautiously approached as Peter and Michelle were talking and were now lying at her feet, all three of them panting and staring at her.

"These boys need their walks. It's OK to walk Paisley with his heart condition, isn't it?"

"Absolutely. Just let him set the pace. I've got to get home and take Pippin for his walk too."

He had decided on a really long walk.

CHAPTER
Twenty-Eight

Peter was glad that Laura had already left when he got home. Less explaining that way. She had gone into the city to attend Festival du Voyageur with some friends. Peter didn't like crowds, so he declined to go and besides, this was a group of her old high school friends, and he always felt awkward around them.

"Pippin!" he called when he stepped in the door. "Do you want to go for a big walk?"

There was the sound of toenails skittering across tile as Pippin rounded the corner from the kitchen. He stopped in front of Peter and looked up at him, head tilted to one side.

"That's right! A big walk on the lake! I just need to get a few things ready first."

Peter moved efficiently around the house, gathering what he needed into a backpack. Then he went to the garage and grabbed his cross-country skis and put them into the back of the truck.

"That's it, boy! We're ready to go!"

Pippin hopped into the passenger seat and Peter started the engine.

"This will be fun and this time nobody will be chasing us!" Peter said it more for himself than for Pippin.

Peter drove into town, but rather than going straight west through to the closest dock, he turned south on 59, drove for a few kilometres, and then turned west on Copernicus Road. This took them past a small cluster of forlorn-looking cottages that had been boarded up for the winter, and then to a dead end at Suomi Beach, where there were a handful of saunas, none in use at the moment.

Peter took out his binoculars and trained them southwest. From this angle he couldn't see the ice fishing hut he had seen from the higher vantage point at Michelle's, but he could see the distinctive clump of ice ridges that it hid from view.

He estimated about five kilometres based on what he had seen through the telescope. Maybe five and a half. Speed was difficult to calculate as it depended so much on the snow conditions. If he was lucky, he'd find snowmobile tracks going the same way and be able to follow those. That would allow him to do ten kilometres an hour easily, maybe even 12. So, it would take no more than 30 minutes to get there.

"Ready, boy?"

Rhetorical question. Pippin was always ready. And they were in luck. Within minutes of heading out onto the lake Peter spotted snowmobile tracks coming from shore just a little south of them and appearing to head out toward the ice ridges.

It felt warmer out there than the −18 °C promised in town. It helped that it was a cloudless and windless day, and it helped that Peter was working hard to ski fast. Pippin loped along effortlessly beside him. For a long while it didn't look like the ice ridges were getting any closer. Distance and size were always deceptive on a flat, monochrome surface. That time they skied across to Gimli, Peter got Tom to set a whisky bottle on the ice and then ski further out and stop to pose in such a way that through Peter's camera, it looked like Tom was leaning on a bottle as big as he was. With nothing to give perspective, you never knew whether an object was truly large, or just close.

The snowmobile tracks dodged the largest ice ridges, threading a reasonably smooth path through the rough jumble. Then suddenly the hut was in view, about 200 metres away. It was a large one, painted matte black in stark contrast to the gleaming white all around. The door and a window faced the path. Strings of frozen fish hung beside the door. A snowmobile was parked out front.

There was no sound other than the squeak of Peter's skis.

Peter stopped and pulled his backpack off to get his binoculars out. As he was doing this the silence was broken by the creak of a door opening. Peter, still fumbling with the binocular case, looked up, startled. A person in a dark blue skidoo suit and white helmet climbed onto the machine. He, or possibly she, was slightly heavy-set and a bit shorter than the average man.

"Hey, stop!" Peter shouted.

The person glanced briefly at Peter and then started the snowmobile. The noise of the engine ripped through the air. In a matter of seconds, person and machine were gone behind the hut, heading northwest at high speed.

When Peter recovered from the shock, he put the binoculars away and skied quickly to the hut. The door was unlocked. It had a plaque that read, "www.prairieoceanerentals.ca," with a logo that featured a smiling cartoon fish. He opened it cautiously, motioning Pippin to sit outside.

The hut was about the size of a small bedroom. There were Plexiglas windows on three sides. The fourth side, opposite the door, had rough plywood shelves from floor to ceiling, filled with a mix of canned goods, sacks of flour and rice, a few tools, a coil of rope, several rolls of duct tape and a stack of well-used paperbacks. Fishing supplies were on a separate set of shelves beside the window on the right. Clothing hung from pegs beside the window to the left. A kerosene heater with a blinking red light occupied the near corner on the left. The floor was rough pine planking with a large, round hole in the centre. The only furniture was a small sleeping platform — being just boards you couldn't really call it a bed — to the left of the hole and two chairs to the right. The chairs looked like garage sale finds, having likely graced a suburban kitchen in the 1950s.

Peter called Pippin in. He sniffed around for a moment before coming back to sit in front of Peter and watch him curiously as he dug around in his backpack.

"Here it is," Peter said quietly to himself. From the bottom of the pack, he had extracted a crumpled white T-shirt in a clear plastic bag.

It was the Newer Waves T-shirt Tom had given him.

Pippin kept watching.

Peter pulled the T-shirt out of the bag and held it out for Pippin to smell. Pippin sniffed at it intently and then, evidently satisfied, stopped and looked up at Peter. The look was one of naked anticipation. Pippin knew what was next and began to tense.

"Seek!"

Normally more preparation and training to the specific scent would be needed, but Peter was so confident that this was the equivalent of 1+1 for Pippin that he didn't worry about it.

He was right.

In under a minute Pippin was sitting at attention under the clothes hung on the peg. Peter got so excited that he almost forgot to check out the windows. But nobody was out there. The snowmobile was not visible anymore. But these were Tom's clothes — therefore, that was Tom on the snowmobile. The person in the blue skidoo suit had been the right build too.

He had been right. Tom was alive and was hiding out in the rented ice fishing hut, being smart enough to avoid his regular hut or the hunting cabin. Peter considered that this implied at least a little bit of advance planning as he would have had to have rented and positioned the hut before disappearing. Interesting.

Peter gave Pippin his liver reward and then sat down at the table. He took out the paper and pen he had brought with him. He began to write.

Dear Tom,

I can't tell you how happy I am to have my suspicion confirmed that you are alive! I know what's going on and I can help you.
I'll come back tomorrow, probably around one, and we can talk.

Your friend,
Peter

Strictly speaking that wasn't true. Peter didn't know what was going on. Not entirely anyway. The shape of the whole thing was forming in his mind like a cloud that shifted from the shape of a rhinoceros to a Buick to Cuba to . . . something. The something was almost there. Almost clear. But claiming certainty would be more enticing to Tom. And enticing Tom was key to creating actual certainty.

On the ski back to shore Peter was suddenly struck by a mental image of Kevin parked beside his truck, waiting, fuming, getting ready to handcuff Peter for interfering. But this was impossible. First of all, Kevin had no way of knowing Peter was out here. Secondly, even if he saw Peter here, Kevin wouldn't have any idea that the hut had anything to do with the investigation. Kevin would have to find out soon, but not today. Peter would talk Tom into turning himself in and then he could figure out a story for

Kevin about how this all came to pass. But those were details he would worry about later, and besides, Peter would be a hero at that point for having facilitated Tom's surrender, so all would be forgiven. Even Laura would forgive him.

CHAPTER
Twenty-Nine

Laura was going to be out most of the day, so Peter had the house to himself. Uncharacteristically, he didn't have any plans. He still had a couple of chapters in *Alone on the Ice* and there were a few emails he had been meaning to write, but neither of these felt right for a sunny holiday afternoon.

Maybe he should go down to Winnipeg and meet Laura and her friends? No, that was still as bad an idea as ever. Laura was somehow able to flip between introvert and extrovert settings, whereas Peter was stuck on introvert, especially when it came to people he didn't know very well and who chattered loudly about subjects he wasn't interested in. Better to make a mug of rooibos tea, sit quietly for a bit and watch the nuthatches zip back and forth from the trees to the bird feeder. Then, after 15 or 20 minutes of that, he could get his notebook and work on sketching out theories again. Maybe with music. Oscar Peterson? That seemed about right.

He had no sooner settled on this plan than his phone began to vibrate. He was on call for the holiday. But it wasn't a client. It was Kevin.

"Hi Kev, how's it going?"

"It's going good. Look, Pete, can you come down to the station?"

Peter's chest tightened. "Oh? What's up?"

"There's news about Jawbone and I have a question for you." Kevin sounded friendly enough, so Peter relaxed.

"Yeah, sure. Now?"

"Now's good."

The station was quiet. Peter assumed that the other officers were out on calls or patrol, and perhaps some had the holiday off. Kevin met him at the door and walked with him to his office, which was even more chaotic than usual. In addition to the drifts of papers on the desk, and the overstuffed bookshelves, there were now several cardboard banker's boxes, filled to bursting, stacked haphazardly on the floor. Kevin picked his way through them to get to his chair.

"Sorry about the mess, Pete." Kevin grinned. Both of them knew that he wasn't sorry in the least. "Coffee?"

"Oh, no thanks. I'm good."

"You sure? Made it fresh myself just now."

"I'm sure, thanks."

Kevin shrugged in a suit-yourself kind of way and poured himself a mug.

"So, you've got more info on Jawbone?"

"Better than more info, bro. We know who he is." Kevin sat back as he said this and smiled broadly.

Peter waited for him to say more, but Kevin was obviously enjoying keeping him in suspense. "So, are you going to tell me?" he finally asked.

"Park Junwoo."

"Who? Korean, from the name, but do you know anything more?"

"Some. He's a gangster. Or was, I guess is more accurate. Belonged to an organized crime group in South Korea called the Seobang Faction."

"Wow." Peter's mind began to race, making connections in previously blank spaces.

"Yeah, wow. That's what I said. You really sure you don't want any coffee?"

"Really sure. So, any idea what a Korean gangster is doing in small-town Manitoba? And more specifically, in Tom Pearson's swine barn?"

"That's really why you're here, Pete. I was hoping you could help me figure that out."

Finally, an acknowledgement of his usefulness. But maybe it was more Pippin's nose Kevin needed than Peter's brain.

"Of course. Anything I can do."

"Cool. Then tell me what you were really doing in the trees at Tom's place last week."

This was not the conversation Peter was hoping to have.

"I told you . . ."

Kevin cut him off. "Cut the crap. Laura told me that you found an odd piece of paper with Korean writing on it. She said you found it in town. She mentioned it when I stopped by to check on you guys this morning. I told her about Jawbone's ID and she told me about the Korean note. Where did you actually find it? Not in town, right? At Tom's, right?"

Peter paused for a moment before answering. He looked down at his lap, and then back up again at Kevin. Kevin didn't look angry, just serious. "Sorry, Kevin. You're right. I did find it at Tom's. Pippin tracked it based on scent traces I collected after the break-in at the clinic. You know, where the burglar cut himself and bled."

"OK. I won't ask you why you withheld this evidence, but I will ask you to produce it. And by the way, ask is a polite word for something else."

"Of course. I can get it right away. But I memorized the first part. I got Anne Shin to translate it for me."

"Oh?" Kevin began rummaging on his desk. "Hang on a sec." Kevin pulled a pad of lined yellow paper out from under a teetering pile of files, which then collapsed, cascading onto the floor.

"Shit. OK, shoot. What do you remember of the translation?"

Peter looked at the ceiling as he brought the numbers and letters into focus in his mind's eye. "First line is '3.5 black 52,500, 4.1 white 123,000.' And the second is '2.7 white 81,000, 6.4 black 96,000.'"

"Really? That's it?"

"There were a few more lines, but Anne said they were all the same. A small number with a decimal, the word black or white, and then a larger number ending in zeros."

"OK." Kevin narrowed his eyes and chewed on the tip of his pen as he thought.

"Anne thought that the larger numbers probably represented money. Dollars or won."

"That makes sense." Kevin nodded as he continued to chew on the tip of his pen.

"So, maybe the weight of something and the value. The big number with black is exactly 15,000 times the small number, and with white it's double that, 30,000."

Kevin began rubbing his beard. Peter knew that this and the pen-chewing was what his brother-in-law did when he was deep in thought.

"Hmm," Kevin said. "Cocaine is about a hundred bucks a gram on the street, so a hundred grand for a kilo, but wholesale is in the 20 to 30 grand ballpark. So, coke is definitely a possibility."

"That would explain white, but what about black? Is there a cheaper black cocaine?"

"Ha, no!" Kevin stopped rubbing his beard and looked at Peter. "But hash is black. It's only worth four grand or so wholesale, but for street value 15,000 is close."

"Why would he list hashish at the street price and cocaine at wholesale?"

"No idea. And nobody I know uses black as code for hash. White for coke, yes, but not black for hash. But maybe in Korea?"

"Maybe. And why in Tom's barn? Do you have any evidence Tom was involved in drugs?"

"None, but that could just mean not yet. We're going to get the canine unit up with their drug dogs and see what we can turn up in his house and property."

"And how did you make the ID for Jawbone?"

"He was on an Interpol list. The gold teeth helped a lot, although there are a lot of criminals with gold teeth."

"No surprise."

"I guess not. And then the clincher was from Border Services, which showed him entering Canada in October." Kevin jabbed his finger at his wall calendar as he said this, although it showed February, illustrated with a photograph of two polar bear cubs.

"So, he's been here a long time!"

"Yep. And we think it's a they, not a he." Kevin grinned as he let this bombshell hit.

"They? As in the non-binary pronoun, or as in more than one Korean gangster?"

"More than one Korean gangster, although I have no knowledge of their gender identity and preferred pronouns, so maybe both?"

"Jesus." Peter sucked his breath in.

"No, Jung Min-Jun. But it also starts with a J, just like Jesus, so you're close!" Kevin was known for rapidly flipping from stern to jovial and then back to stern again. He explained that it was a Viking trait genetically linked to his red hair. Whenever he said that, Peter reminded him that Laura was as calm, predictable and steady as the Red River in July. Kevin would shrug and say that the gene was obviously on the Y chromosome.

"Right. Jung Jin-Mun . . ."

Kevin interrupted: "Min-Jun, *Min-Jun*."

"Jung *Min-Jun*. Fine. What I wanted to ask is how you know."

"Border Services again. Park and Jung arrived together . . ."

Now Peter interrupted: "You know those are their family names, right? Koreans write their family names first, then their given names. But carry on." He smiled at Kevin.

"Really? Interesting. But not relevant as cops like calling people by their last names anyway. For example, if I decide to bust your ass, I'll say 'I busted Bannerman's ass,' not 'I busted Peter's ass.' Sounds more professional that way, don't you agree?"

"Sure. But go on. Park and Jung arrived together . . ."

"They arrived on the same flight and, according to the Korean National Police Agency, Jung is also linked to the Seobang Faction." Kevin drained the last of his coffee and said, "Man, that was good!"

"But I take it you have no idea where he is."

"Roger. No idea." Kevin got up and walked to the door. "I've got to go to the can. Too much coffee, I guess. Sit tight."

After Kevin left, Peter couldn't help but crane his neck to see what was on Kevin's computer monitor. It was just a screen saver of a bare-chested fireman with a Dalmatian. He quickly scanned the papers on the desk and the floor for anything of interest, but none of it had any obvious connection to the case. As he did so he wondered whether he should tell Kevin about probably having found Tom. He originally planned not to tell him until he saw a clear path to how Tom's innocence could be proved, but then sitting there talking to Kevin, he began to feel squeamish about keeping important information from him. But as soon as he heard Kevin's heavy footsteps approaching the office door again, that squeamishness evaporated. He sat back in his chair and composed himself to look casual. Kevin shot him a curious look as he walked back around the desk to his own chair.

"So, Pete," he said, and paused to take a sip of coffee. "So, black F-150 guy. I think there's a decent chance it's Jung."

"Elton's killer."

"And pork fiend. The same, yes. I've got some photos. Have a look and see if you can identify him."

Kevin began to rummage among the files on his desk.

"But as I've said, I never saw his face."

"I know, I know, but just in case something sparks . . ." Kevin said, trailing off as he leaned over to look at the files that had fallen off the desk, ". . . something."

"OK, but a description of height and build would be more useful."

"A-ha! Here it is!" Kevin brandished a manila file folder in the air like a trophy. "Right, so let's have a look. Here are his pics." He handed Peter a couple of mugshots and several more photos that looked like they had been taken from security camera footage. Most were blurry and seemed useless to Peter, but one was relatively clear and showed a man walking toward the camera.

"Yeah, that could be him. Short. Wide shoulders. Slightly bow-legged."

"Cool. Regardless, every cop in Canada is on the lookout for him now."

"What happened to the F-150 seen west of Winnipeg?"

Kevin shrugged. "Gone. Happens sometimes. There are so many minor roads. Amateurs like those kids hotwiring cars are easy to find, but a pro can hide for a while. It can take a lot of work and sometimes it just comes down to a lucky break, but we always get them eventually."

"Always? You said something different before, when Tom disappeared."

"OK, almost always." Kevin chuckled. "But we try damned hard to live up to our rep."

"I suppose 'almost always gets their man' sounds lame."

"It does."

"But you don't think I need to be worried?" Peter shifted forward in his seat and placed his hands on Kevin's desk. Kevin began rubbing his beard again. He also did that when he was nervous.

"I didn't say that. Maybe worried's the wrong word, but you should still be careful. We're pretty confident he hasn't returned to the New Selfoss area, but I can't guarantee it."

"OK. I'm always careful anyway."

Kevin raised an eyebrow.

CHAPTER
Thirty

Pippin was delighted to see Peter when he returned home. He was always happy when either Peter or Laura returned — running up to the door, tail wagging, big doggie smile on his face — but he seemed especially happy today.

"Do you think we're going somewhere again?" Peter said as Pippin bounced back and forth in front of him. "Wasn't that long enough on the lake this morning?"

Evidently it wasn't. Some days Pippin seemed to draw from a bottomless well of energy, with exercise only sharpening his desire for more. Peter often mused that the world's energy problems could be solved if we figured out how a dog could possibly be so lively and run so far on what looked like so little food. A dozen Pippins could probably power a house. But there would be all sorts of practical obstacles, of course.

"I'm sorry, boy, but it's getting late, and I'm beat. But if you're good, we make a few rounds of the yard after supper, OK?"

Pippin's bouncing settled as Peter's tone of voice told him that nothing exciting was going to happen right away. He stayed in the foyer, watching the door, still smiling, tail still wagging, even as Peter stepped around him into the living room.

"No Pippin, she won't be back for another hour or two. And when she gets home, I doubt she'll be keen on a big W-A-L-K either."

Pippin waited a couple minutes longer and then gave up. He padded over to where Peter had settled in his armchair and curled up near his feet. Merry was already in Peter's lap.

The euphoria he had felt on finding Tom had completely dissipated and been replaced by an unsettling feeling of dread. Kevin's reassurances had not done anything to tamp this feeling down. And the feeling had a basis in logic. Jung had been after something when he chased Peter. Why would he give up so easily? He had come all the way from South Korea for whatever it was. And he was a professional, so changing cars would be a snap. Maybe he always had two? Maybe that dark grey CR-V seen on Rod's surveillance video was him too? Perhaps Jung and Park had a falling out and Jung killed Park? It had to be about drugs and Tom got mixed up in that somehow. But why import drugs from Manitoba to Korea? Isn't it easier just to get them directly from Colombia or wherever?

His mind was whirring like a spinning top — rapid circling and jerky random movement with no destination. This was frustrating and pointless. Maybe tea would help. He gently nudged Merry off his lap and went into the kitchen to put the kettle on. As he did so, another unsettling thought asserted itself. If it was Tom on the lake, why did he take off when he saw Peter approaching? With the distinctive bright yellow MEC jacket Peter wore when he skied, Tom must have known who he was. Maybe he was just out of his mind with fear and paranoia.

This line of thinking got his mind whirring again and the tea did not help. Peter paced for a while and then settled on re-watching an episode of *Game of Thrones* to distract himself until Laura came home.

His phone rang at just before 3 a.m. He usually left it on vibrate, but when he was on call, he worried that it would not be enough to wake him up. Fortunately Laura was a very sound sleeper, so it didn't bother her. He rolled over and picked it up.

It was Peggy Dinsdale.

He answered in a sleepy voice as he stood up and slid his feet into his slippers. "Hi, Peggy?"

"Peter, I'm so sorry for calling this early, but I didn't think it could wait until you opened."

"That's OK. Is something wrong with Emma?" The basset had been doing well on her meds for Addison's, but surprises were still possible.

"No, she's fine. It's Martha."

Martha was her Nigerian pygmy goat. Peggy had a small farm just past the edge of town with five goats, two Swiss dairy cows, a donkey, several ducks, a few geese and at least a dozen chickens.

Peter was more awake now. "What's wrong with her?"

"I think she might need a C-section. She's 142 days now and she's been pushing since just after midnight."

"OK, I'll be there in 20 minutes."

Peggy's farm was a postcard of white picket fences, an old wooden farmhouse with a wrap-around porch and a big red barn. It was as pretty in the winter as it was in every other season. Tourists often stopped to take pictures of it, especially if the photogenic donkey was out front.

"How's she doing?" Peter asked as Peggy opened the barn door for him.

"Martha's the toughest one of the five, so she's hanging in there, but I can see she's struggling."

Peter nodded as he knelt down in the straw beside the small black goat. She had a distant look in her eyes and did not seem to register his arrival.

"I should have called sooner, but it was the middle of the night and . . ."

"It's OK. She'll be fine."

Peter bent over and with a flashlight had a careful look at Martha's hind end. Then he reached into her, murmuring, "Easy, girl, it's OK."

Peggy watched him, arms crossed, her face a picture of worry and exhaustion. She looked completely different without her makeup and hair done, wearing a loose plaid shirt, down vest and jeans instead of a tight sweater with leggings or a short skirt. He liked her better this way.

"Crown first breech. But the kid's alive. It'll have to be a C-section," Peter said as he washed his hands in the bucket Peggy had set beside Martha.

"But head first is good, isn't it? Why is it stuck?"

"It's head first like this." Peter put his chin down against his chest. "And the front legs are swept back, so the shoulders are wider. Also, it's a big one."

"Oh, OK. Do you have everything you need?"

"Yes. I was expecting to have to do a caesarian. Calves I can turn sometimes, but not kids. I'd have to train a monkey with small hands to do that!" Peter chuckled, but the joke went right by Peggy, who had turned her attention to Martha, stroking her head. He heard her softly saying, "Uncle Doctor Peter's going to look after you, don't worry."

"I'm going to give her a mild sedative and then freeze the area. Sometimes we need to do a general anesthetic, but she'll be fine with a local." Peter didn't tell Peggy that Martha had been pushing for so long that he was worried she'd be too weak for a general.

The overhead lights in the barn were off, but Peggy had set up a spotlight for Martha's pen, which had half-walls separating it from the rest of the barn, where the other animals could be heard shuffling and grunting in the dark beyond the small world of yellow light centred on the little goat, her doctor and her owner. The sweet hay smell was comforting, as was the particular animal quality of the warmth in the pen. Peter worked in silence and Peggy focused on stroking Martha's head and occasionally whispering in her ear.

The silence was broken when the fluids and membranes had been cleared from the kid's nose and mouth and it began to bleat. This was like a pin pricking a balloon and the whole mood changed from tense and focused to relieved and joyful.

"Thank you, Peter, thank you so much!" Peggy said as she rubbed the kid down vigorously with a towel. Then she brought it to Martha's nose.

"My pleasure. When something like this goes well, it makes it all worthwhile," Peter said while placing stitches.

"I hope you can still get some sleep tonight before you have to go into work!"

"Yeah, I think so." But he doubted it. It would be 4:15 by the time he finished and then with clean-up and so on he likely wouldn't be home until 5, which was only an hour before wake-up time anyway.

Peggy thanked him several more times before he left. She also apologized twice for her appearance and looked at Peter in a way that made him feel uneasy. The old Peggy was back.

Peter looked forward to the short drive home. There would be no traffic at all, not that there ever was much in New Selfoss, and the town would be silent and asleep, which always made Peter feel like he was in a movie, where he had special powers to keep moving through a world compelled to sleep through some other-worldly force. That might be a lonely feeling for other people, but it wasn't for Peter.

As he turned onto Linnaeus, his headlights swept across a car heading the opposite direction.

It was a dark grey Honda CR-V.

Common enough, but what caught his attention was that the driver looked like Brian Palmer. He only got a split-second glance of a face lit by the dashboard lights of the CR-V, so it wasn't a clear view, but nonetheless, Peter was sure that it was Brian.

Brian had a CR-V?

Peter had no idea.

He was always driving an Audi or a Range Rover when Peter saw him. But then Brian lived in a big new place that he had torn down three bungalows to build, and this place had a four-car garage, so who knew what else was in there.

What was he doing out so early? Dental emergency? But his clinic was in the opposite direction.

Peter briefly considered honking and giving a friendly wave, but he decided against it.

CHAPTER
Thirty-One

The morning was rough. As much as Peter had made his peace with being called out in the middle of the night, it still destroyed him. He needed his sleep. Eight hours was ideal. Seven was acceptable. Six was tolerable every now and again. Less than six was intolerable anytime. Last night he had gotten just under five hours. Intolerable. Peter drank two cups of strong black coffee at dawn rather than his ritual tea to increase his caffeine level and allow him to function at work, but he did so ruefully, knowing that it might interfere with his next night's sleep, setting up a domino sequence of bad nights. The half-life of caffeine may be six hours, but that meant that a quarter of it was still in your system in 12 hours and an eighth in 24 hours. He estimated that his coffee had 120 milligrams of caffeine per cup, so the 240 milligrams total would still leave about 50 milligrams in his system by bedtime. Too much. Not enough to prevent him from falling asleep, but enough to degrade the quality of the sleep. Ugh.

Laura listened sympathetically, although she had heard Peter outline this caffeine physiology every time he got called out at night. His brain was very agile, but it also had some remarkable deep grooves worn into it.

"Well, you saved that little goat's life. That made it worth it, right?"

"I suppose."

Before going to work, Peter called Kevin. A blindingly obvious thought had come to him as he was drinking his coffee.

"Hi, have you got that Korean note handy?"

"Good morning to you too! But yeah, it's in the evidence room. I can get it. How come?"

"There are 11 sets of letters and numbers, right? The four Anne translated and seven more."

"Sure, if you say so. Do you want me to go get it and double-check?" Kevin sounded bemused.

"No, that's OK. It was a rhetorical question. I know there are eleven sets. Let's say that each represents a pork shoulder or ham or something like that. I had two. We don't know how many Elton had, but I doubt it was nine, so there are quite a few unaccounted for."

"On it already, bro. Even before the note turned up, we'd been working on the assumption that there could be more break-in targets than just you and Marwick. Once we found out that both of you had accepted meat from Tom, we started checking with all his other contacts. There's a lot of them."

"And?"

"Nothing so far. A couple are out of the country though. Snowbirds and vacationers."

"How about Brian Palmer?"

"He was at the top of the list, but nope, he didn't take any meat from Tom. Neither did Brian Windham."

Neither of them spoke for a moment while Peter wrestled with whether to ask what he wanted to ask.

"If that's all . . ." Kevin began.

Peter cut him off. "Can you get a warrant?"

"A warrant? Like a search warrant?"

"Yes, a search warrant."

"For who?"

"Brian Palmer."

"Are you serious? No way. There isn't anything remotely resembling probable cause, unless you know something you're not telling me."

Peter could picture Kevin's face flushing and his hands clenching.

"He's Tom's best friend. It's just logical that he's the most likely person to have more of the meat and that he may know more than he's said about what happened to Tom. You can't just assume he's telling the truth and leave it at that. It's . . ." Peter paused. ". . . illogical to do so."

"That's not enough to trigger a search, Pete. Not nearly enough. You know that."

The conversation with Kevin drained the last few droplets of Peter's mental energy, so it was fortunate that the gods of veterinary fate were merciful with him that morning. All the clients were pleasant, and all the animals were cooperative. Even the staff was in a good mood, which wasn't always necessarily the case. Kat cleaned and reorganized the lab cupboards, something Peter had been asking her to do for months, and Theresa had baked cupcakes that had been frosted with cat faces, so the three of them enjoyed those during a brief lull, while swapping crazy client stories. And most importantly for Peter's fragile state, nothing arose that was especially mentally challenging. He could function well enough, but he didn't feel he had the mental horsepower to tackle complex problems this morning. Even with the extra caffeine boost, Peter felt like all the little spaces in and around his brain had been jammed with cotton, lending a peculiar, muffled sensation to all of his thoughts.

It was also fortunate that the afternoon was clear in his schedule. There were no farm calls booked and it was still generally the slow time of year, so there were no small animal appointments either. He could ski out to Tom's hut again for the one o'clock meeting he had promised. That was what he needed. Vigorous activity in cold, fresh air was the best antidote to cotton brain. Hopefully, Tom would be there.

Peter's last appointment of the morning was Captain, a Shetland sheepdog owned by Dave and Brenda Einarson. Both of them came in for his appointment because he was going to have an ultrasound to investigate high liver enzymes. Captain looked untroubled by all of this. He always looked untroubled. He was possibly the most stoic dog in Peter's practice. Dave put Captain up on the table while Captain just stared straight ahead. He continued to do so when Peter shaved a patch over his last ribs, and he presumably continued to do so after the lights were turned off as well, although it was too dark to tell.

"So, it looks like it's his gall bladder," Peter said after a few minutes of scanning through a grainy monochrome version of Captain's abdomen. "This is an extremely common problem in shelties, but it's not serious. See here? The black part is liquid bile, which is normal, but the white part is where the bile has thickened and has become sludgy, so it doesn't flow as well."

"Why does that happen? Are we feeding him wrong?" Brenda asked.

"No, it's just a combination of genetics, luck and age. In fact, for most diseases in people and animals, those are always the three biggest factors: genetics, luck and age."

"Can we do something about the sludge?"

"Yes, I can prescribe ursodiol, which is a bile thinner. And . . ."

He paused.

Without warning, the Rube Goldberg machine in Peter's brain had suddenly kicked into motion again.

The cotton around his brain vanished.

He resumed talking, saying rote things about the liver and bile and digestion and so on, but the core of his attention was now focused on the marble running through pipes, tripping a lever, dropping into a little cup, tipping it over and then dropping again on a bell, which rang and caused a bright red flag to run up a little pole.

That was it.

Dave Einarson asked him a question, but Peter had to get him to repeat himself.

"So, he's all done now? I can put him back on the floor?"

"Oh, sorry, I zoned out for a second. Tired from a goat C-section call last night! Yes, of course. I'm done with Captain. He was such a good boy!"

Peter offered the dog a liver treat, but Captain was aloof, or perhaps suspicious.

"Ha, that's funny, he's normally such a glutton!" Brenda laughed.

Peter walked home as quickly as he could without breaking into a run. He had solved it! Now he just had to get to Tom in time. He would change, grab his skis, his pack and Pippin and they could be at Suomi Beach in half an hour. That would have him at Tom's on time.

"Where you guys headed? And why the hurry?" Laura asked as Peter rocketed around the house getting ready.

"Oh, just out onto the lake. It'll help clear the cobwebs," he said as he stuffed an extra sweater into his pack.

"The lake? Really? There's some weather building in the southwest. A Colorado low."

"Right, that's why I'm rushing. To beat that." In fact, Peter didn't know about the storm. He was just suddenly gripped with an even more urgent need to talk to Tom, and with the fear that something terrible would happen soon if he didn't.

"Hmm, well, you've only got a couple hours. It's supposed to hit mid-afternoon. Sixty- to 80-kilometre-an-hour winds and ten to 20 centimetres of snow by tomorrow morning."

"Not really a monster."

He watched as Laura's brow furrowed. "No, not here in town, but enough of one if you're caught out in the open on the lake in that."

"Don't worry. We won't even go out of cell range. I just really need to get out there. You know." Peter finished with his pack and hoisted it onto his shoulder before calling for Pippin.

"Yeah, I know. Just watch the sky."

"Of course. I'm going to ski southwest from Suomi Beach, directly toward the storm front so I can keep an eye on it and calculate my turnaround time."

And he did. After strapping on his skis and adjusting his pack, Peter squinted southwest, past the ice ridges that hid Tom's hut from view. High cirrus clouds, like sloppy white brush strokes, were pushing into the sky from the far southwest horizon. Those marked the leading edge of the system. If it was typical, it was probably moving 40 kilometres an hour, so given the distance, he would have two to two and a half hours. Like Laura said, mid-afternoon. Plenty of time to get out there, talk to Tom and get back.

Peter called to Pippin, who had been sniffing along the edge of a snowbank, and then the two of them set off across the lake.

CHAPTER
Thirty-Two

T he wind.

It moaned and whistled. So much louder all of a sudden.

But the blizzard was still a couple hours away?

His head hurt. It hurt so much.

It was dark.

He was lying on his back.

Moaning wind. Painful head. Darkness. Recumbency. Peter's mind scrambled to sort out these sensations.

It was dark because his eyes were closed. He opened them slowly. It was like looking through a window that had been smeared with soap. Everything was blurry, but in an uneven way, with some bits and pieces clearer. Little patches of colour, like a red tin on a shelf and a blue garment hanging on the wall.

He tried to move. He couldn't. His ankles and wrists were bound. Not rope. Maybe duct tape?

He squeezed his eyes shut, opened them again and really concentrated on focusing.

Damn, his head hurt.

Now Peter could see more clearly. It was Tom's ice fishing hut. He was on the sleeping platform and he was alone.

Where was Pippin?

Peter tried to call him, but his mouth wouldn't open. Duct tape again. The best he could do was make mmm-mmm-mmm noises. That should be enough to alert Pippin that he was awake.

If Pippin was in the hut.

But it didn't seem like he was. Escaped? Tied up outside? Injured? Killed?

No. Can't think that.

Peter tried to concentrate his memory. He closed his eyes again as his head hurt less that way.

They had been skiing through the ice ridges. He remembered that. He also remembered seeing the cabin and seeing that the snowmobile was not there. He had been disappointed and tried to calculate how long he could wait before the storm hit.

And that was it.

No memory of anyone approaching him, or of Pippin barking to alert him, or of anything. Just standing outside calculating time and then suddenly the wind was so loud, and his head hurt, and he was lying down in Tom's rented ice fishing hut. But Tom wasn't there.

Jung had ambushed him.

This is where Jung had disappeared to as well. The lake. Everybody disappears to the lake. But where was Jung now? When was he coming back?

Peter slipped into unconsciousness again like slipping under black water.

When he next woke up, the wind was even louder. The hut shuddered with each gust. Peter wondered whether it would move on the ice.

He looked around.

Still empty.

Still no Pippin.

"Mmm-mmm-mmm!"

Nothing.

Through the windows he could see snow being driven horizontally by the wind. It must be late afternoon then. The peak of the storm.

And then he heard another sound, layered underneath the wind. He strained to make it out. It was a snowmobile. As it became louder and more distinct it sounded like two snowmobiles. Then one stopped and the other continued for a second longer. Definitely two snowmobiles then. There was a third Korean gangster? Park, Jung and . . . ?

Peter decided that the best strategy would be to pretend he was still unconscious. He closed his eyes and tried to slow his breathing.

The door opened. The wind was suddenly even louder. There was the sound of boots stomping.

"Fuck, it's a bitch out there!"

Tom! Not Jung! Didn't he see him on the bed? He was about to make a sound to catch his attention, but something stopped him. Some deep instinct.

Then the sound of the door slamming shut and the wind quieter again, followed by another voice, lower, gravelly. "Fuck! And it's only getting worse. How's our guest?"

Brian Palmer.

What was going on here? Peter's mind scrambled. But he had had it all figured out. It was logical. Every piece fit perfectly. Tom's piece was labelled "naïve dupe," not . . . this . . . whatever it was. Damn it. What had he missed? And where was Pippin?

"He's alive, but still out cold. Stupid fuck."

"You should have hit him harder," Brian grumbled.

"Ha! Maybe."

Tom! Peter couldn't believe what he was hearing. It was like some basic law of physics was being revised live before his ears. Of course, he knew that human behaviour did not follow laws the same way as physics, but having that knowledge didn't make this any easier. The people around him needed to be different. They needed to be predictable and reliable. Most of them knew this. Laura knew it. Kat and Theresa knew it. Kevin sort of knew it, but he liked to mess with Peter sometimes. He thought Tom knew it. Maybe he knew it and didn't care though. Like an extreme version of Kevin. The galling thing was that both Tom and Kevin were popular, more popular than Peter. Is that what people liked? Unreliability and unpredictability?

He could feel his breathing speeding up as these thoughts charged through his mind, so he focused on slowing it and turning his thoughts elsewhere. He suddenly felt someone's breath on his face.

"Yeah, breathing."

It was Brian.

"I should just put a bullet in him and stick him in a deep drift way the fuck out on the lake. He won't turn up until his skull rolls onto Grand Beach in a few years."

Peter's gut clenched.

"There's got be another way, Bri," Tom said, sounding alarmingly tentative to Peter.

"Yeah, the other way is that *you* do it. Should be you anyway, as you've got one under your belt already. No point in both of us being murderers."

"Fuck you."

"No, fuck you. If you hadn't gotten greedy and messed things up with Park, we would be in Panama drinking rum and Cokes or whatever they drink down there."

"Are we going to do this again? Go over all this? What's fucking done is fucking done, Bri. Sorry, but shit happens. And it was need, not greed."

"Whatever. I'm just sick of all this bullshit. If we can get the gall bladders, we can bail to Vancouver, where my guy will set us up with another buyer."

He was right! Maybe he had been wrong about a trivial aspect of Tom's personality, but he was right about what was going on! Tom and Brian were selling gall bladders from poached bears, including polar bears, to the Korean gang and they were going to smuggle them out hidden in pork products! He knew they were extremely expensive due to their reputation as a high-end remedy for a range of diseases from diabetes to epilepsy to heart disease. In reality, bile extract had some use in liver disease, but that was it. And even for that limited use it did not need to come from bears. Poor bears.

The joy of being right momentarily flooded Peter's mind and pushed all other thoughts aside. It was so good to be right.

"And get me the hell out of the country," Tom said.

"Yeah, yeah, I'm working on it."

There was some shuffling and the clink of a bottle.

"OK, just a small pour," Brian said.

"Why? We're not going anywhere anytime soon."

The hut shuddered with an especially violent wind gust, as if to emphasize Tom's point.

"Always better to stay sharp," Brian said.

"Disagree."

There was silence for what felt like a very long time. Peter presumed they were drinking.

"At least shoot the stupid dog," Brian finally said.

Pippin!

"I'm not shooting the dog! I know that dog."

"You'll shoot a man, but you won't shoot a dog? Loser."

"Why don't you shoot him?"

"I don't hurt animals."

"Fuck you."

They both started laughing, but their laughter was cut short by a sudden loud sharp sound, like a firework or the briefest thunderclap.

A gunshot.

CHAPTER
Thirty-Three

"**W**hat the hell?!" Brian screamed.

There was a crashing, thumping sound.

Peter opened his eyes.

Brian and Tom were on the floor. The chairs were knocked over. Rice fountained out of a large hole in a bag on the shelf.

"Jesus! Fucking hell! Is it Jung? It can't be!" Tom shouted.

"It's not Santa Claus, you twat!"

Bang!

Bang!

Two more shots through the west wall. One sent a coffee can flying and one whizzed by Peter's ear. He closed his eyes again.

Shitshitshitshit.

"He's trying to flush us out so he can pick us off!" Brian yelled.

"It's a fucking blizzard out there! That's insane!"

"If we get out the door low, and dive behind the skidoos, we'll be OK." Brian was quieter now, but still breathing heavily and there was a distinct quaver in his voice. "They're better cover than this shithole. We're sitting ducks behind this fucking thin plywood."

"OK. And there's two of us and only one of him."

Bang! Bang! Bang!

Three more shots in rapid succession, this time through the north wall, either side of the window, and aimed lower.

"God damn it! The asshole grazed my boot!" Tom screamed.

"He's circling around to the front! We have to go now," Brian said in an urgent whisper.

"What about Bannerman?"

"Fuck him. If he gets hit, he gets hit."

"Sure. OK, let's go."

Tom! Untie me at least! "Mmm-mmm-mmm!"

Tom glanced quickly at Peter, whose eyes were now open, but looked away again immediately. He was carrying a rifle. Brian had a pistol.

"One, two, three, go!" Brian shouted and they burst through the door, rolling to the right where the snowmobiles presumably were.

There was a frenzy of screaming and shooting. The door was left open and swung back and forth wildly in the wind, but Peter could see nothing and had no idea what was going on. He began to try to shift himself to the left, to the edge of the platform, hoping to fall to the floor and roll under for better cover.

He was just about to topple over the edge when Pippin came tearing into the hut. He had chewed through a length of rope looped around his neck.

"Mmm-mmm-mmm!"

Peter dropped to the floor. Whump.

Pippin ran over to him and began sniffing him all over, making happy yipping noises.

More shots — at least a dozen — were fired outside while the blizzard howled but the shouting had stopped until suddenly there was an anguished scream followed by a loud, "Fuck! Brian!"

Peter's wrists had been bound in front of him. He held them up to Pippin's nose and looked him urgently in the eye. "Mmm-mmm-mmm!"

Pippin looked back at him and began to sniff the duct tape.

"Mmm-mmm-mmm!" Peter lifted Pippin's lip with the side of his duct taped wrist.

Of all the oddball things I should have trained him to do and didn't, Peter thought. *Please, please, please . . .*

Pippin licked the duct tape and then, after an agonizing pause in which Peter was sure they would both be hit by bullets and die, he began to nibble at it.

Peter couldn't believe his eyes. "Mmm-mmm-mmm!" If he had been religious, he would have been praising God fervently at that moment. A genuine miracle. Worthy of a pilgrimage of thanks. But he wasn't religious. Instead, he fervently praised Pippin's intelligence. The dog just knew. Thank . . . dog.

Within seconds Pippin had torn through the duct tape and Peter's hands were free. Peter ripped the tape off his mouth and from around his ankles. "Good boy, Pippin! Good boy!" Then he freed his feet and crouch-ran to the door.

It was like looking into a blender making a vanilla milkshake. The world was a chaotic white swirl. The wind had swung around to the east, so the snow was pelting Peter directly in the face. For the moment, however, there was no shooting or screaming. Peter shielded his face, crouched lower and grabbed the door so it wouldn't hit him as it swung crazily. He peered carefully to the right.

Tom was behind a black snowmobile with his rifle resting on the seat, trained on where the ice ridges would be. Peter couldn't see anything out there.

Then he saw Brian. He was slumped behind the other snowmobile. A large red stain fanned out from his head, soaked into the snow. It was the only colour in this black-and-white world.

Peter squinted into the needles of driving snow, trying to see what Tom saw. Or maybe Tom didn't see anything either.

Two shots rang out. One ricocheted off the black snowmobile's engine cover and the other smashed through the plexiglass window of the hut.

Tom fired back, apparently aiming based on sound clues alone. He reloaded, and as he did so another shot came out of the east, this one ripping through the seat of the snowmobile.

That's when Peter saw it. A fuzzy black shape floated into view like an apparition at the very edge of visibility in the white tumult of wind and snow. Tom must have seen it too.

A shot. And then a scream.

Tom shot three more times in rapid succession.

Nobody shot back.

Tom began to step carefully and slowly toward where the apparition had been.

Peter looked at Pippin. This was their chance. Sprint to the left and detour around the ice ridges before tacking straight east. They'd be gone and out of sight before Tom noticed. There'd be no tracks for Tom to follow in this storm.

Fortunately, they had left Peter's boots and jacket on, although his gloves and hat were missing. Ski boots weren't ideal for running in, but there was not enough time to put the skis on and he didn't want to chance the keys not being in the snowmobile's ignition, or it not starting immediately. No, they'd run for it.

They dove into the maelstrom. Pippin was twice as fast as Peter but kept him in sight by glancing back constantly.

Then there was another gunshot and a puff of snow exploded between Peter and Pippin.

What!? Jung was still alive and shooting at him now!?

Peter wrenched his head to the side quickly to glance over his shoulder.

It was Tom.

Tom took two more shots at Peter, but fortunately much less well aimed.

Peter tried to run faster, but it was so hard in those boots, on this fresh snow, and into this wind. His head still hurt like a dozen gnomes were hammering on it.

Then he heard the snowmobile start up.

They had reached the first large ice ridge. Peter scrambled up it, knowing that Tom would have trouble with that, hoping that there would be a rough jumble of vertical ice and sastrugi on the other side. Pippin followed with no difficulty.

They were in luck. Peter could only see three metres in front of him, but those three metres would be impassable for a snowmobile. As was the next three metres, and the next after that. He paused for a second to check for his phone, as he hadn't had time to do so until just then. It wasn't in any of his pockets. They must have taken it, or it had fallen out in all the chaos. He and Pippin couldn't hide here long. They would just have to make it to shore somehow and then find help. One step at a time.

He heard the snowmobile howling to the left of him, obviously circling ahead to cut off access to the shore. Then the noise stopped.

Peter and Pippin stopped moving through the maze.

He listened carefully.

There was nothing. Only the wind. Cautiously they began moving again, picking their way forward, sometimes going around obstacles, sometimes climbing over them. His hands were becoming numb with cold. He was going to lose fingers if they were out there much longer.

Was someone moving up ahead, behind the next sastrugi? It was hard to tell. They stood still again.

The wind settled and it became much easier to see. Yes, there was definitely someone there, moving slowly toward them.

Tom. He was on foot.

Tom was very experienced on the ice and, Peter thought with a pang of fear, very experienced with rifles. Was hunting polar bears in the high Arctic much different?

Should we try to hide? Or backtrack? Shit. He had no idea. He was still trying to process Tom's betrayal. It was impossible to think straight. An unfamiliar mixture of anger, panic and sadness had taken over his brain.

Tom had obviously seen them as he began to walk faster. Peter could see him raise his rifle. Peter turned to run, but immediately tripped on chunk of ice. He got up as quickly as he could and looked back toward Tom. The wind had picked up again and the visibility dropped.

Thank god. There was still a chance to run.

And then just as he turned away, he caught a glimpse of light behind Tom. Blue flashing light. At first faint and mirage-like, then strong and real. Then the sound of snowmobiles. Several.

Tom began to run away, to the right. There was shouting. Impossible to hear what through the shrieking wind. Other figures were running too. There was more shouting. Then they all stopped running.

Peter dropped to his knees and Pippin sat down beside him.

A figure approached.

The figure turned into Kevin.

"You butthead!" Kevin said, his facial expression unreadable behind the visor.

Kevin hauled Peter onto his feet and hugged him.

CHAPTER
Thirty-Four

The three of them sat in a semi-circle of armchairs around the fireplace on the Sunday evening after Peter's rescue on the lake. Pippin snored quietly on the floor beside Peter, and Merry was on Laura's lap. The fire was especially bright and strong because Peter had built it with the well-aged birch and oak he saved for special occasions, rather than the usual collected deadfall that sputtered and hissed. Thelonious Monk was on the stereo, and they had just finished a vegetarian cassoulet that even Kevin, an otherwise fervent carnivore, declared to be delicious.

"And this is your good stuff?" Kevin said, contorting his face into a parody of extreme disgust after taking a tiny sip from the scotch Peter had poured him.

"You bet!" Peter replied with a laugh. "The delightful essence of burning tires with an enchanting undertone of old Band-Aids. What's not to love?"

"Christ, Pete." Kevin muttered and then took another cautious sip of the dark amber liquid in the small, tulip-shaped glass.

"It's the sulphur in the peat they burn to dry the malt that produces the burning tires effect, and the old Band-Aids comes from the iodine in the salty sea spray. The Laphroaig distillery is on the shore of the island of Islay, just off the west coast of Scotland.

And those are only a couple of the dozens of volatile compounds in here. You should see the mass spectrograph analysis!"

"If you say so." Kevin put the glass down on the side table and looked over at Laura, who was grinning at him.

"A beer, Kev?" Laura asked.

"Yes, please."

They were all silent for several minutes, listening to the crackle of the fire blend with the quiet jazz. They had avoided talking about the events of the last few weeks at dinner, focusing instead on the weather and the animals and world events and funny reminiscences. What each of them wanted to say hung in the air like a ghost unseen.

Peter spoke first. "So, Kev, Jung talking yet?"

Kevin wiped beer foam from his red moustache and beard and nodded. "Oh yeah, he was out of intensive care on Monday already and was eager to talk when he found out that we had Tom too. And the same for Tom. Both figure if they cooperate, they can shift blame on the other and bargain for leniency."

Peter leaned forward and nodded but kept quiet to encourage Kevin to keep talking.

"The South Koreans want to extradite Jung to face charges there, but that won't happen for a while. I don't know this officially yet, but I've heard that he and Park had actually gone rogue from the Seobang Faction and worked for a billionaire in Seoul."

"Oh yeah?"

"And here's the really interesting part. I don't know the name of this billionaire, but word is that he works with the North Koreans. He's their guy, or one of their guys, in the south who secretly supplies Kim Jong-un and his entourage with all kinds of stuff, including . . ."

"Bear gall bladders!" Peter practically shouted.

Startled by the loud noise, Pippin woke up and looked up at Peter before grunting and settling back down to snooze again.

"You got it." Kevin took another long swallow from his beer before continuing. "Not just bear gall bladders, but polar bear gall bladders specifically. It's one of Kim Jong-un's weird things. I guess he believes that they'll keep him young, or make him strong, or make his dick grow, or something anyway."

"So, I was right. That was the 'black' and 'white' on the note. Black for black bear and white for polar bear. The first number was kilos and the second dollars."

"Yup."

"And the total value of the gall bladders hidden in those 11 pork shoulders and hams is $968,000."

"Right again, Dr. Math. And that's just the value to Jung and Park. Presumably, there was princely markup before Kim Jong-un got them." Kevin downed the rest of his beer, held the empty glass up to Laura and winked.

"Enough to kill for."

"Apparently so."

Laura looked at Peter, pointed at Kevin's empty beer glass and then pointed at Merry, who was back to sleeping on her lap. Peter got the hint and got up.

"Another?" he asked Kevin and took his glass.

"Don't mind if I do."

"What does Tom say happened with Park?" Peter asked over his shoulder as he walked to the kitchen.

"He says it was self-defence, of course," Kevin replied, raising his voice so that Peter could hear him.

"You don't believe him?" Peter called from the kitchen. Kevin didn't answer right away while he waited for Peter to return with his fresh glass.

He took a long sip before going on. "Maybe. Don't know yet. What's clear is that there was an argument when Tom and Brian found out how much the gall bladders were selling for in Korea versus the shitty amount they were being paid to supply them.

They threatened to cut out the middlemen if they didn't get a better price. Apparently, Brian has, or I should say had — rest in peace, asshole — a contact in Vancouver that promised a direct line to wealthy Asian buyers."

"Yeah, that came up while they were chatting in the hut, after casually debating whether to put a bullet in my head. But wouldn't that contact be just another middleman?"

"Yeah, that's what I thought too, but Brian and Tom figured this contact would give them a much better deal than the Koreans. Those two were small-town amateurs with pretentions of moving in international professional smuggling circles. One way or the other they were going to get screwed."

"Didn't work out so well for Palmer."

"Nope."

"I never liked him, and him getting shot probably helped save my life, but it's too bad anyone had to die for gall bladders."

"I guess." Kevin glanced at his beer glass. He was already halfway through. "Jeez, I'd better slow down, eh?"

"If you say so, Corporal Gudmundurson," Laura said, winking at her brother. "I suppose you wouldn't want your illustrious career to be blemished with a silly DUI. You're probably picturing Kristine's face when she has to administer the breathalyzer test on you."

"Ha! Yeah, she could peel paint with her eyes when she's angry!" Kevin laughed and reached for his beer, but then pulled his hand back in mock alarm.

Peter steered the conversation back to the case. "And what about Elton's murder? Jung say anything about that yet?"

"Yeah, self-defence too. All these dirtbags were just saving their own skins. Just a bunch of 'unfortunate circumstances.'" Kevin used air quotes.

Peter snorted.

"This particular dirtbag says that he had cased Elton's place before, which we know is true, and that if he wanted to kill him, he would have done it then . . ."

"That's not logical," Peter broke in. "Nobody's saying this was a premeditated hit. It's more likely that Elton just got in the way and besides, maybe he wasn't even home the first time."

"Right. Well, anyways, Jung claims that he was just trying to do a clean and quiet burglary when Elton jumped him and grabbed the knife Jung had on his belt."

"Fat chance. Have you found the knife, by the way?"

"Nope. But I really doubt a court will buy his story anyway. Too far-fetched. And we've got some other forensics that undermine his story." Kevin looked at his half-finished beer and sighed quietly. "It's getting late. I should probably go, guys."

Peter didn't seem to hear him. "Any idea why he wanted to lure me out there that night? Has he said? I presume he wanted to find some way to squeeze info out of me regarding the whereabouts of the rest of the pork, as Elton didn't have much."

"He hasn't said, but your guess makes sense. He was probably starting to get panicky that he wouldn't find enough of it to satisfy his contract, and that we'd catch up with him before he did. A stranger can only stay unnoticed around here for so long."

Peter nodded. "And have you found the rest of that pork?"

"Yeah, you were right, there was a bunch at Palmer's place. Three more hams and two pork shoulders, I think. He had a high-end security system and there's no evidence that Jung tried to break in there. The last two hams were at Ben Thorlakson's and . . ."

"In the Newer Waves with Tom," Peter interrupted.

"Yeah, that Ben. And he and his wife went to the Dominican right after Tom gave him the hams. Only got back last Tuesday and, sure enough, they had been broken into at some point while they were away, and the hams were gone. We've recovered all the pork and gall bladders by the way. They were at an Airbnb Park and Jung were renting in the city. Pretty clever how they did it. They hollowed the meat out and then filled the cavities with the gall bladders. The gall bladders were all Saran-wrapped to prevent bile from leaking out and discolouring the meat. The plan was to then send the frozen pork to Korea in an innocent-looking regular export shipment."

"A weird example of 'where there's a will, there's a way,'" Peter offered.

Kevin chuckled and shifted forward in his chair and was getting ready to stand up when Laura spoke. "Before you go, Kev, what I don't get is how Jung knew where to look for the pork."

Kevin sat back in his chair again, looked at his beer, shrugged, picked up the glass and took a long swallow before answering. "Here's one place where Tom's and Jung's stories line up. They both say that when they were arguing about the price at one point, the Koreans asked to see the pork, but Tom told them that it had all been distributed to friends because he and Brian were getting worried about having all of that in Tom's freezers and the possibility of a raid by Conservation. Jung used Tom's Facebook friends list, applied a little logic to narrow the list down and began sneaking into houses and checking their freezers."

"Seriously?" Laura asked.

"Seriously. It sounds ludicrous, but he was a pro and hardly anyone here, except Palmer, has a security system, so he was able to go through about a dozen or more. Nobody knew that it had happened. And then in your case, he found what he was looking for and made it look like a proper B&E. Not a dumb guy."

"Why twice at Elton's?"

"Here's where it gets a little convoluted." Kevin drank some more beer before continuing, while Peter stoked the fire, briefly disturbing Pippin. "Tom says that they originally moved all the pork to Brian's, but when Park is killed, they become paranoid about Jung going after Brian and getting in despite the security. Park and Jung had also hinted at having friends like other gang members they could call on. As far as we know, that was a bluff. Anyway, that's when Tom starts really farming the pork out to friends. They probably planned on eventually moving all of it out of Brian's. The first time Jung searched Elton's was just before Elton got the meat. But then a few days later Elton posted a picture of one of the hams on Facebook with the caption, 'Thanks Tom. The other one was delicious!' to tease Tom, so Jung knew he had to go back."

"Crazy!" Laura exclaimed.

"Facebook," Peter muttered, shaking his head, "got Elton Marwick killed."

"I hadn't thought of it that way, but I suppose you could say that," Kevin said. "But anyway, I really gotta go, guys. It's been a slice, and dinner was great. That whisky, well, to each his own, eh? But the beer was great too. Thanks again!"

"Peter, don't you want to say something to Kevin before he goes?" Laura asked, fixing her husband with a hard stare.

Peter looked at Laura and raised an eyebrow. Kevin grinned at him.

"Right, that!" Peter exclaimed. "Didn't I thank you for saving my life already? Well, if not, thank you, Kev. I mean it, thank you."

"Don't thank me, thank her." Kevin jerked his head toward Laura. "If she didn't know you so well, you'd be fish food in the spring. She knew you'd follow your plan to ski southwest from Suomi Beach and then turn around and be back before the storm hit. Only a catastrophe would stop you from executing your plan. I'm just the guy you call when there's a catastrophe."

Peter turned to face Laura. "Thank you. And I mean that too."

Peter and Laura were quiet for a long time after Kevin left. Kevin always radiated the kind of energy that made it feel like a party was in progress when he was there, and then like a library or museum when he left. As it happened, the Thelonious Monk playlist ended at the same time, so the only sound came from the fire. Laura had begun to work on a light brown sweater with a row of tiny green dragons across the chest. As soon as she reached into the knitting bag she kept beside her chair, Merry took the hint and jumped down and padded over to a spot near the fire that she judged as optimal. Not as comfortable as Laura's lap, but it would do. Peter picked up the book he had on his armrest, a biography of the German naturalist Alexander von Humboldt, at least three times and put it down again. Pippin sensed his restlessness and briefly looked at him through half-opened eyes before closing them again.

"Laura?" Peter broke the silence.

"Mm-hmm," she said, not looking up, intent on a tricky part of the design.

"Will you ever forgive me?" He said very quietly, barely above a whisper.

"Maybe. Probably. I don't know, Peter." She still didn't look up. "Kevin has."

Laura didn't respond immediately and kept knitting for a few seconds before setting the needles down and looking up at Peter. Her eyes were glistening.

"Of course he has!" She didn't shout, but she said it with such vehemence that Pippin's eyes popped open. "That's Kevin. Ready to string you up one minute and hug you the next. I'm not like that, and, more importantly — much more importantly — I have a hell of a lot more to lose than Kevin." Tears welled up and strands of her red hair fell in her face as she shook.

"I'm sorry," Peter said, looking at his lap.

"I didn't want to have this argument. I know I can't change you, but why, Peter, why did you get mixed up in this after you promised not to?"

"I just wanted to help Tom. Help my friend."

Laura pushed the hair away from her face and smiled now. "You are both the smartest man I know and the dumbest man. You think that knowing someone for X years plus Y declarations of friendship equals Z degree of friendship. It doesn't work like that. Someone like Tom says that everyone is his best friend."

Peter looked up now. "Even so, I still can't believe he tried to shoot me. The only reason he didn't hit me is because of the blizzard. I had everything figured out. The poaching, the gall bladders, the Koreans, the pork, everything except *Tom*. That was the one missing piece. I should have spent more time with him, then I would have had that piece too."

"I doubt it," Laura said, shaking her head. "You just don't get people. Not really, not most people."

"Yeah, I guess at some level I know that. Have always known that. That's probably why I don't have any true close friends, except you of course."

"And Pippin!"

"And Pippin."

Pippin stirred at the sound of his name. Peter reached down to scratch him behind the ears. Pippin grunted with pleasure and his tail began thumping on the floor.

Then Peter got up, went over to where Laura was sitting and, without saying anything, hugged her as hard as he had ever hugged her. He began to cry quietly. Laura hugged him back and whispered, "It's OK."

Later, long after Laura had fallen asleep, Peter continued to lay awake, the events of the last few weeks running through his mind like a highlight reel. He saw everything again that he had seen, and he imagined the things that he hadn't seen. The images flickered by quickly in a disordered jumble, but as he was falling asleep the memory of the burning barn locked in. His last thought before slipping into a profound and dreamless sleep was, *Those poor pigs.*

Here's a sneak preview of the next
Dr. Bannerman Vet Mystery:

Six Ostriches

PROLOGUE

The fence was gone. Yesterday it was there, but this morning it was gone. He ran toward the opening. Maybe the man took it away. Maybe it disappeared. Much was unfamiliar in this country, so everything was possible. The others stood back. They were cowards. He was the leader for a reason. He could neither see nor hear any danger. This was an opportunity, that's what it was. Let the cowards miss out. He quickly crossed into the new territory and looked about him. The grass was much longer here. And it whirred and clicked and buzzed with many different kinds of insects. Tasty insects. Tasty plants. Paradise. Toward the shrubs it was wetter and there were even more insects and tender-looking shoots. He trotted to this spot and began to peck at everything, gorging like a child let loose in a world made of candy. Then something caught his eye. It glinted in a shallow pond. It was like a piece of the sun. He was so clever for coming here. The cowards would not get this delicious morsel. But it was not delicious. The piece of the sun was beautiful, but it tasted of nothing as it went down his long throat.

CHAPTER
One

Dr. Peter Bannerman and the ostrich stared at each other.

Even though Peter was six foot five, the ostrich was still taller than him, so Peter had to tilt his head upwards to get a good look at the bird's eyes. Caution was warranted around ostriches, but there was a strong fence between them, so he was safe from kicks. A quick sharp peck was not out of the question though. Peter didn't get any closer than necessary.

"How long has he been off his food, Dan?"

"At least a week, and he's hardly been passing any droppings. I think it started when I let them into the new pasture on the east side." Dan Favel, a powerfully built, middle-aged Metis man with an iron-grey brush cut and an impressive moustache, looked mournful. Dan had recently taken early retirement from the Royal Canadian Air Force to start his dream exotic livestock farm. "I thought I was doing them a favour. The grass and bugs were so good over there. Too good, do you think? Did he overdo it?"

"Maybe," Peter said as he continued to consider his patient from a safe distance. "I'll be honest, Dan, this is my first ostrich patient, so I'm going to have to do some reading before I assume that I can just extrapolate from chickens and ducks."

"Do you hear that, Big Bird? The doctor is going to do some studying and then he'll fix you up." Dan's gentle, childlike singsong was in comical contrast with his military bearing.

"Big Bird? Is that his actual name?" Peter asked.

"Yes!" Dan beamed. "And that's Ernie, Bert, Mr. Hooper, Oscar and The Count over there." He indicated a corral on the far side of the house, where five ostrich heads bobbed above the high wooden fence. "But they're all girls, except Big Bird and Mr. Hooper. I figured that ostriches don't care about gender identity. And my granddaughter loves their names!"

"No, I don't think they care."

"Is there anything you can do today while you're here?"

"Well, it doesn't hurt to take an x-ray of the proventriculus."

"The what?"

"It's sort of his first stomach. Pro means before and ventriculus means stomach. It's the first place the food comes after travelling down the esophagus and it's a common place for blockages to occur, at least in other bird species. The gizzard is the next stomach and that's where all the grinding happens. Because birds don't have teeth, big chunks can go down and get stuck before they reach the gizzard."

Dan rubbed his chin. "Sounds like a design flaw. The gizzard should be first."

"Ha! I suppose you could argue that, but the proventriculus secretes digestive juices that soften the food and make the gizzard's work easier."

"Oh, OK. So, you can x-ray now?"

"For sure. I'll just run to the truck and grab my portable unit. In the meantime, can you round Big Bird up, hood him and get him in a position where I can approach his lower neck from both sides?"

"Will do, I'll get Kim out to help us."

Peter walked back to his truck, which was parked in the muddy yard between the paddock and the Favels' house. He enjoyed the momentary break to think. He also enjoyed the soft breeze and the novel sensation of warmth from the late-afternoon sun on his face. It was mid-April and the sun was finally something other than just a source of light. He wasn't a sun worshipper — far from it, in fact — but as much as he loved the challenge and invigorating bite of a Manitoba winter, by April he was ready for a change.

As he opened the compartment on the side of his New Selfoss Veterinary Service truck where the x-ray unit was stored, he paused to listen to the trill of a red-winged blackbird among the cattails in the small pond beside the drive. This was the soundtrack of spring. *And it's going to be a good spring*, he thought. This was not just wishful thinking. It was logical because the winter had been so difficult because of everything that happened after the explosion of Tom Pearson's swine barn. The principle of regression to the mean dictated that it was likely that spring would be more average than winter had been and therefore, in comparison, good.

The x-ray machine was compact and came in what looked like a large black cooler on wheels. He grabbed that and the flat grey x-ray cassette and walked back to where Dan and Kim were herding Big Bird into a squeeze chute by waving blankets at him. This was a funnel of fences where the parallel ones in the "spout" could be adjusted to keep an animal snugly in place. Platforms on either side allowed access from above.

"OK, I've got the hook ready," Kim shouted. She was considerably smaller than either Peter or Dan, but she had been an Olympic gymnast as a teen and from experience Peter knew that she was still exceptionally strong and quick. She was wielding a long pole capped with a blunt-ended hook. While Dan stood behind Big Bird to prevent him from backing up, Kim snagged the ostrich's neck. She managed to make this look both forceful and gentle. And then in a split second she put a hood over Big Bird's head and released the hook. This had the desired effect as the 250-pound bird immediately became calmer, no longer flapping his stubby wings against the sides or flailing his head about.

Peter was impressed. It was like something out of Marlin Perkins and *Mutual of Omaha's Wild Kingdom* with Kim in Jim's role.

"Good job, Kim!" Peter called as he approached. "Now please get him to shuffle forward so he's tight in the squeeze."

This took a little more doing, as Dan and Kim manoeuvred Big Bird back and forth, until they had the squeeze chute settings exactly right to keep him in place. The chute was made of steel tubing and fortunately the gaps were perfectly spaced to allow access to the area Peter wanted to x-ray.

Peter was proud of his new x-ray equipment. It was digital, so he could review the results instantly without having to develop films. This was not only more efficient, but it saved stress on the animals.

"It's good! You can let him go!" Peter called up from his crouched position beside the machine.

"OK!"

This was followed by banging and flapping noises as the chute was opened and Big Bird turned around and ran off, presumably in a bad mood.

"What does it show?" Kim asked as she bent down beside Peter and squinted. Dan joined her a second later.

"See this?" Peter pointed to a whitish blob at the bottom of what was obviously, even to a layperson's eyes, the neck.

"Yes."

"That's the proventriculus. All the white stuff is food, mostly leaves and grass, I'm guessing. It's jammed full. The whiteness shows the density, so it's quite impacted."

"Right, that makes sense. Silly, greedy bugger," Dan said.

"But what's that?" Kim asked, pointing at a bright white T-shaped object.

"Good eye. I was just about to get to that." Peter tapped the screen and zoomed in on the object. The cross bar of the T was thicker than the stem and was shaped liked a squashed pentagon, with the point opposite the stem. "It's metal and about the size of your thumb."

"Wow," Kim said.

Peter tapped some more, zooming further, and then adjusted the contrast. "Now look, you can see that there's some sort of symmetrical etching or design on it. There's no way to make out exactly what with an x-ray, but there's no way this is natural."

"Crazy," Dan said. "I guess he'll need surgery, eh?"

"Yes, I'm afraid so. But it's not a difficult one."

"The previous owner of this property had young kids. That must be left over from some sort of game," Kim said as she and Dan walked Peter back to his truck.

"We'll find out soon," Peter replied as he swiped through the calendar on his phone. "Wednesday morning good?"

"Perfect! See you then."

•

Big Bird was Peter's last patient for the day, so he drove directly home. For the first half of the drive, he worried about some of the technical aspects of the planned surgery. He had never operated on an ostrich before. The general principles of surgery were more or less universal, but he fretted over the potential non-universal aspects. By the second half of the drive, however, he had switched to analyzing the probability that the object in Big Bird's proventriculus was a child's toy. He didn't know much about children, but it struck him as being an odd toy, unless there was a tie-in with the Marvel Thor movie. That was possible. He could look up what merchandise was available. And if not that, then what? New Selfoss had been settled by Icelanders and 51.2 percent of the population still claimed Icelandic heritage, so could it be from Iceland? A tourist trinket brought back by someone visiting their ancestral homeland? Lost and picked up by a magpie or raven?

He was lost in this reverie as he parked the truck, entered the house and petted Pippin, their enthusiastic black-and-white lab-husky-collie mix, so he was startled when Laura greeted him loudly from the living room.

"How was your day?"

"Good. Interesting case at the end." After giving Pippin two treats from his pocket and letting Merry, their tortoiseshell cat, rub up against his leg, Peter took off his boots and went into the living room.

"Oh?" Laura said, looking up from her knitting. "Like interesting for vets, or interesting for regular humans?"

"Ha! The latter. An ostrich at Dan and Kim Favel's place."

"Did it disembowel you with its claws?" Laura asked, grinning broadly.

"Nope."

"OK, only mildly interesting so far."

"But get this, it looks like it swallowed some kind of toy or trinket!"

"OK, that's a little more interesting."

"And it gets better. It's a weird, T-shaped metal object with a design on it."

"Hmm, that is interesting." Laura set her knitting aside and put her hand out. "Let's see . . ."

Peter found the x-ray images on his phone and handed it over. Laura squinted at the screen.

"Hmm," she said. "I'm going to adjust the greyscale and try flipping to negative."

Peter watched from over her shoulder as Laura tapped a few times and then pinched and zoomed.

"What do you think?" he said.

"This is a mjolnir," she answered without looking up from the screen.

"A what?"

"Mjolnir. Thor's hammer. A Norse religious symbol worn as a pendant."